Twisted Threads
A True Story

Leila Merriman

Pen Press Publishers Ltd

First published in Great Britain
Pen Press Publishers Ltd
39-41 North Road
London N7 9DP

ISBN 1 904754 64 3

A catalogue record for this book is available
from the British Library

Printed and bound in Great Britain

Cover design by Jacqueline Abromeit
Geminivision

*My beautiful Mum, thanks for giving me life;
without you this story couldn't be told
and this book wouldn't be written.*

About the Author

Born in Upminster, Sussex in 1934 to a single Irish girl, Leila Merriman grew up in County Westmeath, Ireland with her grandparents. Returning to Upminster after the war she went to St. Mary's Convent Grammer School moving to Southend in 1947. She loved sport and was a champion swimmer. Married in 1956 to a Petty Officer in the Royal Navy, she had two children, one boy and one girl and ten years later was divorced on the grounds of her husband's cruelty.

She married for the second time in 1987 and became very involved in local politics. She was Mayoress of Southend 1987/8 and a County Councillor for ten years. Now retired, her interests are to continue her charity work for a cancer charity plus travelling; antiques; her grandchildren and writing.

Chapter One

"I'll take you home, Mum," five traumatic words I spoke to
my mother holding her frozen hands as she lay in her coffin
in the chapel of rest, a week after her death. She had closed
her eyes and slipped away while I was on holiday. It was the
only thing I could think of to make it up to her, as if I ever
could. All she ever wanted was to know there was someone
to pick up her bits and pieces when the end came. She never
wanted me, her daughter, and, in the end I wasn't even there
to do that. It fell to someone else, my lovely little Mummy
had died alone.

As a beautiful young girl born in Ireland, whenever "I'll
take you home Kathleen" came on the radio here in England
tears would fall gently down her face. Now her life was over,
a traumatic, painful life. This is a true story of real life, not
fiction, and truth is stranger than fiction.

Scattering my mother's ashes on the grave of her parents,
Michael (Mick) and Elizabeth (Lizzie) Merriman, in that
cemetery in the heart of Ireland where she was born was the
only way I knew of showing my love for the mother I never
knew.

*

Lizzie was born in Dublin in 1874. Mick had been born in
Delvin a year earlier, both into working class families. They
married in Dublin in 1894.

Mick was a slim, wiry, good looking man. His eyes were
blue and sparkled. His cheeks were hollow in his thin face.
His hair, black and straight, was combed over his forehead.
There was no doubt he had kissed the Blarney Stone. He

could tell a tale like the best. But he had a very tough, almost cruel, streak in him. A very generous man he trusted everyone except perhaps the village copper. As soon as he could walk he could take care of himself and keep up with his peers. You had to in those days in Ireland. He became an expert at hunting, snaring, shooting and fishing – skills that were to serve him well in later years. It would provide him with a job and provide little extras for the large family he and Lizzie were going to have. He and Lizzie raised seventeen children so his skills were a godsend. There is nothing like a nice fat rabbit, a fresh trout or pike from the river, a plump bird shot from the sky when there are so many mouths to feed. Because of his skills, when it came to feeding the family they were always rich beyond words. In other areas, they were as poor as church mice.

As a young man, his activities did get him into trouble. While out shooting in the woods one day with his friend, Charlie, the gamekeeper from a nearby estate caught them. Luckily for Mick the pals had time to separate. Charlie got shot in the leg. No messing about in those days if you were caught poaching, you were shot on sight. Although Charlie was the one who got shot he got away. He couldn't afford medical treatment and when he died in his eighties the lead was still in his leg. Mick was caught, he turned states' evidence and got a short prison sentence. That was his only break with the law in a long lifetime.

Lizzie was a beauty, quite small and solidly built. Her jet-black hair, parted in the centre and brushed back into a bun at the back of her neck, looked fluffy as it framed a round face. She had the deepest blue eyes, deep set. Lizzie went straight into service from school; even if girls had the brains to be scientists, if they came from poor families they had no chance. Parents couldn't afford to feed and clothe them and looked on them working to help them care for their siblings. Moving out was a daunting experience for the youngsters coming from different social backgrounds, shy, naïve; it was a great cultural shock. There wasn't much choice of jobs either and a lot of youngsters ended up in service in the large estates which was a very frightening experience. Lizzie got a job at Cloyne Castle, Delvin working for Lord Greville and Lady Rosa. Cloyne Castle still stands magnificent today. It is the fourth one to be built and was completed in 1877. At one stage, the Castle was deliberately burnt down. Richard Nugent, the then owner, heard Oliver Cromwell had designs on taking the castle over for himself and his army. Nugent said, "Over my dead body." The story is as Cromwell approached he saw the flames and flew into an almighty rage.

Mick lived practically on the doorstep of the Castle. He was born not more than a couple of miles away. He and Lizzie were destined to meet. They would both be at Mass on a Sunday or if they took a stroll down Delvin's little high street they couldn't miss each other. They married in Donnybrook, Dublin, Lizzie's birthplace, in 1894.

On her wedding day, Lizzie wore the deepest blue blouse to bring out the deep blue colour of her eyes. The blouse had very full sleeves. Bustles were out of fashion in 1894 so the skirt was very plain and flared with a thick belt round her waist. Her stockings were wool and silk with calf length lace-up boots. Her lovely long black hair shone and she wore it in its usual style, in a bun at the back of her neck. Her only jewellery was her wedding ring. In those days, working class girls didn't wear jewellery. Only wealthy folk wore jewellery. But she had an extra ingredient. She didn't need jewellery to make her shine and whether Mick knew or not I don't know, she was blooming because she was carrying twins.

Mick stood tall and looked very smart in his knickerbockers. His jacket was tweed and loose fitting. His leather boots were lace-up ending above the ankle. Thick woollen socks and a garter made him look very dashing. Mick had his hair cut very short at the back for his special day. On his head he wore a tweed hat with a narrow turned-down brim. There was no honeymoon. It was straight to work for the two of them on to the great adventure of life together.

During his late teens, Mick had been working on the construction of the tram lines in Dublin. Now he had a bride and the responsibility of providing a home, he had changed jobs. His new job was as a gamekeeper. This living was something that went back to his very roots. He knew and understood everything about the land and what the job entailed. He had grown up with it since he could walk. His first job was at a large estate at Kello, County Longford. It was there the twins were born – one boy and one girl. The baby girl was given to an aunt to bring up. It was quite usual in Victorian times for a young mother to farm her babies out. Babies would be given to the grandparents, maiden aunts, childless couples or any family member who wanted to look after another little soul.

Mick moved on to the Charterville Estate, Tullamore, County Offey. Another baby, a boy, was born there. He was passed on to his grandparents in Dublin.

One night Mick came across two brothers poaching. There was an argument and in the process Mick jammed a gun in the face of one of the poachers. Luckily, the two poachers managed to run away before Mick could really harm them. Even without a gun Mick was a tough character ready to challenge and tackle anything and anyone. They were lucky to get away, perhaps it was the extreme cold, it was an absolutely freezing night. Next morning, Mick was cleaning his gun and he couldn't run the rod down the barrel. He found the poacher's eyebrow still frozen in the barrel. Mick marched with the gun and the eyebrow to the Police Station and reported the previous night's incident. The brothers were found – one minus an eyebrow. They were charged with poaching and received long jail sentences.

Whether the incident with the brothers being jailed had anything to do with events, Mick didn't stay in that job much longer. He moved on to the Hill of Tara at Lismullan, the

Estate of Sir John Dillon. Mick liked to tell the story about the day Lady Dillon decided to watch operations at the haymaking. Like all ladies of those days, she wore very long clothes and on this particular day a wee mouse found its way up the inside of her skirt. She screamed and she screamed and all the staff ran to her aid. But she would trust only one and Mick was called for. Recalling the incident, he liked to boast that he was the only member of staff who had had his hands up the lady's skirt.

Mick was working hard and his family were growing at an alarming rate. Another seven including a second set of twins had been born. Lizzie nursed all of those babies and was grief stricken when her twins died in infancy.

It was now 1906 and Mick decided to quit gamekeeping. The job was getting more dangerous and more hazardous every day. Poaching was the only means a lot of people had to feed their families. Hungry little mouths to feed can make men desperate as Mick well understood. The gentry loved hunting, shooting and fishing for pleasure and they were slowly taking over the land. Most lakes, rivers, woods and the land were preserved for them. So the poor who desperately needed to feed their starving families were getting shut out completely. Mick had to do his share of poaching to feed his family. At night while on patrol he would sneak a couple of trout from the river and creep off with his ill-gotten goods under his coat, hoping the boss was asleep and wouldn't catch him. By day he had to help his boss try to find some trails that would lead them to the poachers. Mick was busy covering them because they were his.

One night Mick took a pal with him to do some serious poaching. Loaded with game, fish and rabbits tied round and round their waists with rope, they heard a sound in the bushes. They were well and truly caught. Poaching carried a jail sentence, and for the amount they had on them it had to be life.

"What are we going to do?" asked Mick's pal.

"There's only one thing we can do," replied Mick.

Thinking the noise was made by his boss, he raised his gun and fired both barrels in the direction of the bushes. There was a crash, a sound of breaking twigs as the body fell to the ground. Mick ran forward in the dark, heart pounding to find he had killed a horse. That was it, definitely time for him to quit. He had become so desperate he had almost committed a murder. He couldn't believe that he had deliberately raised a gun and fired both barrels at what he thought was a human being. His mind was made up. He was finally getting out of gamekeeping.

Next morning, Sir John was incensed. Not only had those bloody poachers walked off with some of his best birds, they had shot his horse.

"If I get my hands on them," ranted Sir John, "I'll shoot the buggers myself. They won't need a trial."

Mick spent a very awkward day trying to cover his movements.

After that incident Mick went to Westmeath County Council and applied for a cottage. The Council found the ideal site at Cullys Farm, three miles from Delvin and only one and a half miles from where Mick was born. One acre of land went with the cottage, enough ground for Mick to grow fruit and vegetables to feed his large family. The surveyor arrived to do the measuring and stake the ground. All was ready for the workers to dig the ditch, plant the trees and the privet hedge. Mick stood watching the activities with interest. He felt he could do with just a little more land. Being the honest rogue that he was he waited for the workmen to go to lunch. He quickly moved the stakes back giving himself another half acre. When the mistake was found out, there were some very displeased people but it was too late to do anything about it and so it was that Lizzie and Mick moved into their cottage, their first home of their own and their last.

They were to have seven more babies there and they were to die there in that little cottage in Moortown.

The cottage had only four rooms. A plain wooden door stood right in the middle at the front with a window on either side. As you walked in the door you stepped into the living room. There was a door on your immediate left which opened into a big room running the length of the bungalow. Lizzie and the girls slept there. There was a large window on the back wall of the living room looking out over the two barns and a chicken shed. Along the wall on the left was an inglenook fireplace with the fire grate and various pots. A large straw basket held the wood and turf to keep the fire going.

Two large, old, very comfortable armchairs stood each side of the fireplace with many cushions. Against the opposite wall was a long oak table, with benches either side and a large chair with arms stood at each end. Along the wall were various cupboards and shelves. A table cluttered with junk stood in front of the window – there was sewing, mending and knitting, books, all sorts of odds and ends. When darkness fell, the oil light on the big table was lit. That with candles was the only means of lighting the home. Electricity as yet hadn't reached Moortown, nor had running water in the home. At either end of the long table was a door which opened into two smaller bedrooms. Mick and the boys slept that side, if necessary six in a bed, three up and three down. There was a statue of the baby Jesus with a candle burning at his feet on one wall. A picture of the Virgin Mary on another and a rosary hung over a picture of St Patrick. By the door hung a little font with holy water.

When the front door was open, a piece of chicken wire reached across to stop the chickens, ducks, etc. wandering in. Mick would sit on the front step and read the papers, puffing away on his old pipe. He always seemed to be able to afford a bit of baccy.

Where is Moortown you might ask, well it's easy to find. Get to Delvin; take the Castle Polland Road; about a good mile out of town there is a left junction. Take that – in Mick and Lizzie's time it wasn't much more than a dirt track. The gypsies could get their caravans through, so too could Jim Burke when he had to escort a soul up to the Pearly Gates. So too could one or two folks who had cars; the farm machinery plus the slaughter cart could get through. But mostly it was a horse and cart that travelled along that road. Nowadays it seems quite posh in comparison. Travel along for about two miles until you reach the crossroads. Now you are in Moortown; God's own spot on this earth. At the crossroads lived the Cullys and the Fleesons, both farmers; and carry on for about another mile in all. You passed the O'Briens, the Merrimans and the Barrys and a little further on you reached the River Deel. That's Moortown. It's about four miles by three. No high street, no pub, no church, about half a dozen families living almost in the middle of nowhere. Moortown had the beautiful thirty-five acre Lake Dysart, the bogs and the Fraocan berries, all of which I shall get back to later. Lake Dysart created its own history. Dysart Tola was the first of many clusters of settlements created in St Patrick's name. Tola was the man who founded the settlement to bring Christianity to Ireland. Later he was canonised. So Moortown has its very own Saint, Saint Tola, and it was there that Christianity first started in Ireland.

Lizzie and Mick settled in to years of hard work. How Lizzie coped, God only knows. Lizzie kept her beauty and her cheeks were always rosy. She wore an apron, it seemed even when she went out. It had come to the point now that as another baby was born one moved out. Her day started early. The first job was to get the fire going. It had been smouldering all night and needed a pick-me-up. There was always a crowd for breakfast. The old frying pan would be balanced on some burning logs. Sausages, bacon, black pudding, all home-made would sizzle. There would be eggs in abundance. The children would have their chores before school. They would cut some logs with the big two-handled saw. Fetch some turf in to keep the fire going all day. Perhaps feed the chickens. While they were doing their chores Lizzie would be preparing their lunch boxes. It was over three miles to walk to school so their boxes had to last all day. There was enough washing to do for her own brood, and sweeping the house out would be done with a broom made of twigs. Baking had to be done, bread and cakes. Lizzie would make the dough then place it in a flat-bottomed cast iron pot. She would flatten the dough to about an inch thick. The heavy pot had to be lifted on to the crane, then with the tongs she would place the lid on. Red hot turfs would be placed on the lid and later out would come the most delicious home-made fresh bread. Lizzie worked without complaint until she dropped exhausted into bed every night. She loved the very bones of Mick and all her kids.

Lizzie washed the floors for the Barrys, her next door neighbours. Mrs Barry was Principal of Ballinvalley Girls School where the Merriman girls were in attendance. There was always a baby in her belly and yet she would go down on her hands and knees lugging the heavy bucket filled with water. Besides raising seventeen children, Lizzie had six miscarriages but she never stopped working. She did the washing for her wealthy neighbours. Water had to be carried indoors, the heavy pig's pot filled with water had to be lifted up and down off the crane. All the washing had to be done by hand, rinsed and starched and then hung out over the bushes to dry. Lizzie didn't have a clothes line, if there was such a thing in 1906. The ironing was long and hot work. All that material in the skirts and petticoats. Lizzie would build up the hot turfs, place the iron on top to hot up. She had to have her hand protected with rags because the handle was hot. No sooner had she ironed an item then the iron was cold and the whole process of heating the iron started again.

Money was desperately short in their house and washing and scrubbing for her neighbours was the only way Lizzie could earn a few shillings. It was the only way anyone could earn a penny in Ireland in those days. There just wasn't any work. Rent had to be paid, flour for baking had to be bought, sugar, soap, medicines. You had to have a reserve for the doctor or dentist. They wouldn't call without payment. Leather to mend all those pairs of boots in winter had to be bought. Oil for the lamps etc. But the Priest would never be refused. You daren't refuse the Priest otherwise you would rot in hell. With the vast wealth of the Catholic Church, it was amazing the Priest would take your last penny. People in those days were ruled by fear; blackmailed into submission. The Priest preached charity to each other. They certainly didn't practise it.

Lizzie would walk three miles to church Sunday morning then return in the evening for Benediction. There was the Stations of the Cross in the evenings and confession on a Saturday before Holy Communion on a Sunday. I wonder what made Lizzie go – a good woman who never had a cross word to say about anyone, who was always the first to help a neighbour, who was good and hardworking. She never turned a stranger from the door, there was always a piece of bread and cheese and a drink. She spent all her years child-bearing. What made her go out on a Saturday night in the rain, snow, freezing cold to confess? Confess what for God's sake! It would have been kinder of that charitable Priest if he had a word with Lizzie and said something like "Look, Mrs Merriman, I've had a word with God and he said have a rest for a year." Of course he couldn't do that, you had to rule with an iron fist, keep the peasants down. It wouldn't work for Lizzie either.

Religion was like a drug and she had to have her fix. The number of times Lizzie went to church in a week. The collection plate was always passed round. You couldn't not give – all the neighbours watched and noted. Never mind,

God will provide, the poor were always told. He will provide the leather to mend their boots in the winter. He will give Lizzie the strength to keep on her hands and knees, not praying but scrubbing floors with another baby in her belly while she had one hanging on her skirt and while she waited for the next one up the line to start school and the last one to leave home and get work. God will provide. The Priest would always take your last penny without a second thought. The plate will pass round to swell the coffers of the fabulously wealthy Catholic Church but God will always provide for the poor.

Dinner in the evening was a very nourishing meal. There was every vegetable available. The pig's pot would be full of lots of them. Perhaps there would be a couple of chickens. A couple of the kids would run down to the River Deel and catch perhaps a couple of trout. It would all be the best and the freshest. After everyone had eaten their fill, odds and ends would be added, boiled up and the pigs would be fed.

Lizzie kept a sow which she looked after. When the sow gave birth Lizzie delivered the piglets herself. If there were more than the sow could feed, Lizzie would take them into the house and bottle-feed them. They were sold after twelve weeks. She would haggle over a shilling. One pig would be kept which was killed after six months, and that provided the family with bacon for the winter. Lizzie raised a few turkeys to sell at Christmas. It ensured there was a good Christmas for all the kids. They would all have their stockings hanging around the fire, hoping Father Christmas was going to be generous. The stockings would all be filled – there would be an orange, a few sweets, perhaps a ruler or a writing pad, some marbles, some fancy soap for the girls – all sorts of little bits and pieces went into filling up the stockings. Nobody would be disappointed.

Mick worked as hard as Lizzie. Every inch of his land was cultivated. He did it all with just a fork and a spade. Every vegetable he could grow was grown. There were rows and rows of potatoes. There were blackcurrants, redcurrants, gooseberry bushes, rhubarb. Lizzie made all sorts of jams and pies. There were cows and goats for the milk which provided the butter and cheese. Mick didn't have any grazing land. His neighbours kindly let him graze his cows on their land. They just turned a blind eye when he turned his cows into their fields. There were pigs, ducks and chickens for meat, sausages and black pudding. Chickens and ducks to lay eggs. Mick could always snare a few rabbits for the pig's pot, shoot a bird out of the sky or go fishing at either the River Deel or take the boat out on Lake Dysart.

He would always have a calf or a foal to sell locally to raise a few pounds to buy the essentials he couldn't grow. Mick worked outside as much as he could. He did jobs for the Earl of Westmeath (that title is now extinct); he was always in charge of the pheasant shoot and the preparation of the birds for the Earl at Cloyne Castle. Two weeks every year he looked after the hares at the coursing at Loughnea. He was head man and did the same job when they had the coursing in the Black Meadow at Moortown. A mammoth job every year was haymaking. Mick didn't have any land, so every year a neighbour would lend him a field to get his feed in to last the animals through the winter. All the children had time off from school to help get the hay in. It was hard work in those days so it was all hands on deck, neighbours helping neighbours until everyone had the hay in the barns. Then there was the turf to be cut in the bogs during the summer. The sods were stacked to dry. Then they had to be loaded on to the cart and brought home. The poor horses worked hard. They were back and forth along the bog road with their heavy load day in and day out.

Next door neighbours, the Barrys, were rich and influential. The drive up to their white front door was winding and on both sides were rows of wonderful flowers. In the early autumn there were lines of glorious chrysanthemums. The Barrys were very interested in greyhound racing and Mick longed to own a greyhound for himself. He finally acquired one, how, nobody knows but he had great hopes that it was at least going to win the Greyhound Derby. He took the dog to Dublin for trials. What happened at the trials was unbelievable. The dog went the wrong way around the track. Mick was furious with it. On the way home, he threw it in the River Liffy and it drowned. Remember this is 1910, plus times were hard in Ireland and anything that wasn't of use couldn't be kept.

Twice a year, Mr Tighe, a retired Bank Manager, came to Delvin to hunt and fish. Mick was his guide as he knew where the game was. He used to have Jim Growney carry the game. It was said to be a fact that the same James Growney supplied Brinsley McNamara with most of the material for his first book *The Valley of the Squinting Windows.* Mr Tighe lodged in Delvin for his two-week stay and on the night before he left he and Mick would have a few pints in Jim Burke's. Jim Burke was a jolly publican, a real roly-poly character with a wonderful moustache. He had jet-black hair parted in the middle and flattened to his head. He was the undertaker as well as the local taxi and on Mick's night out with Mr Tighe he was sent home in the taxi. In his will, Mr Tighe left Mick all his fishing tackle which was quite an expensive gift.

Jack, Lizzie and Mick's fifth born, was now a young man of seventeen. He had a blazing row with his dad one day. Mick was a hard man, he would think nothing of getting a stick and beating his boys. It was enough for Jack, one hiding too many and he ran away to England and joined the army. He was no more than a child, eighteen, so Lizzie said, when he was killed at Anas, France. Lizzie had never experienced such pain. It was something she was never going to get over and something she was never to forgive Mick for. Every time they had a disagreement she reminded Mick if he hadn't been so argumentative, Jack wouldn't have run away and he would still be alive. It was amazing that Lizzie, who loved the very bones of Mick, could be so cruel. She never once gave a thought as to how Mick felt. It must have been the only unkind thing she did in her whole life.

In 1918 an event occurred which rocked the little town of Delvin. There was an unprecedented groundswell of adversity on one hand and a similar reaction of support and sympathy on the other. It was the publication of the Brinsley McNamara book *The Valley of the Squinting Windows*. People believed that the characters in the book were not fictitious but bore a striking likeness to various local people. Readers set out identifying the locals whom they thought resembled the characters and, as a result, certain people were held up to ridicule which added fuel to a smouldering fire. The repercussions were felt to varying degrees throughout the community but they were felt more deeply within the author's own family. The frustration felt by the absence of the author resulted in the community's anger being vested on his family, particularly on his father, James Weldon, who was the Headmaster of Ballinvalley School.

Master Weldon was a quiet, but strict man who was respected as a good teacher and a fair-minded man. He was a familiar figure. Each evening, after school, he would walk into the village to collect his paper in Tierney's shop and sit on the nearby windowsill reading and chatting with the locals. He had a family of four sons and three daughters and they occupied a lot of his thoughts and anxieties. His wife was a demure, retiring person, adapt at cushioning the family from his displeasure over breaches of family rules. His son, John, was perhaps the one who caused him the most anxiety and he disapproved vehemently of his lifestyle. John was a dreamer who liked nothing better than sitting around listening to the marvellous stories told by the local sages, writing poetry and reading books. In 1909, at the age of nineteen, he shocked his father by joining the Abbey Theatre Company in Dublin instead of pursuing a respectable career in the Civil Service. Master Weldon felt that no good would come of this acting business and that it was a waste of time but he could exert no influence on John. He was as surprised as anyone when the book was published.

Meanwhile, there were groups in Delvin summoning in protest and indignation. Meetings were held culminating in a mass meeting in front of the Market House (now the Court House); copies of the book were sacrificially burnt and a committee was formed to campaign for the banning of the book and to bring retribution on the author and his family. A motion was moved that the Master knew, approved and even helped, in the writing of the book. Goldsmith's description of a village schoolmaster was apt.

The village all declared how much he knew;
'Twas certain he could write and cipher too.

Deputations to the Parish Priest, Father Trite, were frequent, insistent and emotional. Eventually, he gave the master notice of dismissal but this was withdrawn on the orders of Bishop Gaughan. A boycott of the school was then organised with a great measure of success. Transport was provided at junctions on the roads leading to the school to take the boys to other schools in the area. Some parents who did not approve of the boycott kept their children at home as a result of intimidation or to avoid becoming involved in the issue. The boycott was not confined to the withdrawal of children from school. The shopkeepers in the village were, reluctantly in most cases, persuaded by influential customers to cease supplying the Weldon family with goods. Sympathetic friends and neighbours, however, surmounted this obstacle by getting extra supplies themselves and passing them on. The boycott never lost momentum despite appeals from a great many sources and lasted almost three years. By this time, it had taken its toll on the Weldons – physically and mentally – until the master decided early in 1923 to retire. Because his retirement was premature and the school attendance average over the previous two years was decimated, his pension was reflectively reduced.

On legal advice, he took court action against the committee which had organised the boycott, thus ruining his career and depriving him of his livelihood. The case, which was heard in Dublin, lasted almost three weeks and it was evident from the beginning that it was the book that was on trial. The cost of the proceedings was great and Master Weldon was shattered when the jury disagreed and so bringing the case to an end without a verdict. The option of another court action was rejected by a then embittered man, despite offers of financial help and support from various writers in England and Ireland including George Bernard Shaw.

The publicity given to the boycott and the subsequent court case turned the book into a best seller. This resulted in financial reward and international recognition for the author who went on to become President of the Literary Academy of Ireland and Registrar of the National Gallery.

Master Weldon and his wife retired to the handsome Valleymount House, Avoca, County Wicklow. He never recovered from the blow fate had dealt him but the passing years mellowed the bitterness and the anger. Now, nearly ninety-five years later, the episode has faded into the caverns of misty memory as have the people who where the leading characters in the drama. The bookstalls and televisions screens now provide with regular consistency, material much more shocking to public morality. Nowadays, a book like *The Valley of the Squinting Windows* might form the basis of an afternoon soap opera.

Brinsley McNamara sought the help of locals when they were holding a meeting in Martinstown Hall. A large contingent armed with sticks and gels marched from Delvin to "kill" Brinsley. They were met at the door by the Commander of the local IRA, Mick Fox, who wouldn't let them in. It gave Brinsley time to escape through a back window and make his way across fields. He left for Dublin, thus ending his eventful career in Delvin.

Mick and Lizzie were very involved. It was quite clear which side they were on because Mick had quite an intense dislike of Master Weldon. One of his boys had a problem with his teacher, Henry Healy. The teacher was beaten up and received a broken nose. Henry went to the parish priest to make a complaint about the Merriman boy. Father James Flynn told him he should be ashamed to admit he was incapable of handling the kids. The boy in question had to be removed at the request of Master Weldon which enraged Mick.

It was late 1920s now and Lizzie was in her fifties. She and Mick had been married thirty-five years. Her tenth born, Lily, was the first to emigrate to England. It broke her heart as she watched her next three daughters rush to join their big sister with two of her sons. But she drew great comfort from her large family who settled nearby and she loved her grandchildren as much as her own. There were to be seventy grandchildren in all but sadly Lizzie wasn't going to live to see them grow up.

For now Lizzie was happy with life. Hard as it had been it had been a good life and she felt blessed with her wonderful family. A trip to Delvin was always a chance to catch up with a bit of gossip. Something she had time for these days. On this particular day, she was shocked at what she heard. Rushing home she shouted to Mick "Get your coat," as she hitched up the horse and cart. "Get in, get in," she shouted impatiently to Mick who was dithering, wondering what was going on.

A young girl had given birth in Mullingar Hospital and one of her sons was alleged to be the father.

"I'll know straight away if that baby is a Merriman," said Lizzie. "If it is it will come home with us."

It was a disgrace for a young girl to have a baby out of wedlock, but not so for the father. It was a case of give him a pat on the back and buy him a pint. Very little was said at the hospital as Lizzie lovingly picked up the baby boy. She cradled him in her arms as she and Mick made the journey home. He was a Merriman and as long as there was breath in her body she would love and cherish him. He was to be called Brendan.

As for the young girl, the baby never happened. She never married and on her deathbed she still denied ever giving birth.

Chapter Two

Lizzie and Mick's second youngest, Sheila, was probably the cleverest of the bunch. She had won a scholarship to go on to Higher Education but it was impossible for Lizzie and Mick to pay the fees and feed and clothe her away from home. So, at fifteen, she travelled to England to live with her sister Lily and help her in her haberdashery shop. Emigration itself in those days caused great sadness and loneliness. Often it caused frustration because it meant there was no hope in your own country, the land of your birth, the place you loved and where you wanted to be. For Sheila there was a sense of failure as well, she was never going to get the education she deserved and never going to reach her full potential. It was to give her a bitter streak in her life.

Lily was a small woman, very plain. Her hair was frizzy which she wore parted in the middle and tied in a bun at the back of her neck. She could swear like a trooper and was never afraid to speak her mind, please or offend. She had a terrible stutter and always had a hand-rolled fag in her mouth. The fag would be going all over the place in unison with her chin while she stuttered until finally the stutter got so bad she had to take the fag out to breathe and catch her breath. Her husband, Bill, was a Captain in the army. A real red-blooded man who found out, after marriage, that his wife thought the sex act was just to have a child. When they had one that was it, according to Lily. It led to a violent marriage. In those days, it seemed the most important thing for a woman was to be married, off the shelf. It didn't matter if it was Mr Right or Mr Wrong. When Sheila arrived, Lily was expecting her baby so she could be a great help and comfort. Bill was abroad with the army so it really was a godsend for

Lily having Sheila there. Times were hard, the recession was still biting and England was between wars. The big stores were beginning to raise their ugly head and take trade away from the little shops. There was no money to pay Sheila a wage but she had her bed and food. They were simple, easy days and there were now six of the brothers and sisters around the London area. When the shop shut, the cards would come out and there was always someone to make up the numbers. They would play almost right through the night. Sheila didn't have a musical bone in her body or any sense of rhythm. It would be a waste of her time going to a dance. She was like a plank of wood. All the brothers and sisters had this wooden appearance, you could not imagine any of them gliding across the dance floor. She was a very shy, naïve girl and, like her baby sister, Una, very pretty. The two youngest seemed to be the prettiest. Like all her brothers and sisters she was very religious and straight over from Ireland she threw herself into the church and looked to her faith for strength.

Sheila was there when Lily gave birth. You would think with the number of babies her mother had she would know, even in those days, about the birds and the bees or, to put it another way, seeing Lily have a baby you would think she could work out what caused it. How naïve can you be? The baby was a little girl, Lily called her Sheila, after her Auntie Sheila.

Lizzie and Mick were still coming to terms with the death of Jack. Sometimes it was unbelievably quiet in the cottage in the evenings. They had one son, Michael, at home and young Brendan was a great joy. Michael was a cripple. As a young boy he fell of his bicycle and hurt one leg so badly that it never grew. It was half the length of his good leg. Michael never married and he stayed at home all his life.

Brendan was growing fast. He had plenty of cousins to play with. Three of Lizzie and Mick's children were a spit away. Two had settled in Dublin, one in County Meath. All were quite close and all with families of their own. So Grandma and Grandpa's home was always full. Of the six children who had settled in England, one or other was always home. Now and then the children in England sent ten shillings, which pleased old Mick to bits. Sometimes, if times were good, he could stretch to a whiskey at Jim Burke's. Not a lot to ask when you worked hard all your life to bring up his large brood.

It was now 1934. Brendan was at school and Lizzie and Mick could take life a little easier. No more scrubbing floors for Lizzie or taking in washing. She made do with her piglets and her turkeys at Christmas. There was always post; so much news from that large brood of theirs. A letter arrived one particular day and Lizzie read the letter in her hand once, couldn't take in what it said and read it again. She was shocked to her very bones. Her baby, Sheila, only a teenager herself, was due to give birth. Sheila, the cleverest of the bunch. Lizzie had had high hopes for her. If any of her children were going to make it, it would be Sheila and now this dreadful, shocking news. Things couldn't be worse.

Time to get my coat on, thought Lizzie. This time she made the long weary journey to England alone. Lizzie was there a few days before the baby arrived. She had plenty of family to meet her in London and guide her on her way. There could be nothing worse for a girl than to have a baby out of wedlock. It brought shame and disgrace on her parents, her brother and sisters. No member of the family escaped the humiliation. The girl herself was a public sinner; the lowest of the low; the scum of the earth, only fit to be locked away in a loony bin which often happened.

Lizzie was glad to be there on time. She made it known it didn't alter her love for her daughter. Sheila was distressed. She didn't want the creature kicking in her tummy, but having to go through the ordeal of giving birth she didn't want any harm to come to it either. The lay workers who came in daily frightened the life out of the expectant mothers with their endless stories. They told them that if a nun took a dislike to them they wouldn't help them when they were giving birth. They wouldn't assist the baby either. According to the lay workers, many babies died. They also told the mothers sometimes the nuns had customers for the babies. As soon as they were born the baby was whipped away and the mother was told the baby had died. The lay workers alleged sometimes a nun had a baby by a priest. It didn't live; the life would be snuffed out of it and it was buried in the grounds. All these stories upset Sheila. She was glad to have her mother with her. It would be over Lizzie's dead body if anything happened to a grandchild of hers.

Lizzie stayed quietly and reassuringly with her daughter. Sheila had experienced a rough time at the convent and her mother found her changed, as if the very heart, soul and spirit had been knocked out of her. Lizzie would never know nor would she want to know or believe the dark side of the nuns and priests. Lizzie came from a time when it was unheard of to think badly of a man of God. You would rot in hell for eternity if such a thought crossed your mind.

When Sheila arrived at the convent she had this monster in her belly that wouldn't go away, how she hated it. She was shy, naïve and very frightened but she was a devout Catholic and was so grateful to be let in; she felt she was home. Like her mother, if anyone said a bad word about a priest or a nun, she would cut their tongue out. On her arrival Sheila was greeted by the Reverend Mother, she was hurriedly shown into a small room and told to sit down. Very few words were spoken and soon the Reverend Mother was joined by two more nuns. One nun was holding a very large pair of scissors and the second nun was holding a thick leather strap behind her back. Without opening her mouth to say a word to Sheila the first nun grabbed a handful of Sheila's beautiful long thick black hair and started to hack it off. Sheila screamed and lashed out to try to stop this nun touching her hair. A thick leather strap came thundering down on Sheila's arms and in total shock Sheila gave up the fight. She was then forced to undress and a large bandage was bound around her breasts. No mean feat because Sheila was at the front of the queue when breasts were handed out. Sheila had to dress in the uniform which was a dull brown and it was shaped more like a sack. And then she was put to work. No lazing around for a scumbag who had been with a man and brought all this shame and disgrace and ridicule upon the whole family. No member of the family escaped – they were all tarred with the same brush. Sheila a young teenage girl was going to work and pay for her sin and the nuns would see to it even if they had to beat her black and blue.

It was now March and it had been a freezing winter. In the early days, it had been Sheila's job to get up ten minutes before the others and fetch the water from the outside well. She had to fill six jugs and place them by the wash bowls for her room mates. She lit her candle at ten to six and made her way along the hall to the kitchen. As Sheila pushed the kitchen door open and lit the room up with her candle, she saw the floor change colour as the cockroaches darted between the floorboards.

The bell to get up rang at six. Before breakfast, it was Mass. Breakfast was at 8 a.m. It was always lukewarm porridge with lumps and either sugar or milk and always cocoa. Dinnertime the nuns boiled the potatoes in the dirt they were dug up in. Tea time it was bread and butter and Sundays it was bread and jam but no butter. If there was soup for a change it was disgusting, the smell made you sick. Days were spent working and praying, life outside had ended the day you entered the Convent. There was no relief from going to Mass, going to confessions, doing penance for your sins. The enormous area of floors in the Convent had to be scrubbed on your hands and knees. The buckets of water were heavy and had to be carried sometimes along long passages, enough to give a young girl a miscarriage if she was lucky. The huge cloths used to mop up the excess water were very hard to ring out, it made your fingers and wrists ache. All the time there was verbal abuse from the nuns. They walked around looking so pious in their habits, defying the girls to hesitate in their work for a moment. Talking was out of bounds but try as hard as the nuns could there were certain girls whose spirit couldn't be broken. But Sheila wasn't one of them, she was deep in self pity. She found it impossible to cope with the shame and it seemed the nuns treated her just as bad if not worse for giving up the fight. A moan of despair when a nun was within earshot and Sheila would feel the toe of a boot on her body. As the nuns passed they would murmur out loud – "Dirty, disgusting."

But Sheila preferred that to working in the laundry. Leaning over the big tubs of water washing all day with her big belly in the way made her back ache like crazy. Concentrating on not getting scalded with the hot water meant there wasn't time to think. Night times it was a relief to get to bed, just to lie down. If she did have the strength to think, her mind went back to that little cottage in Moortown. Her happy childhood seemed only yesterday; she was still only a child herself. She thought of the friends she had left behind, to seek this great new life. The boys who had chased her around the playground – she wondered what each and every one of them was doing now. If they knew the state she was in they would be so ashamed to even know her. They certainly wouldn't want to be her friend. How she wished she could put the clock back, sit by that big fire with her Mum and Dad and have a cuddle.

Life would never be the same again, this shame was something she wasn't going to be able to put behind her, it would stay with her all the days of her life. Utterly exhausted she slept, but however hard she slept when she opened her eyes in the morning it was still there. That lump was growing, Sheila felt so alone. She desperately missed all her brothers and sisters, she didn't think anyone could be so unhappy and not die of the pain. Each day got harder, the daily visits to the priest to be reminded of the filth you were and ask God to forgive you. The constant fear of the belt if by any chance the nuns thought you were showing them disrespect. The nuns didn't seem to care where it landed. Sheila got a few across the back of the head. One thing Sheila was sure of, when this was over if would be a long time before she ever went into a Catholic church again. She would renounce the Catholic faith with a vengeance. That would make her a complete outsider with her large family, they were all so devout. Her treatment by the priest and nuns had put her off the Catholic faith, a feeling that was to stay with her almost to her dying days.

It was March 14th, 1934, ten past one on a Wednesday morning. Time for me to make my entrance. After two days of labour I popped out. I wasn't weighed so I don't know if I was a small or a big baby. Uncle Pat arrived at the hospital. He wasn't a Merriman but he was family. He was married to Una, the youngest of Lizzie's children. Una and Pat were first cousins. His mother, Winifred, and Lizzie were sisters. Winifred lived in London and she sent Pat to help her sister across London with a newborn baby. Time for Grandma to wrap me up and take me away. I didn't have a mother and that was the way it was always going to be. Sheila would come home to see her parents and I would be ignored. Other than that, our paths would never cross. I still didn't have a name. As Grandma reached the door on her way out with me in her arms, Sheila, without a glance at me, called to her mother, "Call her 'Leila'."

Grandma had a horrendous journey home. It was freezing and the huge waves in the Irish Sea pounded the sides of the boat. It was late when Grandma reached Delvin. It would have to be Jim Burke's taxi out to the cottage. Lovely Uncle Tom was inside having a jar with Mick. He took me out of poor Lizzie's arms. She was exhausted and glad to sit down and relax. Mick got the kettle on straight away. Tom told me years later that I was blue with the cold when I reached Moortown and I cried most of the night. I couldn't be comforted. Perhaps I knew in the first days of my life the grief those two lovely people – my lovely Uncle Tom who was pacing the floor of the cottage with me in his arms and my wonderful Grandma who was resting, exhausted in the big armchair – were going to cause me. The two people who were closest to me on my first night in Moortown, the two people who cared most for me after Mick. Worn out and getting a bit agitated, it was Mick, the wise old owl, who came up with the recipe to quieten me. He opened a bottle of Guinness and put a few spoonfuls in my bottle with some milk. Soon I was fast asleep, wrapped up warmly and laid in a drawer. A little newborn baby. I like to think I was a sweet, warm, soft baby, like all babies. Usually they are cherished and bring such feelings of pride and joy. Sleeping soundly by the glow of the turf fire I had no idea the hate, shame, disgrace I had brought on my family. The wish by them that something would happen to me. Mick and Lizzie cared not an iota for the village gossip, nor, for that matter, their own sons and daughters. They would love and protect me as long as there was breath in their bodies.

It was unthinkable not to take a baby to the church to be baptised within days of its birth. If that baby had died without being baptised it would rot in hell. You would think the baby was a mass murderer. What kind of a religion is that? But then this was Ireland in the 1930s and the peasants, normal people like Mick and Lizzie, were kept at heel by fear. So it was that arrangements were made to have me baptised. For Lizzie and Mick the question was what to call me. Sheila had whispered "Call her Leila." Leila it was and would always be. "But is that a real name?" Lizzie asked Mick. They both agreed I was a true Merriman, what or who the other half was, nobody knew or nobody cared. Lizzie decided to call me after herself – Elizabeth Winifred. So that was settled, Elizabeth Winifred Merriman was the full name given to the scrap of unwanted humanity they held in their arms. It's a good name, Lizzie thought, a lifetime has been lived in that name, a lot of history has passed, I'm giving you, Leila, the only thing I have to give you. I'm giving you my name, wear it with pride. As for the birth certificate, it would be put away in a drawer to collect dust forever. No one would ever guess in a million years the trauma that would unfold twenty-two years later when that piece of paper had the cobwebs blown off. I'm only grateful that Grandad didn't have to witness my distress. Grandad died just after my twenty-first birthday. Sadly, my lovely Grandma died when I was quite young.

As for Sheila, she never felt so alone. There was no one in her large family she could talk to. Her treatment by the priest and nuns would stay with her forever. Lily still provided her with a roof over her head but she was most uncharitable about the whole episode. Stuttering, worse than usual, she finally got the words out.

"I hope someone has d-d-d-drowned that f-f-f-fucking b-b-b-bastard."

Sheila was going to forget the whole thing. Everyone knew, so what. Who the father was nobody knew and nobody cared. Nobody was the least bit interested in that baby. The only comment they would make would be one day if they heard something had happened to IT. They would raise three cheers if someone was responsible for ending an unwanted and hated baby's life.

Sheila now had to move on with her life. She got a job as a live-in barmaid at the Beehive Hotel in Beehive Lane, Gants Hill. She was to spend the next ten years there.

I soon became Granddad's little darling. Now a mature man, he had the time he didn't have as a young man. In those days, babies were arriving almost every year and he was stretched trying to feed them. When I got to walking and would run after him, he had time to slow down and wait for me. He would put his big, rough hand down and reaching up as far as I could I would hold it and we would walk along together. Michael didn't mind the two children either. Although he was a bachelor and had no interest in kids, he accepted us.

Michael's accident as a young man left him with one good leg and a stump which came down as far as his good knee. When he walked he looked really uncomfortable. He would put his stump to the ground and his whole body would come down with it. Then he would put his good leg forward and he would rise up. I suppose he got used to it. It was that way all his life. He had a specially adapted bike with one short peddle which he rode everywhere. He earned a small living mending boots and shoes. He had the front small bedroom as his own. All that was in there was a single bed, a chest of drawers and a few shelves. The shelves were stacked with boots and shoes and all around the walls were piles of boots and shoes. They must have been stacked two or three feet high. People from miles around brought their boots and shoes to be mended and couldn't afford to collect them. Over the years, they had died off and the pile got bigger and bigger. Michael sat on the floor, back up against the bed with a shoe horn on the floor between his legs mending shoes all day. He could never say no to mums who desperately wanted a pair of boots mended for the kids to go to school and couldn't afford to pay or a man who needed his boots to go to work. The few who did pay paid for those who didn't. He always managed to get enough money in to buy the leather, nails and glue to continue his work.

He was always wearing the same grey mac and cap. As long as he had the money to buy his baccy to roll his own and have an occasional night out at Jim Burke's he was happy. I'm told on his rare nights out at Jim Burke's he liked a few pints with a few whiskies. He would ride his bike the three miles home singing his head off. Many a time the neighbours fetched him out of a ditch. When he fell he didn't bother to get up. He carried on singing until he was rescued. He lived on in the cottage after Lizzie and Mick died and managed on his own until he died in his eighties.

Sheila had settled in well at the Beehive Hotel. It was owned by a Jewish couple, Solly and May Jacobs. They never had any children and they took young Sheila under their wing. They would have no idea the trauma she had been through and she wasn't ever going to mention it. The past was behind her. She worked hard and started to enjoy life. She was still only a teenager and with a pay packet for the first time. She could go out and buy herself bits and pieces. Sheila was a beautiful girl and life was going to be good.

She threw herself into pub life, made many friends and enjoyed the camaraderie of the customers. One young girl, more or less the same age as Sheila, became a special friend. She would pop in early evening for a stiff drink before starting her night shift as a lady of the night. Sheila thought she was so pretty, fair-haired with bright blue eyes and the loveliest of smiles, she always smelt divine. She always wore feathers, buckles and belts, beads, long or short, bits of fur or fluff. Sheila being a conservative dresser was quite fascinated by her. This particular evening she strode in as usual, popped herself up on to a bar stool, placed her elbows on the counter and with her chin in her hands she chatted away as usual, privately, to Sheila. "I'm absolutely pissed off tonight," she exclaimed, "I've had to see to a Catholic priest this afternoon, he got on my f-ing nerves fiddling with his dress coat, I thought he was never going to get it out. All the Catholic priests I service are the same, they piss about." Unknown to the two girls a customer was ear-wigging; he was so appalled at the suggestion that a Catholic priest would use the services of a prostitute, he went straight to the police. The young girl was chased out of town. Sheila could believe it was true, she had experienced the darker side of the Catholic church. She knew the nuns and priests were capable of anything. But she knew enough to hold her council; she

had too much to lose and besides she was no match for the
Church or the police.

Solly had a brother, Jack, with a fruiterer's and
greengrocer's business nearby. He was married, but unlike
Solly he had a family – one daughter called Elizabeth, and
his wife was expecting their second. The baby was a boy and
he was called John. He was six months younger than me.
Sadly, Jack's wife died leaving him with a daughter aged
four, a baby, a house to run and a business. He couldn't cope.
He gave up his home and his business, farmed his daughter
out with her aunt and moved into the Beehive Hotel with
baby John. There was plenty of room. He had a job in the
Hotel and with the help of Solly and May he could bring the
baby up.

Jack was thirty years older than Sheila. He was a larger
than life character weighing more than sixteen stone. He was
a very worldly man, silver-tongued, absolutely charming and
gentle and kind. His passion was racing, mainly greyhounds
and horses. Sheila was completely captivated by him and
when I was two they married less than eighteen months after
the death of his wife. They popped over to Ireland for a few
days to see Lizzie and Mick. Sheila was very proud of her
husband and she paraded him around. There were drinks all
round at Jim Burke's and they took Grandad racing. When it
was time to say goodbye, there was hardly a glance at me.
We were, in all sense and purposes, two strangers. Sheila had
one ambition in life now, she was a wife. She was never
going to be the wicked stepmother. She adored young John,
loved him as her own. Between her and Jack, Solly and May
he was thoroughly spoiled. He was the only baby she ever
had.

The Merrimans were known for their pale complexions.
Their almost porcelain skin had little colour in it and they all
had the same blue eyes with straight hair. I had a mop of
curls, deep hazel eyes, rosy cheeks and skin that went golden

brown when the sun shone. I could have been half Mediterranean if anyone had thought about it, but nobody did. Life was just wonderful for me. I had plenty of cousins to play with. Go to the crossroads, turn left, a lovely long walk through the countryside lived one set of cousins, on a farm with lots of animals. Turn right at the crossroads and less than a quarter of a mile lived Tom with his three boys, Michael, Sean and Tommy and further along was Christie and Nancy with their two children. Uncle Tom was closest to me and was to play a major part in my life later. When I met him on the road there was always a ha'penny for sweets.

I grew up very fast and soon learned Grandad's skills. When Mick went to the River Deel to fish it was my job to hold the special net he had to catch minnows. The river was wide, quite deep – six feet – and was very fast flowing. There was an abundance of fish. There were perch, pike, trout, salmon, tench, roach and eel. Over the river was a large bridge. Grandad chiselled out three holes in the stone to make steps so I could climb up and, holding on as tight as I could, look over and watch the river flow. If the swans or ducks were swimming past it was lovely. Later when I was older I would catch the eels myself. I would cut them round their throat, rub salt on the cut and then they would skin easily. The skins would be hung up to dry and would provide extra shoe laces.

Dysart lake covered thirty-five acres. I would rush along the path between the bracken through the wood and scramble into the boat ahead of Grandad. It was lovely out on the lake and as I got bigger I would sit beside Grandad and take an oar.

Quite often Grandad had to go into Delvin on an errand. Sometimes he would take me, sitting in front of him on the horse. Sometimes he was easily led astray and would decide to stay longer in Jim Burke's having a drink. When that happened he would put me up on the horse's back, my little legs only long enough to reach across the horse's broad back and giving the horse a smack and telling it to "Get" it would set off home. I had to lie almost flat to reach its mane to hold on to prevent me falling off. When Grandad got home he would have a bottle of Guinness in each pocket for later. When he did open them he would get my cup and pour some in then top it up with milk. "Best drink you'll ever drink, Guinness and milk," he'd say, "put hairs on your chest."

Everyone – man, woman and child – had to help with the harvest. It was my job to walk around after the harvester rescuing all the baby mice and their nests that the harvester had disturbed. At the end of the day I had probably hundreds of baby mice in an old tin bath. I lovingly gave them to Grandad because he knew a place where they would be safe. If only I had known what really happened to them. Ah, the innocence of children.

Days spent in the bog, cutting turf, were great. The big black pig's pot full of colcannon was put on the cart for dinner. No plates were packed. Everyone sat around the pot with spoons and dug in and ate their fill. Tea was served in jam jars with string tied around the neck and made into a handle. That was really glamorous when you're a kid, something you remember all your life. The first thing I had to do before I could play was fill the baskets with the Franghan berries for Grandma. That's the English pronunciation although there is no official translation. The name of the berries in Gaelic is "fraocan" – they are a wholeberry. They were absolutely delicious.

When the baskets were full I could play. All we kids had were some sticks for bats, a ball and our skipping ropes. Sometimes a couple of the grown-ups would get out a long thick rope and turn it for us. Perhaps there would be as many as eight of us skipping in the rope at the same time. It was just great fun, running free, jumping over the holes where the turf had been cut. We certainly didn't have any problems sleeping at nights.

At one time, Mick had a still in the bogs where he brewed his own poteen. On one occasion, it sprung a leak and the wild geese got to it. They were rolling around on the ground legless.

It was always my job to stone the currants, raisins and sultanas for Grandma when she was cooking. No way would I pop one in my mouth and eat it. No! That would be breaking a trust and I liked Grandma being able to trust me. When I was big enough I could churn the milk to make butter. While Grandma patted the butter into about half pounds, I ran out to the rhubarb patch and picked the biggest leaves. The butter would then be wrapped in the leaves and stored.

One thing that upset me every year was Grandad killing a big pig. He would give it a blow to the forehead and knock it out and then cut its throat. It seemed to me the pig made an awful noise. Grandma had all the big enamel bowls on the ground and all the blood was caught in them to make black puddings. The pig's guts were washed out and used for skins for the puddings. One half of the pig was salted and wrapped in straw and stored under the dining room table. When you sat down at the table your feet would rest on the pig. During the winter months when grandma wanted some bacon she would just lift the straw and cut off a large chunk.

Basically, I had nothing to do all day but play. The acre and a half was my doll's house. I'd be out there for hours, amusing myself, making up my own games. One day I came rushing into the cottage: "Granny, Granny, Granny the cat's had three kittens and the other one won't come out!"

Wiping her hands on her apron Grandma was anxious. "What are you up to now?" she asked kindly as she came with me to have a look. There was the cat trying to give birth to her fourth kitten.

"Where are the other kittens?" asked Grandma.

"They're here, Grandma," I said.

I had taken each kitten as it was born, dressed it in my dolls' clothes and put it in my dolls' pram ready to take them for a walk. But I was being held up, the cat wouldn't have the next kitten. I loved my dolls' pram. It was a wooden box with a handle so I could pull it along. It never had any wheels and my dolls' clothes were bits of material. I can't remember ever having a nice doll but the pram was still magic.

Picking each little newborn kitten up, Grandma unwrapped it and put it back with its mother. Kindly, she told me I mustn't ever take a baby away from its mother. Without their mother they would die. She told me to leave the cat in peace to have her kittens and not to disturb her again, but to peep quietly from time to time and when they were bigger they would love me to play with them. I was too young to wonder if I had a mother when I was born.

The big black pot was the most used pot. All the cooking was done in it. If we were having chicken, Grandma would pick up her big knife, wander out into the yard sort a chicken out, grab hold of its head and cut it off. It would be plucked, cleaned, and popped into the pot with lots of vegetables and would stew over the open fire. Friday was always fish (that was the religious teaching). You wouldn't dare eat anything else. You would probably go to hell in the 1930s if you ate anything other than fish in Ireland on a Friday. When dinner was over, the pigswill would be cooked in the pot and on Friday night the pot would have a good wash out and I would be popped into the pig's pot to be washed.

Weekends, Grandma sometimes went to visit her nearby sons or daughters. It was really exciting walking home in the dark. There was no gas or electricity to light the way, only the light from the stars and the moon. Grandma would tell me stories about the leprechauns, the little people, and the fairies people had at the bottom of their gardens. One night we had stopped walking to listen to some sounds. The moon was very bright and glancing down at my feet quick as a flash I saw a little leprechaun running away – really I did! I don't think I'd had any Guinness in my milk that day!

Finally, the day arrived when I had to go to school. It had been a wonderful five years thanks to Mick and Lizzie. No child could have been more loved or well looked after. I don't think there had been one unhappy moment. I'd never had a smack, there wasn't any need, I was as good as gold and was as happy as the day was long. On my first day Grandma took me in the horse and cart. She rode up to the gate with me sitting by her side, her head held high. I hate to think she felt ashamed. Grandma had sixteen of her children go to that school; these days her grandchildren were there. The teaching staff knew Lizzie well. That first day I sat on the floor behind the blackboard and cried all day. Why behind the blackboard? Perhaps I thought no one could see me there.

Ballinvalley School was built in 1900. It was a two-storey building with a big yard and resting in a few acres. The upstairs had two large rooms which were for the boys. Downstairs were also two rooms for the girls. The infants were in one room and the rest of the school in the other room. There was one teacher for each room. One class would stand up in front and the teacher would give them their lesson. Then they would go to the back and sit down and get on with their work. The next class would come forward for their lesson and they would go to the back. So it went on until everyone was working.

There was no doubt I was a clever child. I'm saying this now not to be big-headed but to get the story right. I soon settled down, very good in class, well behaved. It wasn't a problem walking the three miles to school every day. In the summer we went barefoot as there wasn't money for shoes. The only time I knew fear was when I came across the tinkers camping on the roadside. I would walk past quickly, pressing myself as close as possible to the far edge. I was always afraid they would take me away and keep me. I was relieved when I got past without being snatched.

Grandma was born in Dublin and had made a couple of journeys home. This time she took me with her. We caught the bus in Delvin and travelled the fifty miles to Dublin. Walking along O'Connell Street she said to me, "You know, Leila, nowhere in the world will you find girls as pretty as here in Dublin," and she sang sweetly:

> *In Dublin's fair city*
> *Where the girls are so pretty*
> *I first set my eyes on sweet Molly Malone.*
> *As she wheels her wheelbarrow*
> *Through streets broad and narrow*
> *Crying, cockles and mussels alive, alive O!*

On the street corners ladies stood with broad leather straps round their necks supporting baskets on their front full of oranges. They would cry, "Lovely juicy oranges, tuppence each. Come on, Missus, buy a lovely juicy orange. Tuppence each the oranges." I didn't have an orange but I did climb to the top of Nelson's Column. It isn't there now, it was blown up, more's the pity, because from the top when you are six years old you can see the whole world.

Shortly after I began school, the Second World War started. Gerald (Gareth) the eleventh born of Lizzie and Mick's children had joined up as soon as war was declared. Auntie Una's husband, Pat, had joined up; Tom up the road felt he wanted to do his bit so he volunteered and still remembering her baby, Jack, Lizzie prayed that her family would be safe. It was only 1940 when Lizzie and Mick received the telegram telling them that Gerald had been killed. Lizzie was heartbroken. She looked at Brendan, the boy she had driven into Mullingar to rescue all those years back. Thank God she had him now, she would always have a part of her son as long as she had him. He had always been a great comfort to her and he was especially precious now. She hugged him close as the tears flooded down her cheeks.

"I'll never get over this," said Lizzie. "My heart is broken," and she never did.

Una, in London, like millions of parents were concerned for the safety of her only child. She brought Maureen over to Moortown to spend the war years with Mick and Lizzie. Maureen is four years younger than me. She seemed such a little tot to be left when she arrived. We were the very best of friends. Much later when I married, Maureen was my bridesmaid and she is godmother to both my children. That shows the affection I have for her. But as this story unfolds, we were just two little girls, one with a mummy and daddy and one without. Nothing was ever said to prepare me for the nightmare that lay ahead. But then how could anyone know.

The next big event in my life was my first Holy Communion at seven. I absolutely loved the Catholic faith like everyone in Ireland in those days. I was totally indoctrinated. I knew and loved the Bible and would read it as often as I had time. So preparation for the big day was easy for me. I was playing happily at home one day when Brendan came along. I suppose he must have been six years older than me. He was a very tall boy, fairly well built, strong and muscular. His skin was rough almost flaky and he had hands the size of a bat. He had a lovely smile with piercing blue eyes and jet-black hair. I had always loved him to bits, we were the two Merriman outcasts and we were always together. I followed him around like a puppy. Brendan was a very good boxer and I mean really good. I believe he was a champion and once knocked out an Irish champion. He was always shunting around on his feet, sniffing and snarling and punching the air.

"Would you like to come into the barn and practise sparring with me?" he asked.

I was happy to tag along with him, but as soon as we got there he got this thing out and weed into a cup.

"Drink this," he said handing me the cup.

"No, it's fresh wee. You've just wee'd into the cup and it's still steaming," I said to him.

"Drink it or I'll use your head for a punch bag," he said.

I drank every drop. I wasn't physically sick but for years I felt sick. I could always taste it in my mouth. I hated him and wished him in hell.

At school we practised making a confession ready for the big day. We had to kneel down in the box in front of a small window with a net through which you can see the outline of the priest side-face on, make the sign of the cross and say, "Bless me, Father, for I have sinned. I confess to you Father Almighty that I have sinned exceedingly in thought, word and deed. Through my fault, through my fault, through my most grievous fault." If you remembered all that load of rubbish as a seven-year-old you would do well. Our training made this a very important part of our life. It was a very humbling experience to get down on your knees in front of another human being and confess.

The day came for my first confession. I can't explain the sheer reverence of the occasion. I was totally in awe of the priest. I wasn't really sure what a sin was so, like a silly seven-year-old, I half asked, "Is it a sin to hate someone and wish them in hell?" What I didn't realize was of course the priest could see me and knew who I was and what I didn't know – because it hadn't as yet raised its ugly head – I was the village bastard and I shouldn't even be breathing. His sharp reply startled me. "You are the one going to hell if you talk like that," he said, almost as if my place was already booked. "Say three Hail Marys, three Our Fathers and three Glory Be's.

I left the Confessional Box confused, there hadn't been a word of gentleness or a word of kindness in his voice. I hadn't imagined a priest being unkind, they were all saints in my small mind, but I knew I had been put in my place, whatever it was and I was very sad. I knelt down to say my penance and on a day when I should have felt at peace with the world I was upset. I was the one feeling sick from drinking the wee, yet here I was feeling in the wrong. That can't be right I told myself, someone should have a word with God. I looked all around at my classmates, they were all smiling and looking pleased with themselves. I wondered what they had confessed, perhaps one of them had pulled someone's hair or poked their tongue out at someone. Even at seven before I had made my first Holy Communion I had a feeling things weren't as they should be, I felt distant from my classmates.

Everyone had to take a test to show they had the knowledge to receive their first Holy Communion. I had the highest marks with one or two others, we had to wear a different coloured ribbon from the other girls. I would be at the top, or near, at whatever I did; I was as bright as a button but it seemed even at that tender age fate was conspiring against me. Something I wouldn't understand for years to come. The incident in the confessional box didn't spoil my day. Grandma had done me proud, I had a white dress, white shoes and socks and a lovely veil. It hurts me to my very bones now when I think of my poor dear lovely Grandma and how ashamed she must have been of me. But she couldn't give in, she had to brazen it out. That little village in the 1930s, how they must have talked.

Chapter Three

Grandma was busy early, it was a special day, my eighth birthday. She would probably have cooked me a special googli (my name for an egg) for breakfast. That meant she would have gone out to the hen house and got the newest laid egg. She would have tied brightly coloured rags around the egg and then boiled it. The dye from the rags would stain the eggshell and there would be the prettiest, brightly coloured egg.

Lovely Uncle Tom up the road was fighting in the war. When he was free there would be something from him. Whatever he got for his three sons he got a fourth for me, even if it was only a slice of white bread. Can you believe he bought me a slice of white bread? Have you ever seen anything like a slice of white bread? I hadn't. Spread with freshly churned butter and newly made jam, it was delicious.

One thing you could be sure of there was never a word, card or present from Sheila. At eight years of age I was a very happy secure child. I didn't have a care in the world. Good, extra good at school, I had never caused one moment's anxiety anywhere and had been an absolute joy to my grandparents. What I didn't realize was the tower of strength my grandma was for me. While she stood tall and proud, sheltering and protecting me, no one would touch me. What I didn't realize was my days were numbered. As she fussed about on my eighth birthday, little did I know my wonderful grandma was going to have a sudden heart attack and die. It would send me on a road that was to lead me to hell. The priest was right when I made my first confession when he said, "You are the one going to hell." I didn't want to get there but I did get there. It would be fifty years before I found peace again.

Sheila was now in her mid-twenties and had been at the Beehive eight years. She was a very good looking woman, stunning rather than pretty. She was fairly tall and wore her jet-black hair long, almost down to her waist. She had a gift of knowing how to talk to people. It didn't matter who came into the hotel. It didn't matter what part of the world they came from. It didn't matter what their race, religion or customs were, she would know about their ways and would be able to talk to them. There was an air about her, an air of class, she could put on the voice of a lady and the act to perfection. She was very, very pro-Jewish and defended them on every corner.

She and Jack had become a very glamorous couple. No doubt life behind the bar was hard work but she played even harder, ably assisted by Jack. She was even more involved in gambling than he was. Days off they would get a taxi from Gants Hill to Bray where sister Lily now lived. After a visit to the hairdressers the taxi would continue on to Ascot for a day's racing. After dinner it was home by taxi. There was always a gin and tonic in her hand. Sheila could hold her own with the best of them when it came to drink. Afternoons off would be a trip to the theatre in London. She loved clothes and although she didn't have lots and lots, they were of the best and she only shopped for clothes in the Jewish shops. Eight years on she never gave a thought to me and was happy to leave it that way.

It was a Saturday. Lizzie decided she needed to go to church and pray. Leaving Maureen with Mick, we set out. She seemed tired and weary. When we got to the church she walked right up to the front row. I knelt down beside her and was quickly in prayer. Giving me a nudge, Grandma asked me to go and light a candle for her. I was right in the middle of prayer and didn't want to, not just at that moment.

"If," said Lizzie, "you are going to be naughty and play me up, I shall go home, I shall die and I shall leave you."

It could only be the second time in her life Lizzie had been unkind. With a gentle push, I went forward. Putting the money in the box, I took a candle and lit it. Then I walked slowly back to my grandma and knelt down close to her. I couldn't ever remember a time when my grandma had been cross with me. I looked up at her and snuggled close for forgiveness. That was the last recollection I have of my beloved grandma. It was the thought that was to stay with me always.

When we got home Uncle Christie arrived to take Maureen and I to stay with him and Auntie Nancy and their two children. We loved being there. Their big front room had no furniture, just a playpen in the middle, bare floorboards and toys everywhere. The four of us could play and scream to our hearts' content. It was a two-storey house and half way up the stairs was an alcove, a wonderful place to sit. Even in those days I was a dreamer. I sat up there alone for ages playing with my dolls. I was sitting on the grass outside playing and I realized someone was standing in front of me, their shadow fell across me. Looking up I saw this strange woman and without a word or a smile she held out a purse on a long gold chain. It was white plastic with pale and dark pink roses. I put up my hand and took it and thanked her. Without a word she walked away. I learnt afterwards it was my Auntie Sheila. Even at the young age I was I sensed her coldness. I didn't like her at all.

Christie was the first born of Lizzie and Mick's large brood. He was so strong he could do the work of a man when he was fourteen. He joined the army and didn't like it at all. Right through the war, he supervised fifty men in the bogs of Coolronan, County Meath. He was very involved in sport, always playing handball. At lunchtime he would allow the men to let off steam. Someone always had a ball for a kick about. He would make a makeshift ring because there were always a few pairs of boxing gloves around with Brendan in the family. Christie would be the timekeeper if there were any takers for a knock about in the ring. Sadly Christie died later, a victim of cancer, and Brendan dug his grave as a mark of his love for this man.

After a few days, it was time for Maureen and I to go home. Grandma wasn't there, she had gone to heaven. She had done what she said she would do – die and leave me. I can't think I was that naughty. In fact, I can't think I was naughty at all. I asked God what I had done that was so bad that my wonderful grandma had died and left me. I was heartbroken. I knew that day a light had gone out in my life that would never be rekindled. I learnt that Sheila had been home for two days. She couldn't afford any more time, it was more important to be at the Beehive. She was on the boat returning to England when she got the news that her mother had died. Una was seriously ill in hospital in London. It was six weeks before she was strong enough to be told the sad news.

Grandad now had two little girls to care for. He set about the task willingly, we weren't a bit of bother to him. As soon as Una was fit to travel, she came home to convalesce and get away from the London bombing. It was almost a full house again – Grandad, Michael, Brendan, Una, Maureen and me. There still wasn't any running water in the cottage or a toilet. When it was toilet time, you would go out and find a bush to squat behind. Grass or leaves would act as toilet paper. In the winter or when it was raining, there was a rush for the hen house. That was life in those days, everyone was in the same boat.

It was September, time for Maureen to start school. Una had a word with me. "Now, Leila, I expect you to look out for Maureen on the way to school and on the way home and during the day." At the crossroads we met Michael, Sean and

Tommy. We Merrimans were a crowd on our own. In the evenings, I would read to Maureen. I could say reading was my strong subject but every subject was my best. I missed Grandma, but life went on and Auntie Una was good to me. I loved her till the day she died. Una adored Maureen, as all mothers are supposed to love their children.

So it was I delivered Maureen home safe one afternoon. I might have dragged her through a hedge, ran her through some puddles but I had looked after her. Una had a surprise for her. She had made Maureen a dress. It had a flared skirt and all around the hem Una had sewn different coloured buttons. There were red buttons, blue ones, pink, white, yellow, brown. I had never seen such a lovely dress. I was so envious. I would love someone to make me a pretty dress.

I was still sitting there with my mouth open, dribbling, when Grandad shouted it was time for me to go and fetch the cows. It was just half a mile or so down the road. I knew our cows. We had three at the time for milk and butter. Always careful to shut the big gate after me, I started walking behind the cows as they made their way home. I always plaited their tails, just time to plait all three before we reached the cottage. This particular afternoon as I picked a tail up to plait I said to one cow (I don't know what I would have done if it had answered), but I said to it, "You know Maureen has a mummy and daddy, now I think about it, all my cousins have mummies and daddies, all my friends at school have mummies and daddies, I wonder how I was born without a mummy?"

The penny had dropped. For the first time in my young life, I knew I was different. It had to come sooner or later. That dress with the buttons had made it come all too soon.

Evenings Grandad sat on a bench by the fire. Maureen and I stood on the bench each side of him. We used to spit on his bald head and try to wet his little wisps of hair and make ringlets. He wasn't a bit bothered by us. He would put up with all our tricks. He would tell us stories. We knew they were stories, not true, but we still loved to hear them. That's it, I said to myself, I've got a good idea, I'll make up a story about my mummy and daddy. Of course it probably didn't help the story with them being missionaries in China and trying to bring Christianity to the country. My classmates turned on me, called me a liar and wouldn't speak to me. All I wanted was to be like them. I didn't want a new bike or fancy presents. I just wanted to be the same as them.

After a couple of days being sent to Coventry, I was quite upset. Getting home that evening I saw Auntie Una's red bead necklace on the dressing table. I wonder, I thought, if I take the necklace to school and give it to someone, will they play with me? Una missed the necklace and went mad. I don't know what I expected her to do, maybe tell me to get the necklace back and give me a good smack or tell Grandad to speak to me and ask him to give me a slap. That would be a waste of time, Grandad would rather lose both arms than smack me. So, what did she do? Firstly, she wrote to all the aunts and uncles in England saying I was nothing more than a liar and a thief. Then she went to the Headmistress, Miss Fitzsimmons. Now Miss Fitzsimmons had known me longer than Auntie Una. She knew me as a baby when Grandma carried me in her arms into church; a small village, she had seen me grow up. I had been in her school from the age of five. Never once did I have to be spoken to for being naughty. She knew my grandma had just died. What did this good, holy, kind, loving, Catholic lady do? It wasn't to take me aside and ask me if I had a problem and was there anything she could do to help. No! This loving, compassionate, understanding lady made me stand in front of the whole school every morning and say, "I promise I shall try not to steal anything or tell any lies today," as if I were a habitual liar and a thief. I will never know why Una did that. I could well have done without it. I hated the teacher and wished her in hell. I can't do that, I told myself, or else I'll go to hell. So what, I said to myself. What about the priest, I asked myself, I can't tell him he will send me away with a flea in my ear. What about confessions, I asked myself. I'll have to go "LIE" I told myself, make my confession up. So this was my Catholic faith breaking down.

Weeks had passed. I was still going through the total humiliation of saying my piece in front of the school and I felt totally degraded. It had been a particularly cold morning and, after a three mile walk without gloves, my hands were frozen. Returning to my spot in class I said something to a girl behind.

"What did you say?" bellowed Miss Fitzsimmons.

The shock of her outburst and the suddenness of it frightened me to death.

"I c-can't remember," I stuttered.

If my life depended on it, I honestly couldn't remember. She had frightened me so much my brain had gone dead.

"Very well," she said, "Step up here. Hold your hand out," she said, stroking the cane.

Even today, I can remember looking into her face and pleading, "Please, Miss, I honestly can't remember."

I held out my little hand, red with the cold, I could hardly straighten my fingers out they were so frozen, and the cane came swishing down.

"Go back to your place," I was ordered coldly. I held my head high and wouldn't cry. I couldn't wait to sit down and put my fingers between my knees for a bit of warmth and prayed they would stop stinging. I felt so humiliated and degraded and suddenly felt so alone. That witch wouldn't have done that if my grandma was still alive. Grandma wouldn't hold with old spinsters beating and abusing little children. Grandma would have had her guts for garters.

The witch then turned her attention to the school bully – of course she didn't know she was the school bully. This child had respectable parents, they were virtually neighbours of hers; dealing with her Miss Fitzsimmons didn't have to deal with filthy little bastards. What she didn't know was this sweet little girl would sort out a couple of younger girls. She would give them a whole two pence and send them into the sweet shop. She would tell them to spend no more than one penny, but to mess about doing it. Give her time while they kept the shopkeeper busy to nip around the back and steal lemonade, sweets and biscuits. Then, with one of my cousins and others, she played truant.

"Why weren't you at school yesterday?" asked Miss Fitzsimmons.

"Please, Miss, I was sick," came the reply; butter wouldn't melt in her mouth.

"Where's your note?" was the next question.

"Please, Miss, Mum was busy and didn't have time to write one."

"Very well," said the silly teacher, "try to remember next time."

"Yes, Miss," she said, laughing at the stupidity of the woman.

So, you can be a bully, a real thief, a liar and play truant and get a pat on the back. But then I didn't know, that little girl might be all those things but she had a mummy and a daddy. One thing I knew I never told tales, and hated people who did. So I would take my punishment even if others were getting away with murder.

I wasn't too happy with Maureen. Isn't life cruel – someone upsets you, so you pass it on. When we got to the hedge, where we cut through the fields to save walking up to the junction and along the Castlepolland Road, I took off. I ran as fast as I could and left her. Mind you, Maureen couldn't come to any harm, she couldn't say "Leila" and used to called me "Diddly". All I could hear was, "Diddly, I can't keep up; Diddly, you're going too fast." Bless her little heart, she was a sweetie.

One morning I stumbled over something and, picking myself up, I walked back to kick what I had stumbled on. It was a bird's nest with five baby birds squawking their heads off for food. There was no sign of their parents. I waited around for a little while, couldn't wait any longer, I didn't want to be late. I couldn't leave them there to starve to death so, in my caring way, decided to take the bird's nest to school. I placed it carefully in my satchel. At break time and lunchtime I'd feed the birds and save their lives. Once the class had settled at their desks, there was quiet and suddenly this awful noise could be heard. Miss Fitzsimmons' ears were flapping.

"What's that noise?" she asked as she rose and started walking round the desks. She stopped at mine.

"Open your satchel, Leila," she asked. I stood up and placed my satchel on my desk and opened it as requested and there was the bird's nest with five baby birds.

"Different," she said. I thought she was going to explode. She was the type to go bright red. It started at her chest and travelled up over her chin to her hairline.

"Get back over those fields as fast as your legs can carry you. Put the nest in the exact spot where you found it and when you get back the cane will be waiting for you."

It seemed to me nowadays everything I did was followed by a question, "What mischief are you up to now?" followed by the cane. It had nothing to do with my behaviour. The truth was, I was breathing and good holy Catholics wouldn't tolerate children like me, a known bastard. They were just filth and Miss Fitzsimmons certainly didn't want me in her school but she had to put up with me and she was going to make sure I paid for the disgrace I had brought on my family.

Things didn't seem so prosperous now Grandma was dead. Grandad didn't seem the same. He missed his Lizzie so much. In the summer we got cuts and bruises on our bare feet from the unmade roads. I was sitting on the front door step snivelling one day when Grandad came and asked me what the matter was.

"I've got a stone bruise on my foot," I cried.

"Wait a minute," said Grandad, "I'll get a pin and burst it, get the water out."

"There isn't any water in it, Grandad," I said.

"Well, bloody well sit there until there is!" growled Grandad.

The war was intensifying and Sheila and Jack, rather than have their darling John evacuated to God knows where, sent him to Grandad. John was six months younger than me. He had been totally pampered and spoilt. The first shock for him was to find himself, a Jewish boy in a Catholic country, the only one at the time. He was appalled by the living conditions. He had to share a bed with Michael and on Michael's nights out at Jim Burke's he would roll into bed blind drunk and serenade him most of the night.

John was appalled by our toilet arrangements and our general living conditions, kneeling on the floor and washing ourselves in the pig's pot with not much privacy. But the worst thing for him, and the one thing he wouldn't tolerate, was walking three miles to school. He wrote home to his father for a bicycle. Now it was unfortunate John had a nose that covered most of his face, a lovely Jewish nose, and sadly the kids took the mickey out of him. If he had peddled past on a bike when the little tots had to walk, the children really would have taken the piss.

John didn't stay long, the experience scarred him for life. He returned to the comfort of the Beehive. He couldn't cope with the shocking living conditions in Moortown. In the short time John was with us he was baptised a Roman Catholic, made his first Holy Communion and was confirmed on the same day as myself. My confirmation day confession was a pack of lies. I don't remember what I confessed to the priest but I made up something. Grandad did his best. I had a white dress and veil and black shoes. Fancy having to wear black shoes on your confirmation day. Grandad said it was bad enough having to buy me shoes, he certainly wasn't going to buy an unsuitable pair of white shoes. A lady in Delvin stopped me to say how nice my socks were. Was she being funny? I don't know, but I looked down at my socks and I realized my legs were filthy. I don't suppose I had washed them for weeks. I felt so ashamed.

Grandad didn't have patience any more. In the old days, the pig's extra piglets were brought indoors and hand-reared by Grandma. Now Grandad couldn't be bothered so he drowned them in a bucket of water. I hated seeing that. In the two years since Grandma died, my life had changed dramatically. Out of the blue one day I got my very own letter from Uncle Pat. It was the first time in my life I had a letter of my own. Una suggested I write back. I sat up at the big table, my feet resting on the half pig wrapped in straw, and wrote to Pat with all my news. When I had finished, I signed the letter *Love from Maureen*. Una wanted to know why I had done that. I replied, "I didn't think Uncle Pat would want to get a letter from me. Nobody would want to get a letter from me."

That sums up the low esteem I now had of myself. My confidence was lower than a worm. My mind was very confused. I was a totally disturbed child. I didn't have a mummy or daddy, foster or adoptive parents, brothers or sisters. I was alone. I had no one. Even my wonderful Catholic faith had let me down. I felt all the confidence I had when Grandma was alive had been beaten out of me at Ballinvalley School.

My class had been asked to sing with the church choir one morning for a special occasion. We all rehearsed the hymns for weeks. Finally, the morning arrived and the class was about to leave to make the trip to the church. Miss Fitzsimmons stood up and made a point of calling out the names of the girls in my class but omitted to call my name out. I ran up to her and reminded her she had forgotten me.

"Sit down," she said.

"Please, Miss," I pleaded, "I know the words," thinking perhaps, for some reason, she might have thought I didn't know the words. What else could it be?

"Sit down," she said again.

I was the only girl in the class not to go to church that morning. I thought about my thick curly hair. It probably hadn't been combed for a week. I thought about my face and hands and wished I had been extra careful that morning washing them. But it had nothing to do with my uncombed hair or dirt on my face. I was just filth and I was still breathing. Nothing hurt me as much as I hurt that morning. Miss Fitzsimmons had denied me singing in God's house for no reason other than that I was a bastard. I knew I would never forgive her for that.

Winter times the school was very cold. There was a big open fire at the end of our room. It had to be kept going all day with wood and turf. Children who could bring in a sod of turf every day could just once during the day go up to the fire and have a little warm. I couldn't ask Grandad for a sod of turf every day. He had enough to do cutting the turf in the summer to last all winter. I had got used to looking out for myself now. There certainly wasn't anyone else to look out for me. So a sod of turf had to be obtained every day. I wanted to be like the other children and be able to come to the nice, big, warm, open fire and have a warm. Not much to ask when you are only nine. So as I was labelled a thief, I might as well be one. On the way to school every day I nipped into a neighbour's and stole one. It was the same if I was hungry. I would duck into a neighbour's hen house or barn and grab a couple of newly laid eggs. They would be cracked open with a piece of slate and swallowed in one gulp. To be honest I was never really hungry, stealing food was done mostly for devilment.

I always knew when the war ended Auntie Una and Maureen would go home to London. It never caused me any anxiety. I assumed I would stay with Grandad. I was eleven when the war was over. I loved every inch of Moortown. I dearly loved my Grandad. I had even come to terms with Miss Fitzsimmons. Weeks would pass without an incident and my work at school never faltered. So I wasn't too happy one afternoon returning from school to hear Grandad announce: "You are going to England. I'll come and stay with you for one month; give you time to settle down."

No point I thought asking questions. Arrangements had been made without consulting me, so obviously they weren't going to tell me anything.

My farewell to Ballinvalley School was a subdued one. I wasn't even wished "Good Luck, safe journey, God Bless" – nothing, not one word of comfort to keep in my heart to see me through whatever lay ahead.

Chapter Four

I stood in Delvin High Street opposite Jim Burke's with Grandad, Una and Maureen waiting for the bus to take us to Dublin and on to England. My faithful penguin was with me and I hugged him close for comfort. There wasn't a soul in the street, not one person to say "Goodbye" as I was leaving. I wondered if I would ever be back but I knew I was leaving my heart and soul there. It was the place where I had known true peace and happiness in those first tender eight years of my life with my beloved grandma. It was going to be a lifetime before I found peace again.

We spent easily half a day in Dublin, in and out of large government buildings, queuing to see people, sitting on benches waiting. All the time, Maureen and I were left outside in corridors or small rooms. I heard Una say to one very official looking man, "But this child doesn't have anyone here to care for her. She can't be left with an old man. She doesn't have anyone to sign forms for her either. If we can get permission to take her to England, there will be someone there to care for her."

I was very tired and confused and I hugged my penguin tighter. Who was this someone, I thought. I didn't want to be taken away from my grandad. We'll be alright together, I told myself. I can look after myself now and soon I'll be big enough to look after him. Eventually, the necessary papers to take me out of the country were obtained and we boarded the train for the docks. Grandad sat very close to me on the train and bending down so he was close to my ear, he said, almost in a whisper, "When we get to England, you are to call your Auntie Sheila, 'Mother'."

Now my lovely grandad made a terrible mistake with that statement. I don't know what he could have said to me but he should have made it quite clear to me that Sheila was in fact my real mother. Saying, "When you get to England you are to call your Auntie Sheila, Mother" left me in the air and further confused. I protested, "I don't like Sheila, isn't there anyone else I can call Mummy?" I looked to Una for support.

Sheila met the train in London. She greeted her father and sister with great affection but hardly acknowledged me. Una and Maureen said their goodbyes. They were in London so they were home. We made our way to Upminster where Sheila and Jack had rented a house, not a quarter of a mile from where I was born. It had been raining cats and dogs and was still raining when we arrived at the front gate. The path ran to the side of the house where the front door was situated. The dustbin was across the path from the front door. Something must have been put in the bin which had gone rotten because the path was a carpet of maggots. There were thousands and thousands of white maggots and they glowed in the dark. I thought it was disgusting.

The house was a small, three-bedroom, semi-detached painted green. As Sheila opened the door John ran to greet us. Sheila, who I was to call Mum, led the way to the lounge at the back of the house. Jack was sitting comfortably in an armchair. I had seen him briefly when I was two, he was going to be my daddy. I didn't realize until he stood up what a big man he was. He must have been sixteen stone or more. I remember he was wearing a brown and white striped shirt. He always wore suits with a collar and tie. He rose to his feet and holding out his hand to shake my hand, he said, "Welcome, you are very welcome, little one." It was as near as could be to love at first sight. I felt very grown up standing there shaking hands with this stranger. I felt at ease straight away. I felt there was already a strong bond.

Grandad had the time of his life. His son, Frank, visited from Grays. Son Tom was in London and came to visit. Daughters Lily, Mina and Una and Sheila all spoiled him. There were many days at the races and dogs in the evening, cards, quite a few whiskeys and as many pints as he could drink. All too soon his month's stay was up and it was time for us to say our goodbyes. We hugged each other for what seemed like forever. I was told years later that he cried for a month when he got home.

Mum seemed to resent me from day one. My hair was infested with fleas. She used to spread a newspaper on the table and I would bend over the newspaper and she would roughly comb the fleas out. As they bounced she would catch them and pop them between her thumbnails. She should have understood the situation. She had lived in Moortown longer than I had. But she made such a fuss and would tell me I was a disgusting little child. Amazingly, she considered herself a clever woman but she never once thought of having my fairly long hair cut but preferred to almost tear my hair out every morning. It seemed to take forever to get rid of those fleas.

There was still about six weeks of the school year left and it was decided that I should travel to Brentwood every day where my cousins were at school. There were three sisters there, so alike, and all three had the most beautiful hair. Every morning at assembly, Reverend Mother led prayers for a special intention. Whatever the special intention was, it seemed very important and the children prayed with all their hearts. One morning Reverend Mother came in, all smiles, "Our prayers have been answered, thank God," she said. "This morning we shall say a thank you prayer to God."

It was all very strange for me at the new school. Their way of working was different from Ballinvalley but nothing was causing me concern. I had missed sitting for the scholarship so, after a few weeks, arrangements were made for me to sit the scholarship alone. I had to attend at this large building one Saturday morning. I didn't understand what sitting for the scholarship meant but I do remember being greeted very warmly and being led into a massive room which looked like a study. A large, oval, highly-polished table was in the centre of the room. I was asked to sit down and told when I was comfortable I would be given my papers. I remember how easy all the questions were and I was soon finished. Mum and Dad were told almost immediately that I had passed with the highest marks and I would be attending St Mary's Convent Grammar School in Upminster come September.

All too soon it was time to say goodbye to that school where I had spent a happy few weeks. The three sisters were to appear on the front page of every newspaper in the county. Their mother, Odette, was home. Our prayers were for her safe return from the Nazis where she was held captive and tortured.

Now I faced the long summer holidays. I went to stay with Lily for a couple of weeks. Perhaps she still had designs on drowning me. I met my cousin, Sheila, named after Mum, for the first time. She was four years older than I was and had such a lovely life as it appeared to me at the time. I was so envious of her. She had pet rabbits and played the piano. Uncle Bill was caretaker of an island in the Thames. Their cottage was in the country. It was almost like home, Moortown. You had to run over the fields to the river, jump into the boat and row over to the island. Once there it was great fun playing around the club house, skipping and swimming. Lily had a pair of dark green curtains hanging in the dining room. They had been hanging there so long they were faded by the sun and looked like green and white stripes. Returning from the island one day, Lily had taken them down and made me a dress. It was absolutely appalling. Puffing on her fag and stuttering she said, looking at me resembling a tramp in the dress, "That'll do for you." I felt so degraded.

It was wonderful to have learnt that Michael, Sean and Tommy had followed me over from Ireland. Tom was still in the army and had got married quarters for his family in the army barracks at Sheerness. So I didn't unpack my few bits and pieces when I returned from Lily's. I went straight over to Sheerness. I was always at home there. Auntie Maggie was as good as gold to me. There was never ever any bad feeling and I never felt out of place or inferior. I always felt at home and totally at ease; one of the family. I was to spend many, many holidays there. Those times were the happiest of my young life.

The last couple of weeks of the holidays I spent with my favourite Auntie Una, Uncle Pat and Maureen. Una was decorating after her long absence away from her home. Maureen and I were allowed to help. We were given a bucket of paint and some rags and screwing up the rags and dipping them in the paint we got busy ragging. Una and Pat lived in an upstairs flat in Brixton. The neighbours downstairs were very friendly and asked us down to tea. I hate to think what the expression on my face was like – sitting there were two of the blackest men ever born. I had never seen a black man and I was absolutely amazed. They were eating bananas which I had only seen a picture of in a book. I thought at least they were savages but they were very friendly and I was always welcome to pop downstairs. They had amazing singing voices and they would just break into song and sing in beautiful harmony for Maureen and me. We would sit there, two little girls completely spellbound, and when they finished we would clap excitedly.

During the six weeks' summer holidays, I had heard a little about Mum and Dad's great job at the Beehive Hotel. I wondered why they had given it all up and taken me on. It wasn't until 2001, when I had dinner with John, that he told me there had been a terrible row. Mum and Dad had walked out and they had already been in a couple of places before Upminster. I had seen almost nothing of them during the holidays. I had done the rounds, like a sack of spuds, everyone taking a turn at looking after me.

Now it was time to start my new school, wonderful. I still ached for my grandad and missed him so much but I was so excited. Mum had done her best with a long list of requirements, but she had fallen short with clothes. She had bought only two blouses, two pairs of knickers and two pairs of socks. I now realize what a struggle it must have been for her to have done as much as she did. Everything was so expensive and knowing the truth as I do now about her lifestyle I realize what a gigantic problem it was for her. She must have felt cursed having this rotten little child, as she never missed a chance to tell me, going to Grammar School. I was having the chance denied her and it was off her back, how she hated me.

The first morning at assembly was great. You could fit the whole of Ballinvalley School into just the hall. We, first years, made our way nervously to our classroom and sat quietly waiting for our teacher. In walked this very young lady, quite small, neat and pretty. She was wearing a tweed suit and silk stockings. One leg was a little shorter than the other and she bobbed up and down a little. We all rose, "Good Morning," we all chorused. "Miss Glass," she said, smiling. "Good morning, Miss Glass," we all echoed. It was the start of a very busy day.

For our last lesson, we made our way to the dining room. This was a lesson on etiquette. We had a slice of bread and butter on our plate and the jam pot was passed round. We took a spoonful of jam and with our knife placed it on the side of the plate. Then with our knife we helped ourselves from the side of our plate. It wasn't etiquette to plonk the jam straight on the bread. I thought it was an amazing lesson teaching you how to eat. One of the nuns, probably sensing I was lacking in table manners, leant over and smiling sweetly said, "We'll make a lady out of you, Leila."

How could she have got it all so wrong. But, for now, I was thrilled. I think the most important thing to me was I was like the rest of the girls. I had a mum and dad and I could talk about them just like everyone else. Grandad had written. He had signed the letter, *Your fond and loving Grandad.* He will be so proud when I write home about my new school and how well I'm doing. He will be just so proud.

Whatever anyone said about Mum, she always worked her socks off. She played just as hard, but boy, did she work! She was manageress of a cake shop in the High Street selling wonderful individual cakes. There were rows and rows of them with different coloured icing and cream, trays of different coloured jellies with squiggles of cream and trays of trifles. This was 1945, so the displays were amazing after the austerity of the war years and sugar rationing.

My school was in the next street, so sometimes I would pop in to see her on my way home. There was never a warm greeting. She believed it wasn't her place to flatter, praise or give me compliments. If I deserved anything it would come from elsewhere. The truth was, eleven years was a long time and I was quite a tough little nut. She probably had no great affection for me. I wasn't like John – charming and lovable – a little creep. I was more into giving her a bit of lip and I would get a smack across the face. She would scream at me.

"I don't know where you get your rotten ways from."

I hated being hit, only the headmistress at Ballinvalley School had ever hit me before and I hated her. I think I almost hated Mum.

When Mum wasn't working, she never missed a night at the dogs. If there wasn't a meeting she would find a game of cards. She would be out every night. When it was cards, she would come home at two or three in the morning. Dad never said a word, but it worried me and I would wonder what she was doing.

Dad never did a day's work in his life. He used to clerk at the dogs. Now I don't want to cause anger with bookmakers, tic-tacs or anyone else who works at the dogs and works hard in all weathers to earn a living, but Dad was addicted to gambling and his wages were gone before he even picked up his pen. He had no interests or friends. He lived for the next bet. He didn't drink or smoke, spending money on things like that was alien to him. He could have a bet instead. Saturday morning Mum gave me sixpence pocket money and as soon as she had gone to work Dad would ask: "Can I just borrow that?" and he would take the sixpence out of my hand. He would rush out and put a sixpence each way on an accumulator.

Over the years I realized if he did have a winner he wouldn't settle his debts or pay anyone back or treat anyone to anything. He would keep on gambling until every penny was gone. When Dad wasn't at the dogs his home was his castle. He would potter about doing small jobs. We didn't have a radio so he would buy all the racing papers and read them front to back. When I got up in the morning he would be there with the kettle on. I didn't know for years he was up and about to make sure he got the post before Mum. Someone would always be after him for money and if Mum found out she would kill him. For me they were cosy mornings even if he did pinch my pocket money but that wasn't important. He was a real friend, we could always talk and I loved him to bits. He would travel home from the afternoon meetings to feed John and I. Then he and Mum would meet up at the evening meeting.

John and I were alone in the evenings. I had never been alone in my life. I was terrified of the dark and all the strange noises. John knew how much the night times frightened me and he hit on a plan. He tied a piece of string to my big toe which was attached to his wrist and if I was scared I was to wriggle my toe and he would shout out for comfort. I couldn't sleep until they were home, usually about 11 p.m. Tired in the morning, I couldn't concentrate all day and cracks in my school work were beginning to appear. I was also in trouble for my appearance. I only had the two blouses and socks and they had to stay clean all week. One morning at assembly a nun beckoned me to one side and asked, "Did you have your blouse ironed this morning?"

I thought to myself, my blouse hasn't even been washed let alone ironed.

Sundays was the day we were all at home. Considering I was at a convent, Mass was the last word to be uttered in the house. I was distinctly discouraged, Mum was very pro-Jewish. I was a little bit sceptical myself, but still more for my faith than against. So much so, I took Dad on. Remembering I was a child, no offence meant, but I asked him how he thought a Jew would get into heaven. He got so mad with me he grabbed my prayer book out of my hand and threw it on the fire. It landed on its back and opened out. The pages rose up in the flames. I watched it burn. It was the only thing I had of my beloved grandmother. How I hated him and vowed never to forgive him. But, of course, I did. I was sad at losing that precious possession.

The fish man would came round with his barrow selling cockles, winkles and whelks. I would sit with a pin picking the winkles out of their shells for Dad. I hated those wriggly things but he loved them and would pig out.

Mum was a brilliant cook and when her brothers and sisters came on a Sunday, she would prepare bits and pieces to pass around but she would never offer me anything.

"I'll have one after Leila," said Auntie Una one day.

"She doesn't want one," snapped Mum.

"How do you know, you haven't offered her one?" asked Una.

I wondered many times what was behind me being brought over from Ireland. Who had persuaded Sheila to give me a home and why had she agreed. She obviously had no interest in me at all. She didn't even know how old I was. She asked me my age one day and I told her I was twelve. With that she shoved a book in my hands and told me to read it. That settled my mind. Mum definitely wasn't my mother. If she was she would know when I was born. As for the book, I understood very little of it. All those long medical words. What was it all about and what are periods? When they did start? I was too frightened of Mum to tell her. I got some rags and paper to put in my knickers but they had a hole in them. So I grabbed my only other pair and they had a hole too. Luckily, the holes were in different places so the two pairs together did the trick. I had to be very careful how I walked and made my way to the toilet at every opportunity to change the paper. I don't know, life sure can be very degrading.

Auntie Mina lived the nearest to us. She was just up the road at Harold Hill. She had four children and there was only eight days difference in age between her daughter and me. We were at school together, although not in the same stream. Mum liked to go there. You could be sure the cards would be out and a couple of neighbours would pop in to make the numbers up. I know I definitely never stayed overnight there, I didn't like being there at all. I knew when I got home I'd get a smack. Mum would say, "I'm fed up hearing from Mina how rude you have been to her." I would get a thump! I was amazed. Why should I be rude to Mina and when had I been rude to her? She seemed to be a nasty, spiteful person. It seemed laughable to me but she seemed to be jealous. Why anyone in their right mind should be jealous of me God alone knows. I was the one who had nothing. Mina was to cross my path years later and cause me a lot of trouble and heartache. I'd just like to think if there is a God she got her comeuppance when she got to the Pearly Gates, though I doubt she even got there.

It was less than two years and we were on the move. Nobody explained anything just Dad saying, gather your things up now. We left the house with two cases and Dad dragging all our possessions along the pavement in a sack. Standing on the platform waiting for a train I wondered where I was going now and why. Home for me was to be Southend and now over fifty years on it is still home. But why Southend then? I can only think it was because Dad had a brother, sister and daughter living there. Arriving at our new home, the front door was on the pavement. It opened up into a kitchen-cum-living room with a toilet to the left and one bedroom to the right. All four of us had to sleep in one room which suited me. I was used to company during the night. There was a small bed, a large one and then another small one. That was when I realized John wet the bed. Mum would throw the wet sheet over the wardrobe to dry during the day. There wasn't a back yard to hang anything out so she had no other choice. Then in the evening the sheet would be turned this way and that. You could always smell the urine in the room. My pillow didn't have a cover and as I laid my head down on it for the first time my nose sank into it. I realized someone must have been sick on it because that was how it smelt. I threw it on the floor and slept flat.

My mind went back to Moortown. I missed it more than ever. I thought of the lake and being out in the boat, fishing in the Deel and fetching the cows home in the evening. I was more confused than ever. What was this all about? One good thing every morning for the next two years Mum gave me the train fare to Upminster plus my dinner money. Mum now worked as housekeeper to a wealthy business couple. The gambling lifestyle hadn't changed. Mum had a pound bet that "Sheila's Cottage" would win the Grand National at fifty to one. Of course it did and she came home with the loot, sat on the bed like a child and spread it all about. I'm pleased she sent Grandad a fiver. He would be thrilled to bits. It didn't do anyone else any good because we moved the next day.

John and I were very lonely children. We didn't have any friends. I knew no one in Southend and at school in Upminster I was the scruffy little kid. No one even asked me to a party. I wouldn't have been able to go anyway because I didn't have a dress, nor would I have been able to afford a present. There was no way I could ever ask anyone home. Although I was used to living in a kitchen in Ireland that was the way life was. Here I had been to some people's houses and seen the inside and it certainly wasn't the way we lived. We moved again soon after and I was home from school this day when the landlady called for her rent. I heard Dad talking to her. He didn't know I was listening behind the door. He said something like, "I'm sorry, once again I don't have the rent money but I promise you faithfully next week I shall have it."

"Don't bother," she said. "Just get out today."

The humiliation of it all. I knew Dad did have the rent money but like everything else it had to go on a horse or dog first. Mum would go mad – the rows! One day she chased him down the street with a kitchen knife. If she had caught him she would have killed him.

It was the summer of 1948 and we moved again to what was to be our last home together as a foursome. It was a turning point for me because Mum said she wouldn't be paying the fares to Upminster. I would have to go to school in Southend. I was deeply unhappy at not being allowed to stay at St Mary's. I might have been poor and confused but it was the only bit of stability I had in what was a sad life. There was never any thought of failing or giving up. Although my work had declined I was never unhappy in class. With the help of the nuns and the teachers there I would have pulled through. My recollection of the nuns was one of affection – they may have been a bit tough at times but no more than was deserved. It was still a very stormy relationship with Mum. It had never softened. In fact, I think it had got worse. With Una's words still fresh in her ears, I was always the liar and thief. Apparently, I suffered from hallucinations. Everything was my fault and last of all I was mentally disturbed. Too true, too true, I was disturbed but there was nothing wrong with my mind. I was just confused and very unhappy.

Too unhappy to give any thought to how John was coping with it all. He had been brought up in a very privileged lifestyle. He was so spoilt and cosseted he couldn't cope with Moortown which was paradise to this. I suppose it helped him to be with the mum and dad he had always known. For me I didn't know who these two people were. People would say, "Aren't you like your mother!"

In fact, we were like peas in a pod, the only difference was our colouring. Sheila, with her pale, almost porcelain skin, and me very dark and rosy-cheeked. When I looked in the mirror, I saw Sheila in myself. When I laughed I could hear Sheila, my actions and ways were just like hers. In fact, I was so like Sheila I could almost have been a virgin birth. But no way was she my mother, Grandad would have told me. Sheila would have said something herself, somebody, somewhere would have said something. But the strangest thing of all, I never asked and that is the root of all the trouble, big trouble that was to come. I never asked, why didn't I ask? Was I in total fear of the woman? Was there such a wall between the two of us that it was impregnable? Was I so afraid of the consequences, the rows, the accusations? Sheila (Mum) was always talking about herself, how clever she was and if she had been given a chance she would have scaled the heights. It never entered her head that perhaps she could give a word of encouragement to a little girl who quite frankly was falling to pieces.

Our new home was over a grocer's shop in Westcliff. On the top floor were two dingy rooms, one for me and one for Mum and Dad. The stairs down to the landing were narrow and covered with scruffy lino. Off the landing was a large lounge and double bedroom where the shop owner and his wife lived. Along the landing was a small room for John, a bathroom and toilet we all shared with the landlord and landlady, and a kitchen. We four lived in this little kitchen; it was the basic – a table, four chairs, sink and cooker with a couple of cupboards. Next door was a posh butcher's shop, it was spotless in the front for the customers but they would have died if they went around the back. The butcher, very Jewish, while preparing the chickens would chuck their heads and feet out the back door into the yard. It was littered with old boxes and all sorts of rubbish and overrun with rats. It was absolutely appalling, how they kept the rats from coming into the shops I don't know.

September – it was time for me to start at my new grammar school in Westcliff, St Bernards. With Madame Mildred. Looking back to the confused child I was, I would liken Madam Mildred to Miss Fitzsimmons and a touch of the nuns my poor mother had the misfortune to run into. I had kindly been given a second-hand St Mary's blazer, not knowing that I wasn't going to return to the school. I unwisely cut the badge out of the pocket and it looked appalling. I didn't have a new tie but one had been left hanging in the cloakroom and I grabbed that. From day one I knew I was beaten.

My first morning I made my way to the back of the class, there perhaps no one would see me. I knew I was different now. Dirty! I could smell myself, so I perched myself on the very edge of the seat as far away as possible from the girl next to me. Lunchtimes were a nightmare, I was now in a very affluent area, the girls talked about their parents' yachts, their posh cars, their holidays abroad. One girl had been to Capri, I mean who goes to Capri – that has to be the bestest thing in the whole world. The girls had their horses, I could ride bareback when I was three but somehow it seemed different now. They all went to ballet lessons, and had loads of friends. On the way home they rushed to the little shop to buy magazines, sweets, etc. I crept by hoping I was invisible. Now and then I had a halfpenny to buy a stale cake.

It's easy now to criticize, but there didn't seem to be any support. There was no concern for my welfare or my misery. I walked in in the morning, spent the day there then walked out in the afternoon. I can't remember anyone ever speaking to me, I was just invisible. John was first to break rank, he ran away to sea, unable to bear the intolerable life anymore. His fifteenth birthday was spent aboard a Merchant Navy ship in port in Egypt The large crew gave him a party to remember all his life. They ordered a crate of rum, a crate of Coke and a crate of ice. His birthday present was a tall, very glamorous, long-legged, long-haired blonde to do as he wished with. After a few drinks the blonde took him to bed. He couldn't believe her beautiful breasts and he was encouraged to dig in and help himself. John was totally inexperienced with women but his instinct was to let his hands wander, down, down, until his hands were round a pair of "BALLS". Totally shocked he ran through the mess screaming to the laughter of the men, their feet banging on the floor and their hands thumping the table. He collapsed on the quayside with the effect of the drink where he slept the night away. At least he will remember his fifteenth birthday.

My fifteenth birthday was slightly different. I had survived one term at school and had started back in the New Year. In the March I would be fifteen and, as March approached, on the way to school one morning I just stopped walking, stood on the pavement and told myself I couldn't face another day at school the way things were. I would take a leaf out of John's book and get a job. I never went to school again. Instead, I went to the Job Centre alone and they offered me a job in a factory. I really didn't have factory work in mind but it was all they offered me and I was too scared of not getting a job to say anything. On my birthday, I walked along the front at Westcliff, the tide was in, the sun was shining and it was a lovely day. I felt I didn't have a friend in the world. I know I didn't have a bean in my pocket but I was determined things were going to be OK. I set myself a task. Whatever it was I would achieve one thing in my life.

It was amazing the school never got in touch with Mum and Dad to inform them that I was missing. It shows what a waste of space the school thought I was. It was three weeks before Mum realized I had stopped going to school and was working. Her immediate reaction was, "What have you done with your wages?"

They were there, quite safe, I wouldn't have dared spend them. My pay was two pounds fifty per week. I can't remember how much Mum wanted for housekeeping but it opened up a whole new ball game for Dad. Every Saturday morning without fail he would borrow a pound to go to Hamlet Court Road and get some food. It didn't leave much for myself to spend on the normal things a young girl needs. I know that in all my teenage years I never once bought a record or a magazine. I still don't buy those things today.

The girls in the factory must have thought I was a peculiar girl. I didn't smoke, didn't drink, didn't use make-up, didn't chat the boys up, didn't go out evenings or weekends, never went to the pictures. I was amazingly quiet and wouldn't say boo to a goose. My only interest was swimming so I joined the local swimming club, long distance was my speciality. I liked being alone in the water. I felt isolated, there was no one there to criticize me or put me down.

We must have spent going on two and a half years in that hole. How Mum stood it I'll never know, but then she wasn't there very much. Friday nights she gave the shopkeeper the rent then she was off out. Mum and Dad's routine hadn't changed in the years since I came over from Ireland. When Mum wasn't working, she was at the dogs or playing in a heavy card school. She came home for just a few hours' sleep. There was nothing at home for her, just a kitchen with four chairs. There wasn't even an easy chair.

Dad and I had this amazing relationship. I never remember him seeing either his sister or his daughter, but for me he was up in the morning with the kettle on, albeit to catch the post before Mum. All morning he sat in the kitchen studying the racing form. He had no friends and never went out, only to the dogs. My job was in the next street so lunchtimes I came home for a cup of tea and a sandwich. It would be ready and waiting. I couldn't afford, and wasn't interested anyway, in going for a pub lunch. Afternoons, if there was a meeting, Dad was there. Then without fail he was home to cook my dinner. He never once said, "Get your own food." Then he would be off to the evening meeting.

One day I shouted up to him as I came up the stairs.

"Is that you, Sheila?" he asked.

Bouncing into the kitchen I said, "It's me, Dad."

"Do you know you sound more like your mother every day," he said.

A perfect time for me to ask the question and settle my mind once and for all – "Is Sheila really my mother?" But, close as we were, I couldn't ask.

Reading now what I've written about my relationship with my Dad over fifty years on, to me it seems like systematic child abuse and cruelty. I was so alone and vulnerable. He basically controlled me by taking all my money. Of course he looked out for me. I was his next bet. My pay packet was a guarantee he could continue with his addiction and like all abused children I would never say a word to anyone, most of all Mum. Sad to think I loved him to bits. He was all I had as family.

Not one member of our large family visited us while we were on the road as I call it, moving from place to place. They wondered about our continuing change of address. They would have had a fit if they had dropped in and saw the conditions we were living in. We did, however, go to the family parties. In fact, Mum was so determined to keep the front up, that on one occasion she got things wrong and rather than miss out we caught a taxi to Sheerness. The fare was five pounds, a fortune to us. She must have had a good win to have been able to afford to do it.

Show and pretence was part of Mum's style. She didn't have many clothes but what she did have were the best. She did most of her shopping at Judith Scotts, an exclusive shop in Hamlet Court Road. She was still very young and went out of our pigsty of a home looking like a woman of substance.

One of Mum's sisters was planning a trip home with her family in a year's time. I'd be seventeen. She asked Mum to join her and I was amazed to hear Mum say we would go. It was understood I'd pay my own way as I was working, but that caused me a problem. I saw very little of my pay packet and didn't have the strength to say "no" to Dad on Saturday mornings. I got over the problem by getting a second job in the evenings. It was easy to keep that quiet and save all my wages towards my holiday without Dad getting his thieving hands on that money.

It was getting close to our trip home. I was fast asleep one night when I was disturbed by two men with Mum in my tiny bedroom. They were searching through my things.

"It's OK," said Mum, "Go back to sleep."

Later I heard her crying and rowing furiously with Dad. She called him all the names under the sun and blamed him for the position she was in. She screamed at him, "I'll probably go to prison."

She told Dad all she wanted to do was go home to see her father and she had to do a burglary to do that because he was so useless. It had been her day off and she knew the couple she worked for had gone out for the day. So, in the middle of the afternoon, in broad daylight she walked up their path, let herself in and removed enough money to pay for her holiday. Now is that desperation? Unfortunately, a neighbour was peeping out from behind net curtains. When the couple heard it was Mum they didn't press charges. If she had asked they would have given her the money, they thought the world of her. They asked her not to come back to work. What they didn't know, nor did I, was that she wasn't going back to work for them after her holiday anyway, she had made other plans.

It was great for me, I was out shopping till I dropped. I bought myself a pale lavender dress, white bag, shoes, gloves and a half moon hat with white feathers that clung to my head. I could afford to buy some black market coupons. Clothes were still on ration after the war. I remember buying a gold mac, well that was a vital piece of clothing in Ireland, and some bits and pieces so I felt great.

Finally, the day arrived and I stepped off the bus in Delvin outside Jim Burke's. It had been six years, the lousiest six years of my life. I had been away too long, and it felt good to be home. My first stop was Ballinvalley School. I didn't know it but I was quite a pretty girl and scrubbed up well in my new dress and accessories! Well, I was unrecognisable. Because I bounced in, "Good morning" I simply gushed, that wonderful headmistress, for the want of another word, looked at me without a flicker of anything on her face. "Can I help you?" she asked. "Can I help you?" – I couldn't believe it!

I can still hear myself today saying to her, "I'm Leila." Her face didn't alter, the greeting was cold and I left after about five minutes. Had she given me the time of day I could have told her I really had screwed up and she was right all along, I really was a waste of space. But to her it was simply a case of the village bastard returning. Sooner we get rid of her the better, nothing had changed. Her greeting, or lack of it, wasn't going to spoil my trip home.

I loved Moortown almost as much as my mother did, she had spent more time there than I. She had completed her education at Ballinvalley School. She knew everyone, just as I did, but now she was a woman of the world, so to speak. There were many gin and tonics at Jim Burke's, rounds of drinks for the old crowd. She flitted in and around like a butterfly. Grandad, she and I took the boat out on Dysart

Lake. Mum caught a large pike and posed on the edge of the lake laughing like a child as she held the fish out as if to say "Look how clever I am." The ladies, aunts and nieces all had to sleep in the one big bed, three up and three down so there was a feeling of closeness; very nice to have a feeling like that with my mum but, of course, I was just kidding myself. Mum had plenty of time to have a word with me if there was anything on her mind. I'd have understood, whatever she had to say, I'd have understood. I was in total ignorance of the shock that was awaiting me when I returned home. If Sheila was my mother surely there was something there, however small, surely she felt she owed me something. Not treat me like a mat to wipe her feet on and walk all over. Somebody had given birth to me, so surely someone owed me something.

One of the Barry's prize greyhounds had just had a litter of pups. Remembering how much I loved animals as a child I was invited down to see the litter. I spent a very happy time there and on leaving instead of going home I turned right and walked the short way to the River Deel. I smiled when I saw the bridge with the three steps chiselled out for me by Grandad. It seemed so small now. I could stand there and rest my elbows on the bridge and look over. It looked lovely and inviting with the sun shining on it as it glistened and flowed along on its merry way. I decided to take a walk along the bank. Memories of Grandma and my cousins were ripe in my mind as I recalled the happy times I had playing along the bank and fishing. I had walked quite a way and looking back to the road there was no sign of life at all. Not a movement of any kind, not a bicycle or horse and cart were passing. It was hot and the water looked so tempting. Sitting down on the bank, I slipped off my shoes, popped my dress over my head and slipped off my knickers. Time to do a bit of skinny dipping, it was glorious. Dragging myself out onto the bank, I stretched out on the soft grass to dry my front and then turned over to let the sun dry my back.

There was only one cloud on the horizon. We had been home for two weeks and I could no longer get out of going to confession and Holy Communion. Grandad would think we had completely lost our way and would be so ashamed. I didn't speak to Mum about anything. She could put her own act on, she didn't need any help from me. As we walked along the three miles to church chatting, I fell back and walked alone. My thoughts went back to my dearly beloved Grandma. I thought of her on her hands and knees scrubbing with all those kids. Top of her agenda was to give more than she could afford to the priest every week. I had come to think of priests as part of a set-up, employed by the Catholic Church, a fabulously rich organisation. They ruled people in my grandparents' time by fear, threats of hell and eternal damnation. The priests took the last pennies out of the hands of the poor without a second thought which made the organisation they worked for even richer. I was none too happy at the thought of going on my knees and confessing my indiscretions to a man hiding behind a curtain under the umbrella of the Catholic Church. So many priests had proved to be adulterers, fornicators and paedophiles. Not, by any means, all priests but there were enough and the Catholic Church's attitude to them made it bad for other priests. What did the church do about those priests, it knew about them. Ordinary people in the street knew, so there was no doubt the Church knew. Did the Church hold them up to ridicule and shame? Did the Church treat them as it treated a young girl whose only sin was to have a baby out of wedlock? Worse still, the innocent newborn baby who had no say in being born. Mother and baby were the scum of the earth and everyone made sure they knew they had brought shame on the family. So what happened to the priests – they were cosseted, sheltered and protected and if they were paedophiles, they were put to work in a children's home. Silence was their main weapon. No one would dare speak out against a man of God, you would have your tongue cut out. I went through the charade of confessions, by now I realized about ninety per cent of confessions were like mine, an act. My only consolation was it made an old man very happy. I still believed in God, totally, but didn't have any faith in his representatives on this Earth.

All too soon the holiday was over and it was time to bid a tearful goodbye to my wonderful Grandad. We held each other close, I didn't know it was to be the last time I was going to see him. It was also going to be a long time before I came back to place flowers on my grandparents' grave, a long time, a lifetime in fact.

Dad had the kettle on when Mum and I arrived home. The kitchen looked scruffier than ever. To dry my clothes, I would put some newspaper on the top of the cooker, fold my clothes and lay them on the paper. They would dry by the warmth of the cooking. God alone knows what they smelt like with the frying. My clothes were still there on the cooker, just as I had left them ready to start back to work, nothing had changed.

I had no bad feeling about work so next morning I was up bright and early. Realising Mum wasn't around I asked Dad:

"Where's Mum?"

"She's gone," he replied

"Gone where?" I asked.

Mum had left to return to Solly and May at Gants Hill. When did she make the arrangements? It must have been before we went to Ireland. She had gone without a word, she didn't even say "Goodbye" or "See you" – nothing. She had just left. I was just seventeen, abandoned again. Seventeen-year-olds in my days were just children. I just sat there staring into my tea in total shock and disbelief when Dad's words interrupted my thoughts.

"When you find somewhere to live I'm going to join your mother," he said.

I think that hurt me even more. All those cosy mornings he had the kettle on and he didn't have the guts to tell me about their arrangements, when they were made. The bottom seemed to have fallen out of my world.

Chapter Five

I was still dazed by the news I had just received. Wondering if I should skip work and go out and try to find myself a home, when the window cleaner started cleaning the windows for the shop owner. He was quite a local character, everyone knew him. He was a small man about 4 ft 10 inches tall with beady little eyes and he wore the thickest of glasses perched on his thin, hooked nose. His hair was just a frizz ball. Actually, I was nosing through my mother's things one day and there was a photo of him. *To my darling Sheila – All my love, Ben.* He was a revolting little creep and I couldn't understand my mother fancying him. She must have been desperate. I tore the photo into tiny pieces thinking if Sheila missed it, she would think Jack had found it. She wouldn't say anything to him.

Ben would chat to anyone and seeing me he immediately started. For something to say, I told him my problem.

"That's solved, you can stay with my wife," he said.

Jack was relieved he could get going and join Sheila. It didn't take me long to pack and when I got round to Ben's wife, Lil, I found out I had to sleep with her teenage daughter. God knows what the daughter thought, but I was a paying guest and money was tight so she had no say in the matter. At the weekend Lil gave me the bill for bed and board. Fair enough, I expected to pay, but it would have cost less in a good hotel. It was more than I earned per week. I paid with a smile and it left me with nothing for the following week. I knew I had to move on quickly. Luckily, I saw a notice in a newsagent's window for a room to let in the next road. I moved straight away.

Home for me was now the upstairs back room in a large house where twelve other families lived. My landlady lived downstairs. She was a very large, larger than life, character. Her reputation was as bright as her brighter than bright red hair. It was alleged she had a string of convictions as long as her tattooed arms, for prostitution. It was also alleged she had as many convictions for keeping a disorderly house. She sat in her back room in a big, padded chair weighed down in gold rings, bracelets, chains, with a cigarette in a long holder holding court. There were always people coming and going. I was there for three years and she was always fair and straight with me.

My little room had a window where I could look out on the garden. There was a table in front of the window with a couple of old rickety chairs. Against one wall was a bed and on the opposite wall was a sink, a two-hob gas stove and a cupboard. The old fireplace had a shelf and there was nothing else in the room. When I could afford it I bought myself a single wardrobe and a rug, on the tally. One of the ladies living there was lovely and very nice to me. She had about four children. She wore her hair rolled around her head and bits all around her head hung down so she always looked scruffy. One day she was telling me that if I was short of money the landlady could set things up for me.

"What do you think of that?" she asked me.

I just raised my eyebrows, shrugged my shoulders and walked away. It didn't worry me if all the guests were on drugs and into prostitution as long as I was left alone.

I was completely alone in the world now. There was no one to criticize me, no more moving on. I knew where I was from day to day. Life was actually quite good. My job wasn't mind-blowing but I was safe there and my swimming was going very well. I had a couple of long swims under my belt and the English Channel was my next big swim. I had a coach and a boat man who accompanied me at times. Weekends, if the tide was right, I could get a good training session in. I would just set off from the beach. It never entered my head that I would be in any danger – get cramp, get stung by a jellyfish or, worse still, get carried out to sea. I knew no fear, silly girl. I was to learn one of life's hardest lessons. On one of my long swims I was so far out at sea; a fishing boat on its way home after a night at sea stopped and picked me up. The two young men on board were concerned and read the riot act. The wrapped me in a blanket, cooked breakfast and brought me home. As we nearly reached the shore they joked: "Let's throw her back in," and I hit the cold water.

"We will look out for you next week," they called as I started out for the shore.

Good as their word, there they were the next week and I was quickly yanked on board. Breakfast was just as good but this time there was an extra ingredient, S.E.X. That was my virginity gone but at least I knew what sex was all about!

Almost as if life was planned, that was my last swim. The rage at the time was Esther Williams – Water Ballet – and it had come to Southend. The Water Ballet team was formed and suddenly swimming became fun instead of a cold, hard slog. The team were a great bunch of girls. Long distance swimming had left me alone with my thoughts, isolated from conversation. There was no one out there to argue with me, undermine me or hurt me. I was alone and that was how I had liked it. But now I was part of a team, having to mix, and life felt so much better.

Every Wednesday afternoon throughout the summer we put on a show at the open air pool on Westcliff seafront. The costumes were very glamorous and the routines were fabulous. I never thought I'd have the confidence to put on a grass skirt and wriggle around in a pool in front of hundreds of people. Invitations came from all over the place. There was a "Miss Lovelies" during the show and when the entries were small the ballet team made up the numbers. One afternoon the American Navy were stationed off the Pier.

Sailors from the Warship were guests of the Corporation for the afternoon. They were short of entries for the "Miss Lovelies" and it was my turn with a couple of other girls to step forward and make up the numbers. I wore a one-piece red bathing costume and this particular afternoon my long, dark, curly hair fell naturally in ringlets. Of course I came nowhere but later on a sailor asked if he could speak to me.

"I thought you were beautiful, you should have won," he said. "Could I take you out?"

We met on the Friday evening at Westcliff Station. We went up to London and dined at a superb restaurant. I was completely puzzled with the various cutlery etc. but tried not to panic. Then we went to the famous Windmill. Well! Famous, I had never heard of it and I was shocked. Of course, it was all very new and exciting to me. As I left the station later that evening to walk the short journey home a taxi driver called out, "I didn't think I'd see you home tonight."

"Goodnight," I called back happily.

Every Sunday I took the Greenline Bus to Gants Hill to have tea with Mum and Dad. I had met Dad's brother, Solly, and May. They never had any children, had worked their socks off all their lives and now they had retired to enjoy their vast wealth. Solly had a stroke and was a complete invalid. May never stopped telling him she hadn't worked all her life for this. May was very thin and straight-laced. She had managed the Beehive Hotel well for ten years so she was one tough cookie. But she had spoilt and loved young John, so she had a soft side. She was so mean when she boiled an egg she knew how long to let the water boil before turning the gas off and letting the egg stay in the water until it was done. Boiling the kettle for a cup of tea, a cup of water had to be measured. Only water needed was to be boiled. It was a measure of Sheila's desperation that she was living with this mean old woman.

The house in Beehive Lane was small – two bedrooms and a bathroom upstairs, a lounge, dining room and kitchen downstairs. It was exquisitely furnished. The wallpaper was flock everywhere and carpets your feet sank into. I didn't know anything about antiques but I knew the ornaments, pictures and glass were out of this world. It was absolutely luxurious.

There was never an invitation to dinner on Sunday, just tea. It would be the smallest of meals – just a sandwich and a slither of cake served on priceless china. I was just about to pop my piece of cake into my mouth one Sunday when May asked me: "How did your parents die?"

I looked at her in amazement. This question had never entered my mind. As I never had any parents why should I ever wonder how they died. Sheila scalded May for asking the child, as she put it, such a silly question. Jack sat silently and afterwards when they were seeing me out neither gave an explanation and I never asked. Only to wonder once again if Sheila was actually my mother. No, she couldn't be, I told myself. Jack certainly wasn't my father, that I was sure of.

From the time Sheila and Jack returned to Gants Hill, Jack's daughter, Betty (her name was the same as mine, Elizabeth, but she was called Betty for short) fed me once a week. It was tragic that her mother had died when she was four but she had led a charmed life. She was sent to a very affluent aunt in Southend. She had no interruptions with schooling throughout the war. She was sheltered, protected and completely spoiled – nothing like me. I had a totally different upbringing. After one or two romances, she got involved with a married man with children and she was determined to marry him. The day he got divorced Betty told me his now ex-wife made her sick. She had turned up in court looking sick and scruffy just to get the judge's sympathy and hopefully get more maintenance. That made me angry, perhaps the woman was sick being abandoned with young children.

It was a very quiet wedding for Betty and Bernie – the bride and groom, two others and myself. We went back to their flat for tea. Betty asked me if I could persuade Bernie to take us to the Kursaal. They had met there and she wanted to make a sentimental journey back.

"You ask him yourself," was my reply.

"He won't do it for me," was her reply.

Dancing at the Kursaal wasn't my cup of tea. I had never been in the place in my life. But a lot of persuasion from Betty finally found me whispering into Bernie's ear.

"Please, please can we go to the Kursaal?"

It was fate again because Bernie said yes. The Kursaal was big, the biggest thing for miles around. It was bright and noisy with a live band. The centre of pleasure and entertainment in Southend. You couldn't help noticing the fleet was in, a large ship was anchored off the Pier and there were dozens of young men in uniform. Towards the end of the evening a young man in civvies asked me for a dance. Luckily for me the dance floor was so crowded you couldn't put one foot in front of the other.

"I'm in the navy but not in uniform tonight," the young man informed me. I don't know if he felt he had to say something to impress me but he certainly didn't. My reply was a bit tart.

"If you think all I'm interested in is a uniform, you are very much mistaken."

They were the first words spoken between me and my future husband. He was a local lad, home on leave. In those days, early 1950s, nobody had cars so the Kursaal put on a free bus to get all the young people home. As we ran for our bus he introduced himself as Alan and asked would I be at the dance next week. The short time we had spent together certainly hadn't been earth-shattering but who knows. When I arrived home alone to my little room that evening life seemed good. At least it had been a different day. I had seen

Betty and Bernie wed and I almost had a date. That was unheard of. I wasn't into dating.

I was nineteen, in those days still very young. I had been alone in my little room for over two years. I made myself a cup of tea and sat at my little table feeling a tinge of excitement. I thought about Alan and wondered. If only I knew the unbelievable nightmare, the sorrow and the cruelty this young man was going to drag me through. They say you have a guardian Angel looking out for you. Mine was having a night off.

Saturday evening arrived, I had decided to join my workmates at the Kursaal, much to their surprise. There was the man himself, we seemed to get on really well from the word go. Alan was fairly tall and lean. According to his official statistics he had auburn hair and green eyes, he had a lovely set of teeth – a horse would be proud of a set like that. They went with a lovely smile. He was so easy going and just very nice. I thought he was gorgeous.

After going out for about three weeks, it was time to ask Alan home for a coffee. If he was surprised to find home was a little room in a multi-occupied house he didn't say and didn't seem inquisitive at all. I chatted away about my mother and father, Sheila and Jack at Gants Hill and told him I visited them every Sunday. Perhaps next week he would come up with me.

The next Saturday, plans were made for Alan and I to go out in the evening. That morning I was pottering about in my room when about 11 a.m. I heard a gentle knock on the door. Opening it, I couldn't believe my eyes. There stood Sheila. We looked at each other without saying a word for a few seconds.

Finally Sheila said, "I've come home."

After the way she had walked out on me without saying a word. At times it seemed I was the parent and she was the child. We couldn't go back to the life she ran away from but for now the kettle went on. Anything I had, which was nothing, I shared and was glad to do so. In fact, I had often gone without for her.

About teatime she stood up and said she would join Jack for the evening races at Romford and would be back later. But events had taken a shocking turn and she was never to visit that little room again. Jack had left Solly and May comfortable at lunchtime while he went to the afternoon race meeting. He hurried back to Beehive Lane for tea. As he put his key in the door he could smell gas. Running into the kitchen he found his brother dead. May had laid him on the floor with his head in the oven, then she had laid down beside him with her head next to his. She was also dead. Jack's first thoughts, after the ambulance and the police, were for Sheila. He phoned my landlady and asked if he could speak to me. His news was dreadful, absolutely appalling. "Mum has gone to Romford to meet you," I told him. When Sheila arrived at the dog track she heard her name being called on the loudspeaker. Going to the information kiosk she found the police waiting to take her home.

When Alan arrived that evening I was very subdued. But May was no relation of mine so it wasn't as if madness ran in my family. Funny how already mental instability is raising its ugly head. It was almost Christmas and Alan had bought me a present. Presents in my life were very rare so I was absolutely thrilled. There weren't going to be any decorations for me in my little room. No stocking pinned to the chimney for Father Christmas to fill. I would wake up Christmas morning in that bare room all alone. But now I had a present, prettily wrapped, and I was so excited I couldn't wait. So I opened the present there and then. It was a box of hand-made lace hankies. A lovely present which I would treasure.

Next day, Sunday, I travelled as always to Gants Hill. I went by the steam train instead of the bus. I don't know why I changed my routine, not that it made any difference. I was surprised to see a police car still outside the front door with two policemen on guard. One policeman was stretching his legs strolling up and down the pavement. The second policeman was leaning against the fence observing all. Mum and Dad didn't have much to say, nothing had changed only Solly and May weren't there. Walking slowly into the kitchen to put the kettle on, I stood and looked at the cooker, the door was closed. Hard to believe two people had died at that spot only hours ago. A shiver ran down my back. I didn't stay long, the visit was quicker than usual. Dad was half asleep in the armchair, not wanting to wake him I gently kissed his forehead. Mum was anxious to see me to the door. She seemed fidgety; as we reached it she suddenly slipped an envelope into the top of my coat, saying "Take this to Lew," I knew who she meant.

The two policemen watched me as I walked down the path. I smiled, sweetly sick in the stomach, and walked slowly across the road. What if the envelope slides over my boobs and lands on the ground with a thunderous sound. I was scared to death. Once out of sight I retrieved the envelope and put it in my bag. Sitting in an empty compartment, curiosity got the better of me and I had to open the envelope. I held in my hands three of the most beautiful rings I had ever seen. One was a solitaire diamond, big enough to choke a donkey. I wondered why I had been given the rings in such a risky way. Obviously Dad knew nothing about them, they were a little bit of well earned security for Mum.

Sheila and Jack settled down in Beehive Lane to await their fate. Possession was nine-tenths of the law so they thought. There was a Will. May had promised Sheila a fortune to look after Solly. Sheila had broken the contract that morning. She could have lied about it, said someone was ill or made up any story to cover her absence that afternoon. But it would have been of no avail, the Will wasn't signed. Sheila, after I had been prepared to share my home with her without question, told me she would have liked to have me living with them. But she was afraid of the rows I would create with the neighbours. What rows, I wondered? I had now been in the factory over five years and not a cross word with anyone. I lived in a multi-occupied house with some rough people for over three years and never a cross word with anyone. Now a member of the Water Ballet team, a crowd of lovely ladies and never a cross word. What was Sheila talking about? It seemed she never really wanted to make me part of her life. It suited me being alone. I was quite happy.

Later on I heard stories and lies going around about Solly's and May's deaths I was completely shocked. Whatever my mother said or did I defended her to the letter especially if the stories were bare-faced lies. Jack's daughter, Betty, put the story about that my mother helped May with the events of the afternoon and then stole May's best ring off her finger. It was her father who left them and found them later. Mum was in Southend with me. Fair enough, a particular ring had disappeared. In my book Mum had earned something for two years of her life with that nutter of a woman. When I tackled Betty about the lies she said she knew nothing about it. Bursting into tears and accusing me of upsetting her she said she had been protected from all life's little nasties and couldn't cope with what I was saying. As she was a married woman of about twenty-four I thought it was time she grew up. I didn't know until years later that Betty hated Sheila. She was the young woman who married her father. I wish I had known about Betty's hatred, I would have had nothing to do with her. It would have saved me a traumatic experience later on.

Events moved along very quickly with Alan. He took me home to meet his parents. Perhaps women are naturally more inquisitive than men. I prized all the information I could out of them. His mum was a stepmum. His real mum had died when he was young. He originally wanted to go to sea for a couple of years to get away but there was a waiting list. If he signed on the dotted line for twenty years they would take him straight away. So there he was, about two years into the twenty.

Finally the day arrived when Alan and I were going to meet my parents. We chatted away intently as the bus wound its way through the country roads on its way up to Gants Hill. If I was nervous it would only be because I hoped they liked him. I was hiding nothing, there was nothing to hide in my eyes. Now Alan is quite an intelligent man, he was away at sea, seeing something of the world. He wasn't a mollycoddled mummy's boy. He was nobody's fool – or so one would assume. Imagine the scene as we went into the house and I introduced him to my parents. Sheila wasn't much older than me, in fact there were times when I looked older than her. People would ask Sheila if I were her daughter and she would reply, "Actually she's my mother."

So there was this young woman, obviously a Christian and very Irish. There was this mature man, thirty years older, you couldn't miss the fact he was Jewish, very Jewish, even a blind man could see that his nose covered his face. The afternoon went extremely well. Knowing now what I didn't know then, I wonder what was in Alan's mind. Not a lot I would say. He must have been brain dead. He certainly wasn't inquisitive like me. On arriving back on his ship he wrote to my parents, (Mum and Dad) Sheila and Jack Jacobs thanking them for the meal. He also wrote to me. One envelope was addressed to *Mr and Mrs J Jacobs*, the other envelope was addressed to *Miss Leila Merriman*. Everything was wonderful.

Alan embraced the large Merriman clan. He went to Maidenhead to Lily, Bill and Sheila. He rowed over to the island and picked apples. He saw lots of Una, Pat and Maureen. There weren't any members of the large family he didn't know. There wasn't a huge conspiracy of silence. I was me, and had been around the family for a long time. I was accepted for myself with all my human faults. They had long stopped talking about me. Alan saw nothing strange in the different surnames and never once asked a question. It would have been different if he had asked something and I had lied to him. He could have asked just out of curiosity – "Have you been adopted? Did your real father die?" In those days, divorce wasn't an option. Women didn't get divorced. There was no support for them if they did and nowhere for them to go. He could have asked – "Has your mother married twice? How comes a young Catholic girl married an older Jewish gentleman?" There were lots of questions he could have asked but he didn't. He never asked a question. My future husband, the love of my life who was to take me to hell and back, never asked a question.

Wasn't life wonderful. I was a changed girl. I was in love with a lovely man who loved me. All the uncertainties of the past had gone. He gave me such confidence. He loved me for myself, he loved me. There was nothing about Alan, not one doubt in my mind, nothing to give the slightest clue to the horrendous future I was going to have with him. He was gentle, kind, easy going, mentally smart and a real charmer. I was such a lucky girl to have landed a chap like him.

Chapter Six

My swimming was beginning to suffer. Weekends when Alan was home I skipped training and soon got dropped to the reserve team. This hurt too much so I retired from the sport that had kept me sane in earlier years. It was a small price to pay for the happiness I had found. He was the perfect man and any sacrifice was worth it. Two years passed. Trips to Beehive Lane were frequent when, out of the blue, Alan asked me to marry him. He bought a diamond engagement ring and sitting on a bench at the top of Pier Hill he slipped the ring on my finger. We sat there for ages, looking out to sea, completely at peace with each other. Totally in love and committed to each other for life. If only I knew the nightmare that lay ahead. If only I knew the hell. As soon as Sheila heard of the engagement she demanded I come and live with her and Jack. She could contain everything there, protect her little secrets. She would have her finger on the pulse, would be able to organise everything, control it all.

The move to Beehive Lane wasn't a problem for me. My firm got me a very nice job in the West End. I had been with my old boss since I was fifteen, had progressed well there, designing some pieces of jewellery for him and I was the chargehand. Now, twenty-one, it was time to move on. With my brand new engagement ring on my finger it was time to start my new job. Sheila was excited. It was a Jewish firm and she knew I would get on very well with them. My new boss had a young son not much older than myself. He instantly took a shine to me which I found embarrassing. All the other girls must have noticed. The last thing I wanted was to be the boss's pet. He asked me if I would accompany him to the Arsenal Football match the coming Saturday. *No way.*

I wasn't ever going to let my husband-to-be down. He was a millionaire – don't people do some foolish things when they are young. I could be at home now polishing my diamonds! It was a very glamorous job and I loved it. There were some lovely lunches out through work and at Christmas the party was at a swank Soho restaurant. That first Christmas party I had bought myself a black sleeveless dress with a wide red cummerbund. As I was getting ready, Mum came into my room with a brown paper parcel. It was rare for her to do anything like it. On opening the parcel, I found a white, fun fur jacket. It was beautiful. With that over my dress I looked like the cat's whiskers; someone would sweep me off my feet. Mum was pulling out all the stops, but I had a funny feeling she would be delighted to see me split with Alan. I told myself she was just concerned at the length of time he was away at sea and I had chosen a lonely life for myself. There was nothing more sinister than that. She certainly wouldn't come between us because I was *Miss Loyalty Number 1*.

I absolutely loved my job and the people who worked with me. Sheila and Jack (Mum and Dad) were there. I never questioned them. More importantly, I had a fiancé, the house was sheer luxury. What more could a girl want? I seemed to have it all. Life seemed a long way from Moortown, from the poverty and that little girl of eight who lost her grandmother and lost her way along the road. The months passed happily. There was only one fly in the ointment – Jack started meeting me off the tube and borrowing the fares to the dogs and enough for a bet. Sheila was back to her card-playing ways and back to her gambling. They didn't work, there wasn't any rent to pay but the gas, electricity and phone bills etc. had to be paid. Where was the money coming from for food and clothes etc? Mum was still young and beautiful and stayed out all night. I always wondered what she was doing. Jack never said anything.

My wages were now very good, so I didn't mind giving Jack the few quid every day. I was saving very hard for the wedding and as I didn't have a bank account I was saving my big money at home. It didn't enter my head to hide it from Jack. My only concern was to keep it safe from burglars. In my bedroom was a large old fashioned chest of drawers. My woollies were in the third drawer down. It wasn't very original, but safe, to hide my money between the folds of my jumpers. The day came for me to have a spend up. As it was, I was going without little extras young girls need by giving Jack the few quid every day. On opening the drawer one day and plunging my hands in amongst the woollies I realized there was nothing there just a note which read *Sorry, I had to have it.* What do you say, nothing. I felt so desperate it had taken me nearly a year and it was all gone. It was never ever mentioned.

We were still in the 50s so it was rarer then for an Irish Catholic woman to be married to a Jewish man. It was never talked about between Alan and myself. Still not one question about the different names. There was never any remark by Alan that would lead me into saying something about my parents. If he had said any little thing I could imagine me saying, "Well! You know I'm not sure if Sheila is my mother. Jack certainly isn't my father. How could he be? He's a Jacobs, I'm a Merriman!" It seems even strange now there was never anything said because one day Alan came home and said he wanted to become a Catholic. "Whatever for?" I asked. He had spent a lot of time with my cousins and his answer was that our wedding day was going to be perfect. He wasn't going to deny his bride her right to a nuptial Mass and a nuptial blessing by having a mixed marriage. I was going to have the full rights of the Catholic Church. I wasn't particularly impressed; a mixed marriage, Catholic and Church of England didn't worry me at all. I had long since been disenchanted with the Catholic Church although I definitely believed in God.

The day came when Alan became a Catholic. Did that mean to him that he believed we were all God's children created in his image? I mean this is a man who had deliberately become a Catholic. It was time now for meetings with the Priest to discuss the wedding. Of course, the Priest asked us our future plans. We both said, a home first, a car and later a family. The Priest exploded. "You're not thinking of using those filthy contraceptives." He could have said nicely something like – "You know the Catholic Church forbids birth control." He sent us home with a flea in our ear. Sheila phoned to complain to him and he told her, "It had to be said." Fair enough, but it was the way it was said. Next visit to the Priest we assured him we would not use anything. What a hypocritical, two-faced lot the Catholic faith is. It just makes liars out of people. At the end of the day, if people believe in God then that's the important thing, leading good decent lives and trying to be a good person.

The wedding plans were well under way. There wasn't going to be a honeymoon. Alan had just started a two-year posting ashore at Portsmouth. We had got a couple of rooms in a large house, occupied mostly by service families. My firm drove down all my possessions. They were sorry to lose me (it had been a great time working there) and they couldn't do enough to help. They acted as though they were losing a member of their family.

Working in London, I had all the big shops to browse through. My wedding dress was very fancy – satin, lace, frills and bows. I had always wanted a tiara, so a tiara it was. Now I had to watch the pennies. The silly bits of underwear I had planned to buy were left on the shelf. If I had wanted to take my workmates out for a meal that was no longer possible.

It was going to be an Easter Monday wedding. Sheila had pulled out all the stops and, most importantly, taken care of everything. If she hadn't been so protective and had left bits of paper lying around for people to see she would have got her wish. There wouldn't have been a wedding. She had baked a three-tier cake and prepared a wonderful spread. The family started arriving on the Good Friday. Uncle Tom was there to give me away. He had always been there for me. As a little girl, I remembered when I met him in Delvin. There was always a ha'penny for sweets at Tierneys. Jack wasn't coming to the wedding. He couldn't miss the afternoon's dog racing. That wasn't a problem. Michael, Tom's oldest boy, was best man. Beautiful Maureen was to be bridesmaid. She would look lovely in her dress and all the boys would swoon over her afterwards. I loved my cousin to bits but I was always envious of her. Una and Pat arrived. Lily was there with a fag in her mouth, stuttering and swearing like a trooper. The cards were being played day and night and there would be a fight over the kitty if it reached a few shillings. The whiskey and gin flowed. The frying pan sizzled the whole weekend. Family crashed out for a nap where they could. The youngsters sat up all night singing songs of home. One or two played an instrument. It was a great weekend.

Finally, the wedding morning arrived. I was almost sick with excitement and nerves. Almost ready, I passed to look out of the window. There, to my amazement, pacing up and down on the opposite side of the road was Alan. He looked wonderful. In a way I was pleased to see him. He is here for the wedding. Of course he would be, I said to myself. He wouldn't let me down, my lovely husband-to-be. He would never let me down. I didn't have a doubt about anything in my mind. We had been together three whole years. We must have written a million words to each other, discussed every subject you could imagine and knew each other though and through. I had often felt let down in the past but today was for real – no doubts, just certain of a wonderful future. I still wasn't sure if Sheila was my mum or not. Dad I just accepted. After today I'd be away from them. They would be in the background. I wondered if my darling grandmother and lovely grandad would be sharing my happiness. It would have been fantastic if they had lived to see this day.

Putting a final dab of powder on my face in the mirror, I saw a young girl about to start the most wonderful journey of her life with a wonderful man by my side who would never let me down. If only that were true, if only. The clouds above were black and about to burst thunderously. I was completely unaware of the events that were going to unfold that day. Something unbelievable was about to happen which would scar my life forever. Something so unbelievable that as long as I lived I couldn't see how it happened and something I was never going to get over.

The wedding car had arrived – a white Rolls Royce, of course. Sheila could put on a show. On the journey to the church, the car had to negotiate a roundabout. Sitting there in my beautiful dress, holding tightly to my bouquet, I was conscious of the shoppers stopping to have a peep at the bride as they do. With my lovely Uncle Tom at my side I wished the car would go round the roundabout several times. I wanted to savour every moment. The family had done me proud. It was a small jealousy between the cousins who had the most immediate family at their wedding. No one missed my day. They were all very proud.

The service was beautiful and very nerve racking and I was glad when it was all over.

What's in a name? I had my own now, Mrs Leila B. We had just exchanged our wedding vows *"In sickness and in health, for richer or poorer, for BETTER or WORSE..."* or whatever. On Alan's insistence on a nuptial Mass and nuptial blessing, it was done with the full might of the Catholic Church, no second best for him. He had just embraced the Catholic Church with vigour where all children are God's children. The marriage certificate was signed and now we faced the walk down the aisle. The smiles of approval from all around. The hustle and bustle of the photographers and then home for the reception. All smiles cutting the cake, still not a sign of the nightmare that was to unfold later that day.

It must have been about then that he took the marriage certificate out of his pocket and looked at it for the first time. He had changed and was so nasty to me that I crept up to my room and climbed into my bed to have a good cry. Nobody missed me the whole afternoon. They were all having such a good time. Even my new husband didn't check on how I was, even the Priest, who had popped in for a large brandy, didn't bother about me.

It was time for us to catch our train so somebody came bursting in. "Oh, there you are." Nothing about the fact that I had been missing all afternoon. I got myself together very quickly. I might have had just a little thought – What was the afternoon all about? – but in the panic of getting everything together there wasn't time to think about anything. Loads of hugs and kisses from uncles, aunts, cousins and friends. Some guests insisted on coming to the station to see us off. Some were too well-oiled to be able to stand straight. Others were just anxious to get back to their game of cards. The train pulled into the station. More hugs and kisses, calls of "Take care of yourselves," "Good luck." We boarded the train to start a journey that was to see me in hell for the next ten years.

Chapter Seven

We had a compartment to ourselves. Happily, I sank back into my seat. There weren't any bad thoughts about the afternoon. I wasn't going to expect sunshine and roses all the way. Incidents would happen from time to time. So the afternoon had been quickly forgotten. Now, for the first time, I was alone with that lovely man I had just married. It was a wonderful feeling and I couldn't be happier. Alan didn't sit next to me to put his arm around me and whisper words of comfort. Instead, he had sat opposite and as the train started to pull away, he sat bolt upright, ashen, with a look of thunder on his face. He started to undo the buttons on his jacket. With one hand on the left side of his jacket he held it open. Reaching into the inside pocket with his other hand he took out a piece of paper. Handing it to me and looking as though he was going to explode, he said to me, "Explain this!" I was quite taken aback. Trying to keep my composure, I took the piece of paper from him. Opening it up I realized it was our marriage certificate. I read it quickly.

"Explain what?" I asked him.

"Read it again," he said through clenched teeth.

So I read it again. *"Elizabeth Winifred Merriman"* – Yes, that was the name I was given at birth. Alan, was who he said he was, everything else read alright. *"Father unknown"* – Well, that's not surprising. So what, I thought and looking at him I asked again.

"Explain what?"

Sitting opposite me was the man I had that very day married. A man who had just taken a vow, for better or worse, till death us do part. I thought he was going to explode. He was so mad.

"I've just married a fucking bastard! Who the fucking hell are you?"

I sat stunned. He might as well have hit me over the head with a hammer. I was shocked to the core.

"I'm me, Leila, I'm me," I said pleading with him.

"Who the fucking hell are you?" he shouted. "Whose fucking blood have you got in your veins? You're a liar, a cheat, a conniving bitch. You've tricked me into this marriage. I'd NEVER have married you if I'd have known."

Leaning towards me in a very threatening manner and frightening the life out of me he asked, "Do you know what we do with bastards in the navy?"

I sat there absolutely stunned. If I was capable of reasoning with myself I would have just stood up and with quiet dignity, pulled the communication cord, stopped off the train and walked away. The nightmare lasted ten years before I stood in court and got a divorce for cruelty on those very words.

This book is about Sheila and me, not Alan. Because of the concern I have for my two children, those ten years will be glossed over and just a flavour will be given. A lot will be left out. This book, after all, is the story of my life and those ten years are a very important part. What happened to me then made me what I am today, proud of the journey I have trodden, proud of what I have achieved and proud of how far I have come.

The biggest problem I soon found out was, it didn't matter how violent the rows were, Alan still wanted his rights as a husband. At first I would think, he really loves me, wants me, needs me. I would convince myself a man doesn't sleep with a woman just for sex. Give him time, he really would like me and trust me. He would realize none of it was my fault and that I was an honest person. When we are old and grey, sitting by the fire, surrounded by children and grandchildren we would laugh about this. We would say remember our wedding day – weren't we stupid. But Alan was never going to forgive and forget. As the days, weeks, months, then years passed, his anger, bitterness and frustration grew deeper and deeper.

Fortunately, or unfortunately, whichever way I look back on it, before I had time to fully unpack the Suez Crisis started and Alan was posted abroad for eighteen months. It was fortunate in as much as it was a cooling off process and it gave us time to have two children who had to be born. Unfortunately, it did nothing for me as a wife. A long absence gave me time to build up a resistance. Our letters being censored did nothing to help. It would have been a strain writing anyway but when you know a stranger was reading what you were writing it made matters worse. In one letter Alan wrote: *I am keeping my head down. I'd rather be a live coward than a dead hero.* That figures, I thought, a live coward. Any man who beats up a woman is a coward. So the seeds of doubt were well sown in my mind from day one.

Within six weeks of the wedding, I was back home, back with Mum and Dad, back in my old job. Nothing had changed, only now I was married. Now I knew what a terrible mistake I had made. I would keep my secret very close to my heart. No one would know the truth. No one would know I was a battered wife. Times were tough. It was like three strangers living under the same roof. We never talked about the important things. Alan was desperate to find the answers and couldn't believe I knew nothing. He still believed I tricked him into the wedding. He believed, no matter what I said, he believed I knew, had always known. There was no way I could approach Sheila. If I ever hinted anything, she would fly into a rage and scream: "Go away from me. Haven't I got enough on my plate without having to cope with a mad woman!"

That was one thing Mum and Alan had in common, one thing they did agree on. I was totally mad. Alan believed because I was born out of wedlock I was absolutely no good

– rotten to the core. He honestly believed he could have me certified, put away in a madhouse. He really believed because I was all of these things I would one day just die. That would have suited him fine. I used to wonder how I would die, how did he think I would die. There wasn't anyone fitter or stronger than I was, so it wasn't going to be easy for me to pass away.

The eighteen months flew and Alan was due home. The business with Solly and May's estate was nearing an end. Travelling to the docks to meet Alan I wondered what things were going to be like after such a long time. The docks were crowded, the band played. Although I was feeling apprehensive, it was a tremendous sight seeing the warship coming home and you couldn't help feeling excited. We were all straining to get that first sight of our loved ones.

It went without saying, I had played it straight while Alan was away, being loyal and faithful was second nature to me. So it came as a shock to me one day, when Alan had been home some time, that he asked me if he could have a look at my private parts. He told me I wouldn't be able to go to work for a while and that I had to see a doctor. I had crabs. What the hell are crabs? I soon found out what he was like away from home. It was another nail in the coffin. He was the one who reckoned I was no good, yet you don't behave much lower than him.

Cousin Sheila was next to get married and she asked me to be her matron-of-honour. All those cousins, always someone getting married. It was the first time I had been asked to be bridesmaid. I was thrilled. When the invitation arrived, Mum said I had been asked because I was ugly. All the cousins were beautiful and cousin Sheila didn't want anyone to outshine her on her day. I travelled to Maidenhead alone the day before, no way was I going to be late on the day. The hotel was very nice and, after a leisurely breakfast, I made my way to Auntie Lily's to prepare for my big moment.

How I envied cousin Sheila on her wedding day. Her husband's parents owned a garage and it was obvious they were financially well off. The reception was at a very smart hotel and was a lovely affair – not like my home-made do. His mother wore the most gorgeous mink coat and was dripping in diamonds. Sheila was four years older than me which put her in her late twenties. She had done well by waiting, what a good catch. A year before her death we had lunch in a very smart restaurant. We were both financially secure then so we ordered the best. I had long been trying to talk her into putting her life story down on paper. Like me, she thought the children would be upset. I knew by now quite a lot of her story, and if I thought mine was traumatic it doesn't touch hers. Chatting over lunch that day, she told me about her violent upbringing. Something I find very hard to believe. Even in her twenties if she came home late, her father would order her upstairs and, as she walked up the stairs, he would thrash her legs with a cane. In the end, the violence was so bad she vowed that the next man to ask her to marry him she would accept even if he were a tramp.

The man she did marry, Gordon, was in his thirties. He first asked her out because he needed a lady companion to accompany him to a presentation dinner. It progressed from there. Now cousin Sheila was one sexy lady, always up for a laugh and with a terrific sense of humour. She thought it a bit odd that he never touched her and put it down to a combination of respect and shyness. The first bombshell came before they were married. Sheila had noticed that her husband-to-be had a lot of illnesses and he asked her to accompany him to the doctor. He had some sexually transmitted virus and the doctor wanted to check that she hadn't given it to him. Sheila was appalled. This was the 1950s, so gay man and the illnesses they carried weren't in the vocabulary of ordinary people. She told me that day over lunch. With all the signs, she never twigged. It was when she was in hospital having her baby he was cautioned for offences against boys. The news shattered her life. She vowed when her youngest was eighteen (there were two children) she would walk away. He continued with his men lovers and she kept her word. She walked away. When she first approached a solicitor for a divorce, she was told her husband having an affair with a man wasn't grounds. She did get her divorce in the end. The whole experience put her off marriage ever again and she lived alone for the rest of her life. Gordon had dozens of lovers through the years. His favourite haunt was Bournemouth. He would stay away weeks at a time, scouring the gay bars there. Sheila kept her finger on the finances mainly for the children's sake.

Almost on his death bed, Gordon fell passionately in love with a twenty-six-year-old man. He gave this lad a great time – swanky hotels, smart restaurants, designer clothes. Gordon mentioned to Sheila one day that he was going to give this lad control of a sixty thousand pound insurance policy so he could learn about finance and responsibility etc. It took Sheila five minutes to get to the solicitors and block it. On hearing he wasn't going to get his hands on the sixty grand, the young man did a runner. Gordon was distraught. He cried on Sheila's shoulder. "I love him. Please get him back for me." He couldn't understand that a diseased-ridden skeleton of a man, as he was then, was only wanted for his money.

Sheila had started to put it all down on paper. We spent hours on the phone. Sadly, she died prematurely.

About a year after Sheila's wedding, there was a mega row in my family which over forty years on hasn't been resolved. Sheila never let me down. She was always there for me. So it was a privilege to have spent the time with her a year before her death. Sitting in that smart restaurant, we were two ladies in our late sixties, very much at ease in each other's company. She was shocked at the story that she had asked me to be matron-of-honour because I was ugly. On the contrary she said, all the cousins were jealous of my beautiful dark looks. We both had had a bad life but now at the end of the day we were at peace with ourselves. We laughed about the film moguls turning our life story into a blockbuster.

"Who would play you?" Sheila asked.

I said I fancied Julia Roberts.

"No, no," said Sheila. "She wouldn't be nearly pretty enough."

How we giggled and did each other's confidence the power of good. We had come a long way since Sheila's mother, Lily, asked why I hadn't been drowned at birth. Sheila was surprised at the ignorance of our aunts and uncles. Most of them seemed so uneducated and they never developed any social graces. I told her she was being hard on them. She hadn't grown up in Ireland as I had and I saw things differently. Our aunts and uncles were born at the turn of the century into a poor family. They never had a chance to make anything of themselves. They were all of the old brigade – bigoted Catholics indoctrinated with the religion. Mind you they wouldn't sit next to a black man or woman in church. For me, it was good to see her. Someone up above told me to get in touch. A year later when I learned of her death, I was very grateful for the lovely memories.

Alan's next posting was at Chatham, just across the water. We had two rooms with a lovely lady. She was spotlessly clean. When the coalman dumped the coal down the shoot into the cellar, she went into overdrive. She asked me to go down into the cellar and sweep the coal to the side, sweep up all the dust, then wash and polish the parts of the floor not covered in coal. I agreed with Alan on that one, I was mad to do it. While we were there, Sheila and Jack moved back to Westcliff. They had their pay out from Beehive Lane and were set for life, so I thought. However difficult things were they were all I had, they were my only family, so I was anxious to get home and have a nose! Life was difficult with Alan. It was like treading on eggshells all the time and never knowing when the next smack would materialise.

At the first opportunity, I made for home. Funny how a place I had never seen was home. As soon as that ship pulled out of harbour, I was gone. Arriving at the front door it looked impressive. Sheila and Jack had rented a downstairs flat in a very old house so the rooms were huge with great high ceilings. Standing at the front door, you looked down a straight hallway to the back bedroom. The huge lounge was in the front and had a big bay window. Everything in the room was red – red carpet, red curtains, big red suite with red cushions. The dining room was next – red carpet, red curtains, dining room suite with red seats on the chairs. The kitchen and bathroom was painted red and white. It was a lovely large flat but red throughout. I vowed never to have red in my home. The important thing was at last Sheila and Jack had a home. They could settle down now and hopefully grow old together.

I was staying over for a couple of days. The big back bedroom was mine. Little did I know that later it would be home for Alan, myself and a baby. In the morning, Jack came quietly into my room and handed me a box of chocolates. That was a surprise. It wasn't Jack's scene to give presents.

"Could you just lend me fifty pounds?" he asked.

That was a lot of money to me at the time, but what worried me was he had just received a pay out from Beehive Lane and here he was broke and borrowing already. The future looked bleak for Jack.

Chapter Eight

Next stop for Alan and myself was Rosyth in Scotland. We had a lovely flat over a shop next door to the swimming pool in Dunfirmlin. I always wondered why at naval bases I was stuck on my own out of town. Most of the other naval wives were housed at the base at Rosyth. They had each other for comfort and support while I was very lonely and alone, especially at nights when the shops shut.

The ship was out at sea for weeks on end and time dragged particularly at weekends. Sundays I would take a long walk in the beautiful park in Dunfirmlin, making sure I was home before it was dark because I was frightened of going indoors if it was dark. I knew no one and wondered what secrets my husband was hiding, whatever they were he was going to great lengths to keep me from finding out. I never came in contact with any of the other wives, there must have been hundreds and hundreds of other wives, yet I never met one of them.

To pass the time and may I say, keep myself sane, I went job hunting. First I got a job selling Christmas cards in Woolworths, then I got a job at the wool factory Paten and Baldwins, This is absolutely no criticism of the factory, they were very good to me. My problem was after three years of marriage I was pregnant. Around the huge factory floor were very large tubs. They soaked the sheep coats in the tubs to clean them and remove the oil. Whatever was used the smell made me vomit but that was down to me. The alternative was to stay at home with not a soul to talk to; perhaps that was the plan, that I would die of loneliness.

The great big looms were awesome, I thought I would never be able to master them. All those strands of wool spinning around, all having to be kept under control, all whizzing into balls of wool on the pegs. It was a very early start and January and February in Scotland was freezing, I'd go home every evening to a cold empty flat, bolt the door and not move until the next morning. My other problem was the language; of course everyone was speaking English but the accent was so broad I couldn't understand a word anyone said to me. That didn't really matter, my whole day was spent trying to master the loom.

Across the road from the flat was the dance hall. Saturday nights I'd sit on the arm of the chair and watch the young people coming and going. They all seemed to be having such fun, laughing and hugging each other as they went on their way. Every Thursday evening two people from the Salvation Army knocked, I told them I didn't have a lot of time for them. They said that wasn't important and insisted on calling anyway. They sat together on one side of the fire and just talked. I realize now they probably sat together because the flat was cold. I thought they were odd people and wondered why they came and what they got out of it. Looking back I realize they could probably see the picture, and understood just how lonely and lost I was. I don't think at that time any human being could have been so lonely and miserable.

Odd from the very start of my pregnancy I travelled home to Westcliff to see my doctor for my antenatal appointments. Almost as if I had a premonition, playing football Alan broke his leg and was airlifted to the naval hospital in Portsmouth. That was the end of that posting.

I do have one lovely memory of Scotland which will stay with me all my life. I don't know who the people were, I had never heard of them before nor did I ever hear of them again. Alan and I were invited to spent the New Year with them. The place was huge, in its own grounds, and there were dozens of people there. It was a real Hogmanay, the first footing, a huge turkey with all the trimmings carved at midnight, a few drams of the local bevy were drank. After dinner everyone played games, the Hula-Hoop had just reached the shops, all the grown-ups showed themselves up trying to do it. Everyone fell about laughing. I was expecting, and by three in the morning I was feeling a bit groggy so I quietly asked the host if there was anywhere I could lie down. I was shown into a beautiful room where everything was in Chintz and lace. I slept like a log, Alan wouldn't have missed me if I had gone home. But I did have an admirer, he knew I had gone to bed not feeling too good. Apparently he checked on me now and then. Suddenly he got the urge to wake me up but couldn't find a reason. Then he had a brainwave. It was early morning, snow up to the ankles, he went outside with a jug, milked a cow and came into the bedroom with the jug of warm milk. Making enough noise to wake me, he offered me the warm milk. He didn't know I was already suffering from morning sickness. The milk turned my stomach over and I was sick all over the beautiful bedclothes. I must have been the only person not drinking that night, yet I was the one to show myself up. That was the only time I have celebrated a Scottish New Year, I shall always remember the kindness and the generosity of the Scottish people.

It was five days later when Alan and I got home. I had to pack and travelled home to Mum and Dad again. I wasn't too thrilled at having to share with them, plus Alan when he came out of hospital, plus a baby. The thought of all of us together was horrendous. Alan hated Sheila like poison. He thought she was the wickedest woman on this earth. All she had done when she was a naïve young girl was have a baby. But, of course, the problem wasn't so much having the baby it was the continuing secrecy. Just as he was recovering from his broken leg, he slipped in the bathroom and broke an arm. Not that I wished him any harm, but I said a little prayer.

"Please God, make it his bleeding neck next time!"

Sheila and Jack were in business now. They had rented a corner premises. Jack had his betting shop at the front and round the corner Sheila had her café/restaurant. They were in heaven. Jack was in his glory gambling all day and Sheila had always wanted her own restaurant. Lily and Bill moved down to Westcliff to help her. This was going to be a great success.

It was a baking hot summer, my bump was getting bigger. To pass the time, I got a job on the biscuit counter in Woolworths. I suffered miserably with lumbago but ploughed on. I thought how hard I had worked since my wedding day. In Portsmouth, it was a grocer's. Chatham, it was the Phillips factory. Rosyth, it was Woolworths and Paten and Baldwins. Never a big spender, I didn't smoke or drink and never visited a hairdresser. Most of my spare cash was running on a horse or a dog – they were still running as far as I was concerned.

Finally, at seven months, the day came for me to give up work. I found myself alone all day; after the two shops closed there was always a race meeting, a card school or the casino. Out of the Beehive Lane money, John had been lent the money to set himself up in a carpet business. Evenings Sheila would give him the petrol money to take her and Jack to the dogs. When there, she would give him five pounds to have a bet and treated him to eats and a drink. This was most nights. There was always something going on somewhere. After all that, Jack would come home broke and was on the borrow. John was broke as well. He could tell a sob story like the best. Like his dad he hadn't worked out that you don't make a living gambling. John went bankrupt and owed Sheila and Jack two grand.

Nobody was interested in housework – well, they were never at home. I was so mad at the life they were leading that I took it out on the furniture. The place shone. The answer was to leave everything as it was and live in a mess but that wouldn't suit me. Feeling fed up with it all one day, I was just over seven months pregnant, I walked round to see the other half of the comedy act, Betty. It was a surprise to see Bernie open the door. He was home in the middle of the day and she was out. That wasn't a problem, I had known him very well for nine years now. I went inside happily and plonked myself on the settee which luckily for me was right by the door. Suddenly, he leapt on me, he literally just attacked me. I managed to push him off and get to the door. Then I ran. I could hear him shouting, "Come back Leila, come back." Reaching the end of the road, it was only a short distance, I stopped to check if it was safe to do so and check how far behind me he was. He was still on the other side of his gate, leaning over. I never spoke to him again as long as he lived. He died in his fifties. He went outside one day to clear the snow away and dropped dead. Suddenly, I didn't go around any more. When my baby was born, I didn't phone. I stopped sending Christmas cards and when Bernie died, I didn't get in touch. I still see Betty. She lives probably less than a quarter of a mile from me. Conversation is very polite, not once has she ever said anything. It would be pointless for me to say anything to her. She wouldn't understand what I was talking about. She would probably tell me she has had such a protected life, she knew nothing. Then she would burst into tears and tell me, "You're upsetting me."

Alan was home when the baby arrived – well, up the road in a pub. In fact, when he was home most of the time he was in the pub. He never ceased to criticize and his conversation stopper when he got mad, which was on a regular basis, was "Whose fucking blood had that baby got in his veins?"

The baby was a cracker. All mums think their babies are beautiful and he certainly was. He was dark like myself, dark hair and dark eyes.

"Can't you accept it's good blood?" I would ask Alan.

"No, I fucking well can't," he would shout, fists flying and then off to the pub. One day I was so pissed off I marched into the pub to confront this man Alex my husband was spending all his time with. I reminded him that Alan was a married man with a young baby and Alan was spending all his money on beer. The chap looked me in the face and with a sneering grin said, "Darling, if he doesn't want to be at home with you, there's nothing I can do about it."

How humiliated and low can you get. I felt awful.

The great friendship between Alan and Alex came to a sudden end. In the early days of our marriage Alan had got himself a very nice car. No travelling on the bus or train for him, it was good enough for me though. Once again Alan got a posting overseas and he asked Alex to sell his car for him, which Alex was happy to do. Well, of course he wanted commission, no messing around, he wanted his commission. Alan told him to F off. Alex wasn't having that and he told Alan if he didn't pay up he would take him to court, which he did and of course he got the money he was entitled to. It is unprintable what Alan had to say. Once again I wondered what was in his mind, to think he could get away with it. I honestly think Alan thinks there is a rule for him only and another rule for the rest of us.

The coming summer when Stephen was between nine and fifteen months old, Alan got a six-month posting overseas. Jack was getting deeper and deeper into debt. He had taken some very large bets and hadn't paid them off. Insurance policies were being sold, all the piggy boxes were raided. He was begging and borrowing. As always, he came to me. I just didn't have the amount of money needed to bail him out. I did have some money, but it would make very little difference. Now that I had my son, I decided it was time to look after myself. So I told Jack the kitty was empty. Even if I had given him my last penny, he would still be broke, so I have no regrets.

It was a lovely warm Sunday and I thought I would have a day out with my son. Have a picnic on the cliffs, walk along the seafront, perhaps sit down in a deckchair and watch the world go by. My first stop was the restaurant, a cup of tea with Sheila. Sitting at a small table alone with Stephen, right by the counter I was deep in thought. Jack walked in, he didn't see me sitting there and I can't believe I never spoke to him. I must have been so deep in thought that I just looked at him and said nothing. He could have been a total stranger. Sheila hadn't spoken to me either, she was busy preparing dinner. Jack called to Sheila. She left the kitchen and came out. She didn't see me, or if she did she didn't acknowledge me.

Jack said to her: "Please don't make me do it, please don't make me do it."

"Go home and do it," was all Sheila said to him.

Jack still didn't see me and he walked out, head down without speaking another word. It didn't seem a very interesting conversation to me, it could be anything and nothing. I watched him walk away. He walked like an old man, totalling dejected. I let him go without calling out. I can't believe I didn't rush after him and walk along the road. I couldn't help him out of his financial troubles but I could have offered some comfort. Instead I did something I never did – clear off for the day and leave him totally alone.

It was quite late when I got home, well late when you have a young baby. There was no sign of Sheila, God alone would know where she was. Jack was asleep in bed. I saw to Stephen, then pottered about all evening. Jack never stirred. Looking in on him once or twice my instinct was not to disturb him. If I thought anything, it would be at least he is getting some rest after all the sleepless nights he has had lately with his worries. Normally I would have whispered something like "Are you awake, Dad, fancy a cup of tea?" But that evening – nothing.

Finally, it was time to get myself to bed. During the night the baby stirred and woke me up. The light was on in the long hallway, and peeping through my bedroom door which was ajar I saw Sheila sitting by the little table where the phone was. She had the telephone directory in her hand. I gave no thought to what she was doing. She appeared to be just sitting there. I got back into bed and went to sleep.

It was the usual early start with the baby, 6 a.m. and he was letting the world know he was around. All my bedroom lights went on and then I heard Sheila on the phone to the emergency services: "I've just woken up and I can't wake my husband," she said into the phone.

I quickly picked Stephen up and went out in the hallway. I suspected she had been sitting in the hallway all night. But self-preservation told me not to say anything. I had nowhere to go with my baby. Jack was still lying the way he was last evening, unconscious, and that's how he was taken into hospital. Later in the morning, I phoned the hospital to ask how he was.

"Are you a relative?" I was asked.

"Yes," I said, "I am his daughter." Well, he had always been the only dad I ever knew.

The doctor was very hostile. "Do you know your father has taken sixteen sleeping tablets?" he asked as if it were my fault.

"No," I said, "I didn't know. I'm absolutely shocked."

I had the sense not to say a word to Sheila. The outburst of abuse I would get would be unbearable. All those hallucinations I was supposed to suffer from, it would be something else I had imagined in my mad mind. I couldn't confide in my husband either. Better keep this to myself. Thinking things through, I asked myself – am I seriously suggesting Sheila demanded Jack went home and killed himself and then sat up all night without having a change of heart, wait as long as she could (which would be when I woke) hoping it would be too late. No, never, I told myself. It didn't happen like that. But I knew it had.

When I got to the hospital, Jack was in a deep coma. I leaned close to him and whispered, "It's me, Dad."

He responded immediately and frightened the life out of me. I ran to get a nurse, amazed that there was any life there. I leaned over him again and pleaded with him.

"Please, Dad, please," I said, "Don't die like this, not like this. Please, I beg you."

From that moment, he slowly came out of the coma and three weeks' later he was home.

He lived another five years but his health had suffered. Every time the doctor wrote out a prescription Mum would say, "Another ten years off my life."

I could see her predicament. She was this beautiful teenage girl, seduced by this old man. She had worked her heart out all her life and was still only a young woman. Every penny she earned, he gambled. There were the horrendous years when I came over from Ireland; she had obviously been pressurised by her large family into taking me on, a responsibility she didn't want. She didn't have any love for me nor the finances to keep me. It was a disastrous time for her; finally she ran away. She survived a couple of years of misery looking after Jack's brother and his wife, ran away from that and was given a chance with a few bob from Beehive Lane and what happened to that? It had gone like the rest, running on a horse or dog. Apart from murdering him herself, what else could she do? She was desperate. But why not just walk away.

It was the same story with Alan. He hated me like poison. When he came home and saw me, the hairs would stand up on his arms. I made his flesh creep. He really believed I was so evil I would just die naturally or he could have me committed. Why come home and verbally abuse and physically beat up a woman with a baby? Why not walk away? In both cases, it was the same old chestnut.

RESPECTABILITY. Sheila came from a large close-knit family and wouldn't admit to failing in her marriage. Alan, with all his airs and graces, as a Chief Petty Officer, P.E.T.T.Y – that word couldn't be more fitting – wouldn't want a divorce. It was far more respectable having a poor wife in a madhouse or even better if he was a widow. It wasn't very respectable being divorced. You don't get a lot of sympathy that way.

As for me staying, I was still wrestling with the vows I had taken. It would have to be very extreme before I broke those vows. Remember this was the 1950s and people just didn't get divorced.

Alan's reason for me being around was his allowance book which he reckoned I needed to live. He forgot I wasn't a weakling who needed a man to support me. I had been on my own, fighting my own battles, since I was eight. I didn't need his book. I'd be rich if I had a penny for every time he screamed at me "All you're interested in is my book." I married him because I loved him and until the end I hoped there would be a breakthrough.

Most of my time now was spent looking after Jack and Stephen. I tried to talk to Jack as much as I could but we never mentioned the hospital incident. One day Jack asked me to teach him how to say my prayers.

"Don't be silly, Dad," I said. "Prayers are all the same. There's only one God."

"But I want to make sure I'm going to the same place as you," said Jack.

He became a Catholic which was ridiculous. It didn't impress me. Funny how close we had always been even with all his gambling. I know if he had a chance to put my life on a dog with a fifty-fifty chance he would take the risk. But I honestly loved him.

Sheila was now running both businesses. She was out all day and, as usual, out most evenings as well. So it was great to hear out-of-the-blue that favourite Uncle Tom was coming to visit. I would make a special effort for lunch. It would be easier for him to eat with Mother but no, I wanted to spend some time with him. He had long left the army and was now working in Lyons Corner House. I was anxious to catch up on all the family gossip.

He sat himself down in an easy chair and the first words he spoke were: "How about you and me going into business together?"

Sheila was selling the café to pay off their debts. Once again I was the last to know. She would keep the betting shop and hoped to make a living gambling. Lily and Bill had long left and returned home to Maidenhead. It seemed a wonderful idea – the two of us in business together. So that was that. There was nothing to discuss. We both totally trusted each other and we could talk as we go. One thing was for certain, Tom had never, and would never, let me down. He just wouldn't let me down. I would trust him with my baby's life. So it was settled. Tom gave his notice in at Lyons and to make things even more cosy, he got a flat a couple of doors away from us. We both put in equal amounts of money. Now, for the record, and for the benefit of a large, nasty, jealous section of my family, let's get this straight. When Tom and I talked about buying a café/restaurant, a business, we were actually talking about buying the goodwill of a poxy café stuck on the corner of a side road. We actually each put in three hundred and seventy-five pounds for the goodwill, everything else was rented.

From day one, Tom worked harder than me. He would open at seven o'clock to get the workmen for breakfast. I came along at nine with my baby in the pram, work as hard as I could in the circumstances. Stephen would be sleeping outside or sitting inside in his high chair while he was awake. Then I went home at teatime while Tom would stay open until eleven at night. Not an ideal situation but Tom knew that was how it was. The most important thing to him was to be his own boss. Tom was in his element. At the bottom of the road, just a couple of hundred yards away, was a very large hotel which accommodated the overflow of army wives from Shoebury barracks. Most of the ladies had husbands overseas just like myself. They were in for their cigarettes or just a cup of tea and a chat. They got on like a house on fire with Tom. After all his years in the army, he was on their wavelengths. When I arrived in the morning, there would be a couple in the kitchen helping Tom with the breakfasts and a couple running round doing tables. After I left in the evenings, I knew there was an army of them in to help. I think they thought I just came in for the company. I was quite happy with everything. You know I never even asked Tom how much we were paying them. No need to ask questions, Tom seemed very happy with his life. He was working hard. We were very busy and it was exactly as he wanted it.

As the months passed, Stephen naturally grew and he got more and more restless. It was getting difficult coping with a lively little boy. One day things seemed to be going really well and Tom was in top form. It seemed the time to have a chat.

"Look, Tom," I said, "You seem to have it made. Would it be OK for me to stay at home?"

I had never had one penny in wages. You don't expect pay when you are building up a business. I made it quite clear to Tom that money didn't matter, I didn't want any. Tom honestly didn't mind me leaving and I retired from the restaurant. If I did think of money I would say to myself, one day I might get a surprise and boy did I get a surprise!

Time was flying by and Alan would be home in about three weeks for Christmas. That was the only change in our little family routine. Was it the trigger? Alan coming home and maybe asking questions. Sheila had left for the betting shop. She seemed to be making a success of it. As soon as she opened up, it was in to Tom for a cup of tea and a chat. She popped in during the mornings for more tea, lunchtimes for her dinner and afternoons for more tea. If there was anything wrong, if the café was dirty, or there were no customers, or Tom was down, she would know, Sheila was no fool. She saw her brother many times during the day every day and there was nothing wrong. One thing I know for certain, Sheila and Tom were very close. They thought the world of each other.

Jack and I were having a cuppa, he had missed me when I was on café duty but he had enjoyed having me around since my retirement. Suddenly, our peace was shattered by the sound of the phone. A total stranger informed me the café wasn't open and did I have a spare set of keys. No! I didn't have a spare set of keys and no, I knew nothing about Tom. But I would check his flat. Sheila was on the phone. No! I had no news and no suggestions.

At about 11 a.m. one of the searchers went around to the back of the café, looked through the kitchen window and saw Tom dead on the floor with his head in the oven. Sheila was home in minutes after phoning her sisters with the awful news of their wonderful brother. She was distraught. Soon Mina arrived. There would be trouble now, if there wasn't trouble already Mina was sure to make some. I was right. She laid into Sheila with her fists, called her a whore, yelled that she had been to bed with two men at the same time. What did all this have to do with Tom killing himself? It didn't matter to me what Sheila had ever said or done. Nobody hits or speaks to my mother like that. I threw myself at Mina and dragged her away asking her what the bleeding hell it had to do with her. Pushing her towards the front door I told her to mind her own business. Worse of all I told Mina poor Jack was in frail health and had to witness such a disgraceful scene.

"Poor old sod," I yelled at Mina as a I manhandled her out the front door. We have to listen to her threats, she would make it her mission in life to see Tom's boys get their share. Mina was always jealous of what other people had. She was a lying, spiteful, vile, foul-mouthed woman. Where did she come from, surely she couldn't be a Merriman.

Tom left only one note to me in which he wrote, *This will be a nine day wonder. You will soon find something else to talk about. Make sure you give the boys their share.* That showed the state of his mind – there was no "share" there were only bills.

One of my few regrets in life is that on that day I didn't pick the phone up and phone Auntie Maggie or any one of the three boys. Mina had left me totally shell-shocked. I had a baby to care for and I was left with a real live problem, perhaps one of them could phone me. The days passed and not a word from Sheerness. Mina had done a good job. No news about the funeral. I was so traumatised about it all that I couldn't phone now and face any more rows or rejections. Obviously there were some very bad feelings for no one to contact me, especially as they were part owner of a café. Sheila and I spent endless hours discussing our heartache wondering if we were in any way to blame. How could we, he was a grown man, with a wife and three grown up sons my age. How could we be to blame we asked ourselves hundreds of times. It was upsetting not to have a chance to go to the funeral and pay my last respects. I expected he was buried at Sheerness, after all that was the family home. They wouldn't all come to Southend for the funeral and not one of them call on Sheila or myself. They wouldn't be that cruel, not a word, so he was buried in Sheerness. It sounds silly but I knew in my heart he was in Southend. My lovely uncle was resting close by.

Alan arrived home for Christmas and it was a re-run of when we first met – just before Christmas when Solly and May died, now it was Tom. I hadn't been near the café and, credit where it's due, he took on the task of opening the place up. Whatever went on the day Tom died who knows. In the morning the fishmonger had delivered a box of wet fish. It had stayed on the kitchen table all day. No one had put it away in the fridge. The smell turned your stomach. Alan set about scrubbing the whole place out. It took the whole of his two weeks' holiday to get it fit to re-open. But he had a whole new arsenal of ammunition. He was married to a family of nutters and I was the nuttiest of them all. If it was the last thing he did, he would have me locked away. He complained about his meals, my mother's cooking, nothing was right. It never entered his head to go out and find a flat for Stephen and myself. He preferred to accept the hospitality of these nutters come home and abuse everyone.

Sheila was to get rid of the betting shop and help me out of the mess I found myself in. She made it clear she wanted paying for every second she worked. That was fair enough, she had an invalid husband to support plus a home to keep. The first letter I received was from Tom's landlord saying he had never paid the rent and enclosed the bill. It never crossed my mind to challenge the bill. As if he would have let Tom stay there for six months without paying any rent. Next Tom owed the tobacco company over a thousand pounds. Now we are talking about 1960 so a thousand pounds was a lot of money. There were bills from every quarter. All I could think about was my desire to continue living in the place I loved. To be able to walk down the street with my head held high and not to owe a soul a penny.

Stephen would have to be put in a nursery which was awful. At that time, children waited until they were five to go to school. Ordinary kids didn't go to nursery. It broke my heart. I had never been parted from him. As I walked away, the tears fell freely. It was like putting him in care. When I got back that tea time he was standing in a corner. He had wet himself. He didn't do it again, he was too frightened.

But now it was serious business. I had inherited a mountain of debt. None of it mine, but I had to work to pay it back. Sheila and I rolled our sleeves up and set to. The weeks passed and not a word from Sheerness. A great sadness remained with me. I thought a lot about missing the funeral and couldn't come to terms with the fact that I had done that. Often I asked myself if Sheila was to blame, selling us the café. Then I asked myself if I was to blame staying at home. But those thoughts soon passed because it was a really good business. One by one the debts were settled. Funny, not one of the crowd of army wives came near the place. They seemed to disappear off the face of the earth. Not that it would have been fair to ask them if they could throw some light on his death. Not one word from Sheerness. If they had been in touch and offered some words of comfort the café would have had a different ending.

One thing I knew for certain was I didn't want to work and live with my mother for longer than necessary. One other thing I was certain of was I didn't want to be in the café business and one further thing I was certain of was I didn't want to benefit by one penny from Tom's death. So when the last bill was paid I went to the Solicitors, next the Estate Agents and the café was put on the market for half price. It was sold, remember we are talking about goodwill only for three hundred and seventy-five pounds – my share of the business. Guess what – I heard from those three lovely lads in Sheerness. So, they did have tongues in their heads after all. I grew up in Ireland with those three boys. They were the backbone of my life. We knew, loved and trusted each other. When they said "jump" I knew I wouldn't land and hurt myself. We ran barefoot, wild and free. There was nothing but what we did have we shared. Now they thought there was a few bob. They forgot the rules. They had left me, with a baby, sweating my guts out to settle their father's debts which had nothing to do with me, only honour and now they wanted their share. You meet a few bastards in life, funny that I thought I was the bastard. My Solicitor soon put them straight. If people pulled together when the tragedy happened, if there had been one ounce of support, if that wicked bitch, Mina, hadn't set out to destroy, things might have been different because the café was a gold mine. It was a very sad chapter in my life and today, fifty years on, the rift remains. I never forgave Mina. She is now long dead. All I hope is that when she got to those Pearly Gates she got her comeuppance.

One job that fell to me was to clear out Tom's flat. I wondered why the boys hadn't been along to pick up their dad's possessions. I just put it down to them not being bothered. Painstakingly, I went through his mail trying to find one clue as to why he had killed himself. There was a reply to a letter he had written to Auntie Lily. He had obviously tried to borrow my share from Lily because he wanted to buy me out. Was he planning the deed and wanted to spare me the responsibility of his debts? Lily had written back saying she couldn't help and anyway if the little cow wanted her money (which I didn't, there was no question of it) I could wait.

It was a particularly bad time for Sheila, the betting shop and the café, the spoils from Gants Hill had gone. From the day Mum walked out on me as a seventeen-year-old without a word, until the will being settled took about eight years. Now everything had disappeared and she was back where she had started, only worse. She was that much older and Dad was an invalid. It had taken him less than two years to get through every penny. She now had to work really hard to support herself and Jack. She got a job housekeeping which didn't pay that well. She was in a very serious card school and always had the money to play cards. Jack was frail and almost blind. He would wander to the phone and ring the bookies to place a bet, but they wouldn't accept it. They long knew there wasn't any money for Jack to settle his debts. So Jack would wander back to his chair and sit down very dejected. He never went out and was a very lonely old man.

Alan was back and forth. He no longer had the support of his drinking pal Alex, so he was even more frustrated and bitter.

He hated us all like poison and Sheila hated him even more. What was it with those two, I used to ask myself. We had been married about five years now and life was at a crisis. I spent my days as a lodger in someone else's flat with a crying baby and a sad lonely old man for company. Mother was out day and night. Alan, when he came in, found it easier to start a fight and have a punch-up, then he could disappear down the pub.

The crunch came for me one Sunday afternoon. I had reached the ripe old age of twenty-seven; the years had not mellowed Alan at all, in fact the years had made him even more bitter, so much so he now considered me a health hazard. I had hoped with the baby we would have found something to break the deadlock but every day that passed he grew more angry. I was lost, just lost, totally fed up with the non-stop verbal and physical abuse. I hadn't been sleeping well for ages so, craving sleep, I took Mum's sleeping pills. They had no effect, might as well take a few Smarties, so I took a few more. It was like a curtain coming down. Boom.

Next I woke up in Southend General, with a doctor leaning over me asking me, "Why did you want to kill yourself?" That was the last thing on my mind, but it was just the shock I needed. It was the beginning of the beginning. It was almost the last straw for Alan. He asked, "How much more do you think I can stand?"

It wasn't how much more he could stand but how much more I could stand. I had received my wake up call, my brush with death, as the doctor at Southend General called it, had shaken me to the core. I thought I would never get over the incident, my grandma and grandad would be so ashamed of me. The strength and courage they had shown when they took Brendan and me on wasn't for this. But in a strange way it put an extra bone in my back. You don't go through an experience like that without changing and some good coming out of it. Never again would I shrink from a fight, I would always have the courage to go for what I thought was right.

Nothing was going to help me at that moment with my unhappy marriage. Domestic violence didn't exist, nobody spoke about a thing like that. It was as dark a secret as being born a bastard.

I seemed trapped whichever way I turned, and being married in the Holy Roman Catholic Church was going to be hard nut to crack. No one seemed to be helping me so I was going to help myself. It was desperate measures. Anything that involved leaving Jack was desperate. I was going to buy a house for Stephen and myself. I would look around for a little place. Finally I found my ideal home – a small two-bedroom bungalow and, most importantly, not far from Jack. I would be close and able to visit every day. Alan was away at sea so he got his father to check what was going on. Old Mr B, bless him hurried around. He was quite impressed, no problems at all. Having reported back to his son, I got on with all the arrangements. Visits to the Estate Agent, Solicitors etc. etc. Having run myself into the ground, Alan arrived home to sign the Deeds. As was the case in those days, it was all in the man's name. The Married Woman's Property Act wasn't law.

I moved with my son and I felt I was doing something his father had never done, provide him with a home. It was a very sad day for me leaving poor Jack, but it was a question of my survival. I knew how lonely he was and would be even lonelier. Now I had to think about my son and most important myself. In my heart, it was the end of the marriage. If Alan got a long posting overseas, which he was due, I wouldn't be going. I had at that time taken enough verbal and physical abuse, but it was to be another child and another five years before the final break came.

Chapter Nine

Now there was some serious shopping to do, we had nothing, just the presents that remained from the wedding. I was as much to blame, not doing a running total of outgoings as we went along. We bought a new three-piece suite, new table and chairs for the kitchen, new cannon cooker, bedroom furniture and furniture for Stephen's room, all on the never-never. Plus a huge ornate mirror for the front room, which I was totally against. With the mortgage repayments, all the normal bills plus we already had a car on the never-never, the outgoings were exactly twice the incomings every week. I quickly realized I would have to do something desperate if I was going to keep the roof over my head.

Guess who my first visitor was, even before I had settled in. Jack was on the phone to say Mina had arrived. Nothing had been heard or seen of her since the fight the day Tom died. With all my cousins, she soon heard on the grapevine that I had my "own place".

"Where is she?" Mina demanded of Jack. I was making it quite clear to Jack what I thought of Mina, not knowing she had snatched the phone out of his hand. Nothing would deter Mina, her mind was warped. She was going to make as much trouble as she could. I watched out of my window as she tried to cross the road and I thought why don't you just jump on your broomstick, you old witch. It was a wasted journey for her, I soon showed her the door. I wondered why she was so evil towards me; this had gone on since I was a child. I remembered the hidings I got because she told my mother tales, untrue tales. Perhaps me just being alive was the problem. As a young girl Mina had a baby out of wedlock like my mother. She was a bit luckier than my mother in as much as she was able to keep it a secret from most of the family. Her daughter died; little Carmel is buried in Ireland. Very few people know this until now. I wouldn't dream of making excuses for her, I'm just trying to understand why it was me she took her spite out on. She hated me like poison, even though she didn't really know me. In her warped mind it should have been me who died and not her Carmel.

It was heaven having a home of my own. A nice garden for Stephen to play in. Racking my brains for a way out of the financial mess, one morning there was a loud rat-a-tat on the front door. Standing on the doorstep was a tall, dark-haired man who had the look of Cliff Richards. He would be the same age as myself and he introduced himself as Paul. He had been talking to an acquaintance of mine and had been advised to call. He looked harmless enough so he was invited into the kitchen and the kettle went on. Paul had just left the Merchant Navy and with his pay-off he had bought a café on the seafront at Westcliff. He had been told if he could get me to help him, he would be on a winner.

Poor Stephen, he had enjoyed his time in his new home, now it was back to Miss Cheeseman. I would work nine to five Monday to Friday. It was just after Christmas when Paul opened; it was desolate down on the seafront that time of the year. In fact the first week he was open I don't think we had a customer, so quiet were we that I said forget my wages this week. Paul was married with a family but I considered he was a real friend. As the days got lighter and warmer we got really busy and staff had to be taken on; Paul was on his way.

Evenings, when Stephen was in bed, would be spent quietly watching the TV, knitting needles going nineteen to the dozen. Alan was back and forth, it was amazing how easily rows started. It was a normal Saturday morning, everything was peaceful, nobody was looking for trouble, Alan had to go out and when he returned he asked: "Who have you had in?"

The tone in his voice suggested to me that he wasn't talking about old Mrs Jones next door dropping in.

"Nobody's been in," I replied.

"You're just a liar," said Alan. "I can smell him."

"Smell?" What was he on about now. It was all part of the wear-me-down process actually trying to drive me mad. Then I would get a slap, just a little slap, just to soften things up. Then, because I was playing up, the slaps would get harder. By evening things would be quite violent. By playing up, he meant I was still breathing. Alan really had one law for me and one law for himself. Just by me still being alive everything was wrong, he could do as he liked.

One of my lovely cousins phoned to ask if she could come and stay for a break – she was feeling depressed and needed a change. I was delighted to see her and have her company for however long she stayed. Alan was home and on the very first morning I left him the money to get some shopping, decent chops etc. for dinner. I didn't expect him to have the spare cash to feed my family. They bought a bottle of whiskey and a bottle of gin and spent the day in bed together. There was no dinner when I got home from slogging my guts out. No point in saying a word, it would all be in my mad mind, it had been a really bad weekend. Thank God he had returned to his ship and I was still alive.

It was midday and I was busy getting lunch for Stephen. Now, I will give people the impression I am mad writing this. It's impossible to explain – nothing happened, I saw nothing, heard nothing, felt nothing but I knew someone was there and said something to me. No, that's not true, nobody said anything. I really can't explain; all I knew was that a Dorothy was looking after me and everything was going to be alright. A couple of days later Mum called and I was still looking around expecting to hear or see something.

"That's three or four times you've done that," said Sheila. "What's the matter?"

"I don't know," I said and told her about the happening. "The funny thing is," I said, "I don't know a Dorothy."

"Yes you do," said Sheila. "Alan's mother who died when he was young was Dorothy."

It certainly was a weird experience.

A year or more passed and Alan got a year-long posting overseas. Was that Dorothy doing her bit? A whole year without a fight – heaven. What we wrote about I can't imagine. It must have been very shallow stuff. One thing we definitely never discussed was having another baby. The one we did have Alan didn't know whose blood was in his veins so goodness knows what I would have written if he had said anything about a baby.

It was no big deal for me having Alan away for a year, in those days the phone wasn't used as it is now. So the only contact was letter writing, I never bothered if they weren't very regular, I was too busy working to pay off the never-never. It was hard work in the café but I always enjoyed it. The customers were great and many became friends. Some would come in every morning for breakfast or just a cup of coffee on the way to work. Wednesdays, half day in Southend, I knew I would see the same people down for lunch or afternoon tea and a laze in the sun. Fridays, fish and chip days, was the same; they were a great bunch. There was always the one who fancied his chances, when I cleared away his cup there would be a fiver under it. Next time I'd remember to be a little cold.

One lady customer had a profound effect on me. I liked her and envied her right from the start. Looking back I can't believe she liked me, we were in different worlds – she was so rich and I was so poor. I'd hate to think she was using me as a pretend friend to get at her husband. Pearl was about the same age as myself but that was where the similarities ended. She was tall, slim. Red-haired, fingernails and toenails polished. Her jewellery was priceless and her clothes were exquisite. She smelt divine, her perfume just wafted over the smell of the cooking. She was very Jewish, I do admit having a certain rapport with the Jewish people, then I was brought up by a Jewish man and a very pro-Jewish mother. We did have one thing in common, a lovely smile. We did have something else in common which wasn't apparent to me at the time. With all she had, and she had everything material, she was totally lost and desperately unhappy, perhaps she sensed my despair.

Our friendship only spanned a few months but it had a lasting effect on me. Pearl kept insisting I called on her and eventually I did. The flat was on the seafront at Westcliff and the last time I had sat in such luxury was at Solly's and May's at Gants Hill. Immediately I arrived she picked up the phone and ordered steaks. The butcher jumped into his car and delivered them straight away. It was the same butcher I had lived next to as a seventeen-year-old. I wondered if the rats were still around, but reckoned the cooking would kill the germs. Pearl had one daughter which she adored and thoroughly spoiled, she lived for the kid.

Her husband was someone she didn't say a lot about. He had a gown shop off the High Street, Southend. Pearl herself had grown up in the North of England. I gather she didn't have much as a child and came to London as a teenager to better herself. It was obvious she had married well. From the little she did say I gather her husband's status had grown and her Northern roots of poverty and no education were letting her down in her husband's social circle. She would say things like, "I waited until he was in the bath to speak to him, a bloke can't be pompous when he is in his birthday suit." But she never expanded on her conversation with him. I gathered she thought he was having an affair.

Perhaps if I were in a different frame of mind I would have responded differently, maybe I would have been shocked. But I was a battered wife, my mind was tortured, anything she had to say on the subject of her husband was so tame, to me that is. One Saturday night there was a knock on my door and Pearl was standing there. "Can I stay with you?" she asked. Of course the door was open and she was very welcome. She obviously had had a major row; not wanting to pry and make her feel awkward, we chatted away all evening about anything and nothing. I never even got around to sorting out where she was going to sleep. I mean what was she doing in my pokey little place, her bathroom was as big as my lounge. About eleven o'clock the phone rang, it was her husband, he was on his way to take her home. He didn't step inside my place, he was very polite, a perfect gentleman. As for Pearl I had the feeling she felt she had scored a victory, he had come after her. After all, she would have to have left him my phone number. I went to bed without giving her a second thought, the row couldn't have been all that serious.

Money at home was still tight, in fact most weeks it didn't stretch to meet all the bills, so I had started working on a Sunday. I didn't see Pearl sit down at the table, when I did the greeting on both sides was warm. "Just a coffee, please," she said. We chatted away between customers, sadly it was a Sunday morning and I was busy. As always I gave her every second of my time that I could. She looked lovely, calm and relaxed, wearing her beautiful jewellery. She explained she had taken her daughter to a friend for the day, so she could have a lazy day on her own. She paid and left with her usual lovely smile, she said "Goodbye" and I watched her for a few seconds as she walked away.

A few days later I was walking along the road and a stranger stopped me. This lady asked me, "Are you Pearl's friend?" I said I was. "Well, do you know she is dead?" she asked me. She had walked home from the café that morning, closed the kitchen door, put a towel along the bottom and gassed herself. In those days people kept their troubles to themselves, I certainly never talked about mine. Divorce was something people couldn't cope with. Still I ask myself, why didn't she say something that Sunday morning? I phoned her husband, I felt he was holding his own. I had the impression he was thinking, piss off and mind your own business, but he was far too well bred to do such a thing.

I've often wondered about the little girl, I'm sure she has had a good life, financially. I'm sure there was a stepmother waiting in the wings to take Pearl's place, which she could never do. That little girl will be in her mid-forties now, I wonder if there was anyone to tell her about her beautiful mother, I doubt it.

The year flew and he was due home again. God, doesn't time fly. It had been an uneventful year for me. Saturdays I'd take Stephen to the park, perhaps to the zoo. Whatever families do at Saturdays, but there was always the loneliness of being on your own. You couldn't help notice families together, talking, laughing, Dads doing their bit. I longed to be like them, a family unit, but not with Alan. I knew if he was home it would be nag, nag, nag, slap, slap, slap. I didn't want anymore of that. But I longed to be happy. For now anyway Stephen and I plodded on by ourselves, I'm sure he was missing out not having a dad to guide him, but there was nothing I could do about that anyway.

The job at the café had gone well, it was hard work and hot in the summer but I was grateful to be able to work and keep the house going. Paul now opened until midnight or later. He did the evening shift and had a manageress/cook for the daytime. Patricia was an amazing woman, she was just like my Uncle Michael in Ireland. One of her legs was half the length of the other. It was fascinating seeing her bobbing up and down in the very small space, but no way could she cope with the work, her disability hindered her. I needed the job so I worked my butt off to keep things going. Patricia wasn't a pretty woman, not that looks come into it. She had been abandoned by her husband and she was very bitter. One day she made a mistake, sent out four salads without washing the lettuce – they were covered with creepy-crawlies. I was so rushed of my feet I didn't notice. Anyway I wasn't in the habit of checking her meals, I accepted they would be perfect. There was no reason for anything to be said, mistakes happen all the time and they are soon put right. But Patricia in her twisted mind blamed me and let out such a torrent of abuse at me, I just walked out. Probably good timing, Alan would be home in a few days and for what it was worth, he would have my full attention.

The relationship between us was still very strained. One day without any previous discussion he declared in a very gruff voice: "I want a daughter."

Why he should want another baby amazed me. It could only be a front, away so often he had the wife, two kids, car in the garage. I just wondered which of us was mad. It certainly did nothing to bring us closer because it was weeks later Alan had to ask, "Have you got any news for me?"

"If you are asking am I pregnant, then yes I am," I replied, and thought, poor me.

There weren't any hugs and kisses or rejoicing just the bare fact, I was having a baby. I could never understand how a man could beat a woman up and I certainly couldn't understand his thinking about this baby.

Almost from day one I was ill. I was sick morning and night. It was a good job I had taken a heavy dose of sleeping pills earlier. I was right off tablets after that day, and wouldn't take one to save my life. The sickness was unbearable, but still no to a tablet. Thank God, I might have had a Thalidomide baby if I had taken the prescription. More pressing was the state of the finances; to add to our troubles there was a baby on the way.

The only job I knew was the cafés but I couldn't go back to Paul, he still had his disabled lady in charge. So I walked along the row of cafés; most of the people I knew, so it wasn't too difficult to ask if there were any jobs going, doing anything. I did feel a bit like a worn-out tramp, pregnant, asking for work, but things were very tight and I couldn't afford to be proud. I came to the very last café, last chance. I had no idea what I could do next if I was unsuccessful. The last café was owned by a lady called Peggy and she took me on. I would work nine to four, Mondays to Fridays for five pounds a week. I didn't tell her I was pregnant, I was already suffering from sickness. When she handed me the first plate of cooked breakfast to take to a customer, tears came to my eyes, I felt so awful. The smell turned my stomach over, I don't know how I prevented myself not being sick all over the place. Peggy must have thought I was a surly young girl; I was so sick and so miserable, but I had to shoulder on.

Peggy herself was a very bright, bubbly character, tall, blonde, very athletic, played tennis, drove around in a sports car and had lots of friends. She was a bit like my mum in as much as she worked hard and played just as hard. Every day she fed me sausage and mash for lunch, months of sausage and mash but I was very grateful. I don't know if my diet was deficient but I craved chocolate and would pig out on peppermint Aero. I had the luxury of a washer-upper; at Paul's I did all my own washing up. The little old lady at the sink was called Tilly. She was mentally retarded and her family dropped her off every morning; she spent her whole life standing at that sink. You could say her family got rid of her but she was as happy as a lark and always had a big smile on her face. Tilly was such a poor old lady in a way. She always had the same flowered dress on with a wrap around apron. Even on the hottest of days she wore thick woollen socks, her make-up was sweat. She was bent over and would shuffle along but there was a twinkle in her eyes. To her life was good and she knew no better. Tired as I was I would always give her a hand if it meant a rest for me or giving her a little support I would give her a hand and a little hug. She would smile exposing the only tooth she had in her head. She was such a lovely person and she stood at that sink almost to her dying day.

Eventually it became obvious I was pregnant – very – I had worked through the heat of the summer, every week I expected Peggy to give me the sack, she never did and I never gave in. I would leave home every morning at 8.30. Push Stephen in the pram uphill about a mile to London Road, struggle to get across the main road, down Crowstone Road, about another mile to the railway line. I would physically pick the pram up and get over the line, then down to Miss Cheeseman's, drop Stephen off and walk down to the café. It would probably be a full day on my feet without a break, except to eat my sausage and mash. Even that would be interrupted because someone would want something, more bread and butter, etc. Then at four o'clock the process would be repeated.

I kept my appointments with Dr Pearson. "Now then," he would say to me, "you are taking things easy aren't you?"

"Yes," I would say.

"You are leading a lady's life, breakfast in bed?"

"Yes," I assured him.

"Well," he said to me, "I can't understand this. I'm warning you as things are you aren't going to make this pregnancy." I just couldn't afford the baby without working. So I pressed on, doctors don't know everything anyway.

Time was passing, the days were getting colder and the nights were closing in. It was 1962 and it was one of the coldest winters on record. It was dark when I picked Stephen up from nursery and started to push the pram up to the railway line. He would run over while I struggled with the pram, then it was the uphill climb to London Road. My bump was big now and I had difficulty holding my water. No I didn't have difficulty, it was impossible, I couldn't hold my wee. It ran out as I pushed the pram up the hill, all down my tights. By the time I got to London Road I was soaked. It was so cold that winter the wee had practically frozen on my legs before I got home. Finally, just a week before Christmas, Peggy and I called it a day.

Still plenty to do before Christmas, my worry was would I be well enough to cope with the cooking, etc. He would be home in hours, I was dreading it. The home had to be run as efficiently as Her Majesty's Ships. Dust under the bed wouldn't be tolerated. Still presents to get, I was absolutely exhausted.

It was a bitterly cold day. I didn't have anything to put on my legs so with them bare I pushed the pram to the shops. Alan wanted some photo frames for his dad. I searched around for the right ones. Still no present for Alan. We had just bought a brand new three-piece suite and we needed some covers for it. In a shop window was just what I was looking for. Money was tight. I was cold and tired. I'd get the covers for his Christmas present. He would understand. After all it's the thought that counts.

Christmas morning he had got me a gold charm for my bracelet; it was a whistle. "I thought you would like this," he said. "Next time I beat you up you can referee and blow your whistle." I wasn't quite sure about the present or his sense of humour, but I didn't have to wait long for the fight. He undid his present, the covers and he went stark raving mad. "Call this a present!" But it wouldn't have made any difference; if it wasn't the covers it would be something else. The only certainty was that there would be a row. Thank God when the day came and he could sod off back to the ship, leave me in peace to try and hold on to this baby.

January 14th came, it was bitterly cold and the snow was inches thick as I struggled with the pram against the wind to keep my antenatal appointment. "You are doing well," the midwife informed me but as I struggled home with the pram I felt so awful the tears streamed down my face. Taking things quietly at home that evening I knew I wasn't doing well at all. I waited until the morning and I gave my midwife a ring.

"I only saw you yesterday afternoon," she told me, "and you are fine, but I will be in all morning if you need me." I thought what a silly cow she was, I had rung because I need her now. And I felt quite panicky. The amazing thing was after saying she would be in all morning she left the house to take her daughter to school. Luckily for me she was thinking, that lady is quite sensible, if she rang it would be for a reason, I'll just make a quick detour and check. She was just in time as I opened the door I got that feeling – if someone stops this world going round, I'll jump off and I was gone. Now it was her turn to panic, she got the doctor out of morning surgery. He was down in minutes, I think he had always expected that phone call. Mum arrived at the same time, to add to the confusion. Of course Mum would never go quietly. She threw herself on her knees on the floor and screamed to God, "Please don't take her, she hasn't had a life, take me, please." Mum could always be trusted to be dramatic and put on a show.

I heard the doctor say, "If nothing else this patient will die of the cold." With that the midwife opened my wardrobe to get something to keep me warm. I remember thinking how neat I had stacked my bits and pieces. Later the doctor told me at that time he thought I had died. The flying squad arrived, with orders not to give me any bumps on the way, crawl as slowly as can be. The doctor told Mum as long as I remained pregnant it was fifty-fifty whether I would survive. He also told her they wouldn't do anything at the hospital to save me at the baby's expense. But he said the baby was in the worst position now because it had been starved of oxygen during the time I was out.

Matron met the ambulance, I heard her say, "We haven't lost a mother here for five years, make sure you don't lose this one." All was quiet with me until midday; a lovely nurse was fussing about and I said to her, "Can I breathe out now, because I'm holding my breath to stop the baby coming."

"Don't be ridiculous," she said. "If that baby wants to come you holding your breath wont stop it."

"Okay," I said, "I'll breathe out now." With that the baby popped out – that made her move, shouts everywhere.

I heard someone shout, "Someone get the mother." Not much point delivering a baby one end and letting me slip away at the other end. The little baby was perfect and a real joy, she was taken away, I was sedated and placed in a private room.

A day later I was barely with it, I realized my lovely doctor was sitting by my bed. I was conscious of the fact my mouth was open and I was dribbling. He just sat there for ages, how long he had already been there I had no idea. He just sat and looked at me; finally he said, "I'll remember you on my deathbed, you are engraved on my heart in gold." He told me I had given him One Awful Fright, he thought I had died on him.

I stayed in the private room for five days. The night before I left the staff asked me, "Did I have any requests?" I asked could I spend my last night with the other mums, so they pushed my bed into the maternity ward. It was visiting time, Mum rushed in with some pink carnations explaining that Stephen was outside in the taxi crying so I told her to go to him, I was OK. I knew the baby was crying and one of the mums came over. I told her I knew but I didn't have the strength to hold her.

I was unaware on the afternoon Alan learned he had become a father again; he was asleep and was woken up to be given the news. "Another bastard, that baby's not mine, find someone else," he told the messenger. He had been to sea for a year and hadn't been home long enough to have a baby. Well not one of his anyway. He hadn't noticed how ill I looked or how tired I was, he had no idea about anything. The doctor was right, from day one he said I wouldn't make it and I nearly didn't. I had pushed as hard as I could to get the never-never paid off and in doing so I had risked both our lives.

That first night I was home Alan phoned and was surprised when I answered. He wanted the baby called "RUTH". Where that came from I have no idea, there was no discussion, "Ruth" it was with "Elizabeth" after my lovely grandmother. When he did eventually come home Stephen rushed to the door and excitedly told him where the baby was, he wanted so much to show his dad his little sister. "I'll have my tea first," was his cold uncaring remark. When he did see the baby he said looking at her made him feel sick. Funny thing that, looking at him made me feel sick. Mum and Dad were delighted but poor Dad said he had one regret. He knew he wouldn't live to see the children grow up. He died ten months later in his sleep.

It had been a quiet time for Mum and Dad, Mum was working very hard to keep the home going. Dad was now in his seventies, very frail and he spent a lot of time alone, which made me sad. Mum still played just as hard, no way would she give up her card school or her nights out at the dogs. She turned up one day with two tickets to see the game show, *Take Your Pick* with Michael Miles being recorded in London. Did I want to go, she asked. Yes, I did, I said. I got a babysitter and off we went.

I had an idea she fancied her chances of getting on the show and winning a big prize. Mum had been to the hairdresser's and at forty-eight she was in her prime. She had an air about her and people warmed to her. If she had actually met the quizmaster in person she would have twisted him around her little finger but things don't always go your way. We were shown to our seats about five rows from the front, I sensed she was keyed up.

If you don't remember *Take Your Pick*, there were twelve contestants, twelve boxes, plus box number thirteen. Three questions to answer to win a key – boxes contained either a fabulous prize or a booby. One key also opened box number thirteen. The quizmaster then tried to buy the key off the contestant and the decision was whether to take the money or take a chance. That was the show – how the contestants got picked was the question. Finally Michael Miles came on stage and got the show started.

"I've got a coach party here from Milton Keynes," he said. Cheers, clapping, foot stamping from Milton Keynes because they had a mention. "Anyone from Milton Keynes want to come on the show?" he asked. More cheers, shouts of, "Yes". "Right," said Michael, "I want one of you to stand up and give a commentary on an imaginary horse race." Someone did stand up and they were brilliant. "WE have our first contestant," said Michael.

Mum looked at me, I felt she had gone a bit flat. "That's how it's done," she said, "We don't have a chance, sitting here on our own." Next there was a party from some office, somewhere, they had to be a market trader selling tights with three legs. So it went on, it was hilarious, it's amazing how talented people are. By the time eleven contestants had been picked the audience ached with laughter. One more to go. Looking directly at me and pointing a finger Michael said, "That lady in the red dress with the dark hair."

I put my hand on my heart and mouthed to him, "ME?"

"Yes, you, please would you stand up," he said, I was in such a panic, no way was he going to get me to make a fool of myself, it would take me a second to sit down again.

"What's your name?" he asked. "Are you married?" was the next question, followed by, "What does your husband do?" I told him my husband was in the Royal Navy at the moment at sea. Michael had been in the Navy and he was very pro the services. "Please join us and be our last contestant," he said.

It was so exciting, I couldn't believe it. The make-up lady was fussing around, all the other contestants each more nervous than the one next to them. Me, I was petrified, shaking when my turn came I was sorry I was up there, what if I couldn't answer the questions. The questions were easy and I picked the key to open box seven, my lucky number. Bells were ringing everywhere, it was the key to open number thirteen as well. But first Michael would try to buy the keys from me. No way, I was going to open the box. I came from a gambling family and tonight it was my turn to throw caution to the wind and gamble; if it was a booby so be it. Michael was offering more and more money, the audience were geeing me on, "Open the box, open the box," they chanted. I was quite determined I was going to open the box, kept shaking my head and saying, "No, thank you." The money had gone up to a fortune for me and as I said, "No," again, as the word came out with such determination I saw Mum she was screaming, "Have you gone mad!" Michael made a higher offer and so quick I said, "I'll take it."

Everyone went quiet as he counted out the money in my hand, then I had to open both boxes. Would you believe there was a booby in each? Mum would have gambled but she just didn't want me to take any chances. The show went out in three weeks and I'd be counting the days to watch it. I rushed round to tell Dad all about it, although Mum had already told him everything. He was so pleased for me and said how much he was looking forward to hearing me, his old eyes couldn't see but he could listen. For all his faults he was the only dad I'd ever had, but he didn't live to hear me, he died the week of the show.

The night Dad died was weird. It could just be a coincidence. I woke at three in the morning feeling like death. I was freezing cold yet the sweat was oozing out of my pores. It didn't surprise me to hear the doorknocker going at seven in the morning. I knew someone would be standing there to tell me Dad had died at 3 a.m. Sure enough, John was standing there. Dad had gone at 3 a.m. It was almost as if his spirit had tried to say, "Goodbye." That's a daft thought, it was as if he had left something unsaid and he was trying to say it; too late now he was gone. I went to see him in the chapel of rest. He looked at peace, holding his hand I said to him, "You know I've lost my best friend." I reminded him of the TV show in a few days' time and I told him off because he was going to miss it. But I said, "I know you will be there with me."

The night the show went out Mum sat with me to watch. We had a couple of stiff drinks, I couldn't believe Dad was lying in the morgue up the road. Having been Jewish all his life, he had become a Catholic in the last months of his life. He had said he wanted to make sure he was going to the same place as us. It was still a couple of days to the funeral; I can't say Mum was distraught with grief, she was just a little quiet. I never gave any thought to her future, she was a very capable lady to me. She was young, beautiful, had everything going for her. She had a lovely flat, a wide circle of friends, I just assumed life would go on as it was. I wouldn't have given any thought to her living with me, for one thing Alan would have had a fit. So if she was quiet waiting for me to say something, I had nothing to say. But if the choice came to choose my mother or Alan it wouldn't have been a contest, but at the moment she seemed in control, all was well.

The show was great, next morning out shopping I bumped into a neighbour. "Saw you on telly last night," she said. "You looked beautiful." It was a rare moment of happiness tinged with regret that Dad had gone and a bit of excitement in my otherwise beaten, battered and abused life. When I finally spoke to Alan he said he had watched in the mess with his mates and then he proclaimed, "You looked deaf, dumb and stupid." Bloody cheek.

It was a complete surprise to me when, straight after the funeral, Mum went to live with John. They had always been close those two, always at the dogs, gambling on something or other, they were two of a kind. Not many weeks had passed when she called and told me he was moving and there wasn't a place for her, she had nowhere to go. "Well, you had better come here," I said. "In fact, you should have come here when Dad died." She could always put on an act and still doing the old sob stuff she said, "You never asked." I didn't really have a chance, she had gone in a flash. I never bothered to ask her what she had done with a flat full of possessions. Shortly afterwards, she arrived with everything she had in the world in a suitcase. "You know," she said, "He's had everything."

I didn't bother to ask her to expand. I knew about the two thousand pounds he owed her. In 1964 I suppose that was a lot of money and I expect when she had nothing she would have liked it repaid. It never happened. She sat deep in thought. She was still young. From her attitude I guess she thought her life was over. I made the tea.

"You know," she said again wearily, "I spent all my young life working to support two kids that weren't mine." Mum appeared tired out, confused – sad.

So much for the two wealthy aunts; while I was running around without a pair of shoes on my feet John and Betty were being mollycoddled and spoilt on my mum's back.

Mum settled in straight away. Not that I saw much of her. She was working all day, came home for a good home-cooked meal. Then it was off to the Casino or a card school. She was no bother. What a task it was writing to Alan and telling him we had a lodger. She had provided a home for him for long enough, now the boot was on the other foot.

A year passed and over breakfast one morning Sheila reminded me it was Auntie Una's birthday and Una was forty-something or other.

"Gosh," I said, "Isn't she young."

When I was young – eight, nine or ten – and Una looked after me in Ireland she seemed so old. Now I was a mother of two and Una was only in her forties, she seemed so young.

As I said before, Sheila could always put on an act and with a tear just ready to roll down her cheek she said, "I'm only thirteen months older."

"Well," I said to her, "You are only a baby, you have a whole life to live yet!"

With that, Sheila decided the world was her oyster, rushed out to get a paper and go job-hunting. It wasn't long before she got a job as cook/housekeeper to a very wealthy, millionaire bachelor in London. I never saw his flat but was told it was full of priceless paintings. Soon I learned Mum was spending her day off with a Jewish gentleman living in Basildon. He was a bachelor in his fifties and three years after Jack's death – she was fifty-one, he was fifty-six – they married. It's amazing when she was down I was always there, without question, but as soon as she got going she hadn't changed her spots.

She told me her husband-to-be didn't like children and her grandchildren weren't welcome at the wedding. Harold, we will give him a name, may be a real gentleman. He may be well educated. He may be financially secure but someone who didn't want my children, could get stuffed. So, on the morning of the wedding, I sent them a telegram wishing them all the happiness in the world and then went home and stayed there with my children. It might have been different if it was a huge, posh wedding but they travelled on their own to Brentwood, stopped two people in the street and asked them to be witnesses and then travelled back to Southend for a small reception with about half a dozen people. Where children would have upset things I couldn't see. Of course, after that whenever I and the children saw Harold we couldn't get away quick enough. You can't be happy with someone who doesn't want your children.

Harold was a very quiet and gentle person, easy going. From the old school where manners were paramount. Having a confrontation with someone was not his nature. One evening he was so fed up with the attitude of the children and myself that he actually picked the phone up and told me exactly what he thought of my rudeness to him and my children's rudeness.

"What do you expect?" I asked him.

He was amazed at my reply. He couldn't understand why I hadn't come to the wedding. It had been a puzzle to him. He thought perhaps I hadn't wanted Mum to re-marry and considered it disloyal to Dad. No way did he not want the children. Of course, Sheila didn't let herself down with her reply to him. Back came the usual abuse, she had had to put up with my lies all her life. I suffer from hallucinations and quarrel with everyone. It wasn't long before Harold got the measure of Sheila. It was odd to me that I got on so well with both my stepfathers – me being a Catholic and both men being Jewish. Harold and I became great friends. One day he told me I was all he had. He grew to love the children and couldn't see enough of them. He died in his seventies, and at seventy-three Sheila was widowed for the second time.

Chapter Ten

The months since Ruth's birth were passing and like all babies she was getting bigger. Stephen was just like me, very dark, you couldn't argue who he belonged to. On the other hand, Ruth was pale and looked like no one. She could have been fathered by a total stranger which didn't help matters. It seemed to me that Alan was treating the baby like all the other women in my family. His mother-in-law, he considered, was the wickedest woman in the world. He hated me like poison. You have to smile – he accused me of being a health hazard. He was so allergic to me. Ruth was another female like the two of us. The baby felt it, she might only have been a baby, but she knew. One day he took her out in the car, on his return he threw her at me shouting: "Take her, the little cow's wet all over the seat!"

She did literally shit herself when he was around. On another occasion, I left the children at home while I popped out to the shops. On my return, I found Stephen playing but no sign of Ruth.

"Where's Ruth?" I asked.

She was only a tot, how naughty could she have been. We had a dark oak wardrobe in the bedroom and Alan had locked her in it. I opened the door in a panic. Ruth was sitting on the floor. Her big eyes just looked at me. She was keeping as quiet as a mouse. She knew not to cry. Another time Alan threw a small cuddly teddy bear with such force it took a whole glass window out. You have got to have a laugh sometimes. When he came back with the new window pane he fell and it smashed. It was worth the hiding because I couldn't help myself. But joking aside, things were getting scary. No one would ever suggest that Alan would deliberately hurt the kids but an accident could happen at any time. All it would take would be one unlucky blow or throw something in temper and it would hit the mark. It worried me what I would say to the police if anything did happen. What would the neighbours say. They would whisper amongst themselves that I must have known about the violence and had allowed it to happen. So, in the end, it would be my fault.

From day one of the marriage I knew the day would come when I had to get out of it. In the 50s and 60s Domestic Violence was as much a taboo subject as being a bastard. I think that's a stupid statement, because no one knew about it. If they did they wouldn't believe it. No one talked about it, the police didn't get involved, they literally turned a blind eye. There was no support for the battered and abused wife, there was nowhere for her to go. Women just put up with there violent lives, they kept their mouth and their front door shut. It puzzled me, all this was because I was born out of wedlock, as they say. I didn't ask to be born and had no say in the matter. Yet Alan who considered himself "intelligent" was perpetrating an even worse crime freely off his own back, he was committing it of his own choosing. One thing he forgot in between his rantings like a madman, I was abandoned the day I was born. You grow tough in those circumstances and I considered myself a far stronger character than him, even if he was a Petty Officer in Her Majesty's Navy. I knew I had the strength to support my two children on my own. What life would be like I had no idea, but I knew I would be failing my children if I allowed them to grow up in such violence. Worry as much as I did, I found it hard to make the break and renege on my wedding vows. It was like having a sick animal around. I had to be sure, I needed time to say my goodbyes and make peace with myself over what I was thinking of doing. When I put that sick animal down (i.e. get a divorce) I had to be sure there would be no regrets.

Another year or so passed, we had been married, unbelievably, for nine years. Alan was home on a week's leave. Evening came and we were both slumped in our armchairs, one each side of the fireplace – it was a scene of perfect bliss one would think. Alan was sleeping, half waking up, he had completely forgotten where he was. Sitting up and still half asleep, stretching himself he said, "I'd love of cup of coffee, Margaret."

"Who the hell is Margaret?" I asked, and while Alan was quickly trying to wake himself up and get his act together I said, "It's a pity she isn't here to make it. I've had enough."

He was back to his old self. "Oh! Tut tut, come on now, you know you're imagining things, you know you're mental."

He was quick to say she was just a friend who worked at the base. Actually her husband was his friend (where have we heard that one before) and he liked her kids. Just to prove they were one big happy family at Portsmouth he would invite them home.

"You're not bringing your bit of spare into this house," I told him. That got him back to the usual routine. He would bring who he liked into his house. He reminded me it was all in his name. He told me he would have me committed to a mental house.

"Then," he said, "Everyone, especially me, could get on with their lives."

An anonymous phone call a couple of weeks later told me they were laughing their heads off behind my back.

"No, they're not," I told the caller.

She was welcome to the bastard but I still had to be sure. I assured the caller that I had everything under control. It was a pity Alan didn't have one streak of decency or honesty in his bones. It would have been acceptable if he had just said, "Look, I've met someone else, you have a divorce, I'll leave the roof over the kids heads." He had this crackpot idea that because my father was unknown, that made me insane. He could have me put away or his other dream was that I was just going to die. What of, for God's sake, I was as tough as an old boot. Every bit a match for him. He had nothing to lose now and the rows got very violent.

One evening I was so scared I grabbed the children and ran to the police station for protection. What those two babies thought sitting on that long bench in the station, God alone knows. The police kept us waiting for one hour, talking amongst themselves and laughing which unnerved me even further. I told them I was afraid for my children's lives and my life. They then decided to be kind and offered us a lift home. To protest any further would have made things worse for the kids, so quickly we got into the police car. The policeman escorted us to the front door and knocked. Silently, I stood there with the children beside me. I wanted to scream, fall on my knees, beg not to be returned to the home. I was terrified, but to do that would have been too traumatic for the kids. Alan answered the door, all cool and calm.

"Have you hit your wife?" asked the stupid policeman.

"It was only an accident, I assure you," replied Alan very nicely.

"Promise there won't be another accident," asked the still stupid policeman.

"Of course not," promised Alan with all the charm he was capable of.

The policeman placing one hand on the front door and pushing it wide open, then placing his other hand on my back, firmly pushed me indoors. The children following me in, I wanted desperately to make a last protest. The children would be even more confused and I knew as far as the police were concerned it would fall on deaf ears. Stephen and Ruth were put to bed as calmly as I could, kissing them goodnight. I left calmly and slowly closing their bedroom door. I stood outside their door for a while absolutely mortified. There was nowhere for me to go but to join Alan and face the music. I went into the front room where he was and closed the door behind me. It was as if a button had been pressed, up till then he was in control and now he was a madman.

"How dare you go to the police and show ME up like that." You take the hiding hoping and praying you are going to survive the night.

It is appalling that a human being should find themselves in the position I found myself in. My only crime was to be born. I didn't ask to be born and now my only desire in life was to protect two children who also hadn't asked to be born.

Certainly things were deteriorating very quickly at home. When I laid the table for meals I always laid a carving knife where I sat. I knew what was going on at Portsmouth and I knew Alan wasn't going until he had every penny. I could have accepted if he had gone to this woman with sixteen pounds in his pocket as we had when we wed, instead of him hoping and praying that I would be committed or die so he could have my home for her. He underestimated me because I would fight for my kids as long as I had breath in my body. Mind you, I gave great thought to that carving knife. I'd rest my hand on it for comfort and resist the temptation to plunge it into his heart. I was quite determined there would be a life for me after Alan and actually killing him might have made that life difficult. Also I never wanted to face the children and tell them they did have a father but I had killed him.

As the autumn approached, Alan was getting more quarrelsome and much more violent. It seemed he came home just to have a fight and wear me down. This particular evening, I decided to have an early night and get out of his way. I didn't want a fight. I had two kids to look after most of the time I was alone while he was away so I went to bed to get some peace and quiet. Finally, he got into the bed. I felt two feet flat in the middle of my back and I was kicked out of bed.

"I'm not sleeping with a bastard," he shouted.

I didn't reply, that was alright with me, if that was how he felt I wasn't looking for a fight. On the contrary, I was looking the other way. I went into the lounge and made myself comfortable on the settee. In a rage, Alan stormed in and pulled me off the settee by the hair on my head. I wasn't to sleep in a chair either. He pulled me across the hall into the bedroom and dropped me on the floor. I just had a nightie on and there wasn't any central heating. Without any cover I was to lie on the floor like a dog. I beg to differ, even a dog has a blanket or a basket. Putting the boot in, he told me to stay there and make sure I didn't move. Every time he got up in the night to relieve himself from his drinking, he would put his slippers on and as he passed me on the floor he would kick me as hard as he could. Next morning, tired, cold and very stiff I went into the bathroom to wash. The pain was unbearable as I tried to put the flannel to my face. I tried to bath around my headline but it was too tender where the hair had almost been pulled out of my head. After a while, with gentle dabbing, the warm water brought comfort. Looking at myself in the mirror, I wondered how it would all end. Amazingly, life still went on. Breakfast was cooked as if nothing had happened, but I realized the violence was getting deeper.

We went out for a meal. Anyone would think we were a normal couple. There was just the two of us, so there couldn't have been any outside influences such as another couple where he could accuse me of flirting. It was just us two. On the way home, we had to go down a hill and Alan suddenly leant over, opened the car door and tried to push me out. Was he really trying to kill me? What would have happened if I had fallen out and been run over by a following car? Would he have told the police I jumped or would it have been I couldn't have closed the door and fell out? Once again, I asked the question in my mind and why not just walk away. But, of course, he wasn't going empty handed. He was going to make sure he got what there was to get. Even more amazing, however bad the fights were, he never went without his rights.

I remembered when I was first married I would get a good hiding over nothing and then he would want to make love. I told myself then that he really did love me, needed me, wanted me. One day he would suddenly tell me, that was the truth I told myself. That was one of the reasons I hung in there waiting for the breakthrough. One day, when we were both old and grey and the children grown up and we were grandparents, Alan would say, "Sorry." But the going was getting too rough and I could see there wasn't going to be a fairy tale ending. I would rather have two bloody good hidings than be beaten and then have to succumb to sex.

The end came very quickly (although ten years of marriage with nothing but hassle from day one cannot be classed as quick). As he approached the back door, home for another weekend, he was still my husband so I opened the door to greet him, I just felt his fist in my face – BANG. What was that all about?

"I didn't like the expression on your face," he told me.

I could see it was going to be a fun weekend but didn't know at that moment it was going to be the last. It was the whistle of the kettle that ended a ten-year nightmare. Remember the old fashioned kettles with a whistle on the spout? When the kettle boiled the whistle screeched and you knew the water was hot. Saturday was as usual, criticism about this and that, looking under the bed and finding a speck of dust. I was working full-time with two kids. I would get a punch for dust under the bed. So it went on until I got up Sunday morning and once again an attempt had been made to rearrange my face. The children came in for breakfast, Stephen was old enough to see my face, you couldn't hide it, but all was calm. The carving knife was in place. I stroked it once or twice for comfort. Sunday dinner was all peaceful, happy families were being played to the full. In the afternoon, the children were playing in their rooms, Ruth in her cot. I had washed up after dinner and went into my bedroom to tidy up. In a couple of hours he would be away and I would have survived another weekend. The neighbours would know in the morning he had been home when they saw my face. They were used to it by now. They would ask, "Been walking into doors again Mrs B?"

Domestic violence didn't have a place in any vocabulary, it wasn't talked about. This isn't living I told myself. I really am near the time when that sick animal has to be put out of his misery. Alone with my thoughts, Alan suddenly appeared in the bedroom, pushed me roughly on the bed and without one word helped himself. Suddenly, there was this loud screech, he had put the kettle on to do some washing. In the short time it took to boil he was going to rape me, because that was what it was. There isn't another word for it. He finished what he was doing and without another word got up and left the bedroom. I rolled off the bed and fell on my knees and, resting my head in my hands on the bed, I tried not to cry. I had to be brave for the children. But I vowed it would never, ever happen again. Never again was I going to feel so dirty, degraded, used and abused.

This, surprisingly enough, is not a blow-by-blow account of ten years, it is just a few incidents to try to show the picture. I could never put into words the mental anguish and torment of it all, nor would I want to.

The next morning I went to the Solicitors. I was prepared to go through detail after detail of the rows etc. I had made many visits to the doctors over the years. All the bruises had been measured and recorded.

"Start with the first day of the marriage," said the Solicitor. It was painful to repeat the first day to a complete stranger when Alan had asked me to explain the marriage certificate. He'd said, "I've married a bastard. Had I have known, I'd never have married you."

"You've got your divorce," the Solicitor informed me. The beatings and rows weren't even going to be used.

When Alan was told I was divorcing him, he had a good laugh. He told me I must have my head buried in the sand if I thought I would get away with it. He had just been given a medal for fifteen years' good conduct in the navy, so a nutter like me trying to sue him wouldn't get me very far. In my mad mind I couldn't work his thinking out. From day one of our marriage he had been a pig, he had given me crabs, he had been up in court for not paying his dues. Now he was accusing me of trying to get away with something, one of us was definitely mad. To boast the navy had given him a good conduct medal, shame on the navy. Because I didn't fight back when I was being punched and kicked, he thought I was weak. If I had I would be dead but I was going to fight now. He was about to be given a lesson on the rules in Civvy Street, not Royal Navy rules, Civvy Street rules.

Three months later I got my divorce on the grounds of cruelty. But it was a horrendous three months. Alan made a point of coming home. He would alternate between laughing at me or shouting at me. He would go through the place emptying everything on to the floor, tipping out all the stuff in the wardrobes, emptying out the chest of drawers etc. When he left, the place had been ransacked. "You do as you please," he would say, "but not in my house."

Chapter Eleven

The day of the divorce arrived. I was nervous as I approached the Court House. I wasn't looking forward to seeing Alan and listening to his rantings. As I was greeted by my solicitor I learned that Alan wouldn't be attending. He wasn't going to contest the divorce. That was a surprise, but then anyone who behaved the way he did was a coward and wouldn't have the guts to fight fair in court. Wouldn't want to be shown up for the BASTARD he was. As I took the oath I looked at the Judge and I thought how kind he looked. But as he started asking me questions, I began to get worried. All I could do was tell the truth. Was he biased in favour of men, even service men, maybe he had served in the navy who knows. At one point, I thought he would give Alan the divorce. But it wasn't a contest, who wins or who loses, we were both losers. I didn't much care who got the divorce as long as the marriage was over.

"Perhaps," said the Judge, "your husband has strong views about bastards, has he?"

That seemed both a statement and a question to me. But I answered honestly. I told the Judge, "Yes, he has very strong views."

I told the Judge I felt sorry for Alan. I completely understood his views and didn't hold his views against him. Everyone is entitled to their opinions and views, I said. But I had no idea he felt that way. In the three years we were courting, the word never came up. I explained the two different religions, Catholic married to a Jew and the two different names. Nobody set out to lie to him or trap him, I only wish I had known how he felt. He never asked a question. I often wonder what was in his mind all those years. The Judge sat quietly reading some papers, then he looked up and looked at me.

"This is the worst case of cruelty I've ever come across."

He granted me a divorce on the grounds of cruelty and gave me care and custody of my two children. As he understood an eviction order to get out of the house was coming up in another court he said I had to have something. So he awarded me five pounds a week for life or until I remarry and two pounds fifty for each child. A measly ten pounds to keep his two children, it was peanuts, an absolute pittance. Actually, I didn't want a penny. I wanted him to leave the kids in their home, not to be thrown out in the streets on his orders so he could provide a home for this other woman. Sheila sat through the court hearing and afterwards, quite relaxed, she said she was taking me out to lunch.

"I saw you into this marriage and I'll see you out," was her comment.

Sheila ordered a large steak each and double cherry brandies followed by a couple more cherry brandies. She chatted away, not once did she mention the morning's events or say a thing about the past. Even though Sheila was in a calm, relaxed mood I knew not to test it. One thing Sheila had was a large mouth. She could always afford to go for broke. When it came to it that was one thing she and Alan had in common. Neither of them ever knew when to stop, they always went for the jugular.

With the eviction notice in my hand, I went to the Council. In those days, the 1960s, married women were put out in the streets, homeless and penniless, if that was the husband's wishes. But, of course, in those days that didn't happen very often because people didn't get divorced. Women just put up with worthless lives. We had been in the bungalow only three years but had put down quite a large deposit. I didn't want any financial support from him, all I wanted was for him to walk away and leave the children in their home. Let him and this woman get married with sixteen pounds in their pockets as we had done and work for what they wanted, not take the roof from over the kids' heads. That was the second thing I was never going to forgive him for. If I couldn't have the house I wanted half of every penny he got and I was going to fight. I owed it to MY kids.

The Council offered me a house in Tennyson Avenue, for which I was very grateful. The only thing it was lacking was fleas. It had everything else. No double glazing or central heating, an antique butler sink in the kitchen. The toilet was outside, the back door consisted of the frame so you could lock it and the door was just a few slats of board. The wind blew through when you went to the toilet. The bath had no enamel on it. The first time I put Ruth in it to bath her, she wouldn't sit down so I smacked her legs from under her. Yes, life was going to be hard. The last occupants had dumped a double mattress in the overgrown garden and there were needles everywhere in the long grass. I don't know what happened with the mattress if the stray dogs got into the garden and tore at it. Large holes appeared in it. One day there was a gale and when I got home from work there were thousands of feathers over the neighbours' gardens. Years later, our happy humble home was refurbished, it was lovely. We stayed there for twenty-five years, a lifetime. I had had so much moving around all my life, being settled was everything to me.

The bungalow had been sold. Alan was waiting for his cheque. I was still fighting. It was all in his name and he wanted it all. I was going to get nothing. The problem for him was he had temporarily forgotten I was mad and should be certified. He should have remembered. He had spent years trying to drive me bleeding mad. In my madness, I reckoned I might as well keep fighting in court spending the proceeds from the sale of the bungalow. The weeks passed, I wasn't in any hurry. He was screwed up trying to beat me. Finally, he stormed home and shrieked at me: "If you keep going the way you're going, there'll be nothing left."

He wouldn't dare hit me now, we were divorced. It was time for me to be in control of my life. So I calmly told him: "I'm going to keep fighting and make sure I get half of your nothing. That's how mad people think, isn't it?" I said to him.

That was the last I heard of it. He gave in. I was amazed that the Judge gave me half. It was only the second time in the country that it happened that way. Now the married women's property act is in law so women don't have to go through what I had had to go through. In a final settlement the court gave Alan the car while I had the furniture, I was grateful for that. At least I had a start.

My heart was full of hope. Although my worst nightmare had come true – I was not only a bastard, now I was divorced and alone again. Life was going to be bitter sweet, bitter because I was on my own with two kids. Sweet because I was free, no longer would that bastard come through the door and completely humiliate and degrade. Life would be going to be hard but it would be a good life.

One day I sat the two children down for a chat. Not that they understood one word of what I said, they were too young. I told them that there couldn't be anything else that was bad ahead. "We are at rock bottom," I said. "We can't get any lower which means there is only one way to go – that is up!" I promised the kids I would do everything in my power to make things a success. I would work as hard as I could. In return, I wanted them to work just as hard. I only have one ambition in life I told the children, on my deathbed there is one thing I want to be able to say, "I gave my kids a chance" – no one ever gave me a chance.

One thing I was quite determined about, I was not going to take one penny from Social Services. The children (when they both got to school) had the ten pence for their dinner money in their little hands. I got them around on my own steam, no free bus passes. I had felt different all my life, I knew how it screwed a soul up. It would be over my dead body if my children were made to feel different at school. I had the ten pounds a week the court had given me and I would earn the rest. I would scrub floors, peel potatoes, wash up, whatever it took.

Six weeks passed after the divorce and I hadn't received a penny from Alan. I don't know what he was thinking, he was probably in a rage; he didn't get the bungalow. But if he thought he would get out of paying he had a nasty lesson coming. I would have preferred to have told him to get stuffed but I needed that bit of support the courts gave me. I phoned him and got her, she already had her feet under the table. If anyone had told her I was a mouse who could be walked all over she was going to find out otherwise. I reminded her when she lay on her back for my husband (which he still was) she knew he had two children, one a baby still being nursed. I made it quite clear to her that before she got a cigarette in her mouth my kids would eat. I was so mad I could have ripped the two of them to pieces. They were welcome to each other but not at my kids' expense.

I had been back working with Paul throughout the worst times. He would just give me a look and ask, "Are you alright?"

"Yes," I would say, all bright and breezy.

We three had settled down in our little home. Stephen doing well at school and Ruth with Miss Cheeseman. Every morning Miss Cheeseman brought her little charges for a walk along the sea front. Ruth's big eyes stared at me as she passed the café, although I smiled and waved there was never a smile from her. She held on to the side of the pram and walked along, looking back until I was out of sight. I have never forgotten the look on her little face, almost as if she was never going to forgive me and you know what, I don't think she ever has. I could easily beat myself up and go down a guilt road. I was such a hard mum and I made so many mistakes but I believed at the time I was doing the right thing. We didn't have to be so poor, there was help there from Social Services.

Time was passing, that's a funny thing it always does; Stephen was seven and Ruth was four. I had to pop into St Helen's school to see Stephen's headmaster, Mr Grimes. He was a charming man, and I liked him very much He was concerned about the children and wanted to know how I was coping. He understood the major problem of getting the two to different places every morning and picking them up in the evening. "Look here," he said, "just leave Ruth here with Stephen, she won't be on the register for another year but we will look after her." That was brilliant, the world was suddenly very bright.

I will just say I didn't want to waste my life. I wanted to do something with it, achieve something. After my experiences, I would be good at marriage counselling. I would certainly understand people's problems so that was what I would do. I joined the marriage guidance, I think it's called Relate now. Everything was doing fine, the meetings were good, it was achieving my ambition, giving me an outside interest. There were loads of books to read. The next task for me was to talk to a panel for ten minutes on Oral Sex. Now I know I'm wrong – I'm sure there was a reason for it. The experts will say we have to sweep out the tough from the shy etc. but I couldn't see what that had to do with people's problems. Whatever the explanation was I didn't hang around to find out. Remember this was 1960, and although I had been married ten years I had never heard of oral sex let alone experienced it. I couldn't talk on the subject for ten seconds let alone ten minutes. I felt they had lost a good candidate for the job of counsellor.

Next, I joined the Labour Party. Meeting there didn't suit me either. Then I joined the Conservative Party. That was the start of a twenty-five year roller-coaster ride.

It was an early Saturday evening shortly after the divorce when the phone rang. They, Alan and his woman, were on their way round to take the children out.

"They're swimming in the Gala tonight," I told him.

"We'll be there," was his reply as he put the phone down.

We, I thought, suddenly feeling very nervous. I sat in the back row at the pool feeling very odd. My children's father here with another woman. This was the sixties and divorce was still very uncommon. She's got some nerve, hasn't she got any shame I asked myself. All the other mums and dads had been my friends for some time and it felt very embarrassing. There was an empty seat next to me as fate would have it. Turning round to see if they had arrived I saw the blushing bride-to-be standing at the back behind me looking as if she owned the place. I beckoned to her with my first finger to come over which she did. It was the first meeting between the first and the soon-to-be-second Mrs B.

"As you've insisted on coming here tonight, would you please sit on this seat," I said to her, patting the seat beside me. "You're making my bleeding nerves bad standing behind me," I told her. Hasn't she got any shame, I asked myself.

This woman duly sat down and looking at me she said, "The trouble with you is you don't understand Alan."

I looked at her in utter amazement, "You're quite right," I replied, "You're quite right. I'm afraid I don't understand BASTARDS."

I could almost have laughed out loud. I didn't understand! Bleeding cheek. Who the bleeding hell did she think she was! When I had calmed down I couldn't resist a sideways glance. She looked a lot older than me, her skin was dull and colourless, there was nothing pretty about her, even her clothes were matronly. It certainly wasn't her looks that had won him over. It wasn't a lack of the other either because he never went without; I didn't have a choice. She must have felt she had died and gone to heaven. After all Alan was still a very handsome man, if you liked that sort of thing. Outside she stuck something like a cigar in her mouth – smoking, UGH! Alan's pet hate.

A short time passed and Alan phoned again. They were going to have the children for a week at their new home. He hardly knew the kids. It wasn't a case of "would it be convenient?" or "would I mind?" He still acted as though he had the upper hand. It would be over my dead body was my first private reaction but I knew it was one argument I wouldn't win. Alan would go back to the courts and he would get visiting rights. Then he could always use it as a weapon against me and I didn't intend giving him any ammunition. But I was distraught at the thought of parting with my children. One could go and one would stay back. I thought that was the answer. But which one would I part with. In the end, mustering up all my strength, I packed their favourite little bits and pieces and when Alan arrived I gently pushed them out the door with a big smile and calls of "Have a lovely time" etc. Then I sat on the stairs and cried for hours.

The week passed and not a word from the kids. It would be too much to hope that that woman, who had kids of her own, would say to my children, "Give mum a ring." She must have known I would be worried. Would I find out they had changed their names and disappeared? You get all sorts of weird thoughts when you're in a state. Finally, on the Friday evening, a week later, I thought I was entitled to phone. Alan couldn't accuse me of interfering after all these days so, heart in my mouth, I dialled. I hadn't expected him to tell the children to give me a ring. Somebody of his character I wouldn't expect any kindness from. Such a relief, yes, they would be home tomorrow. I spoke to both kids, all bright and breezy but I could hear the tension in their voices. Suddenly they were home, favourite tea in front of the TV. No questions asked. I wasn't one bit interested in those two people. I was just pleased to have us back together.

It was weeks later, Stephen had gone to play football. Ruth and I were walking down the High Street.

"Mummy," said Ruth.

"Yes, darling," I replied.

"If you knew how naughty Daddy was you would never let us see him again," said Ruth.

My ears pricked up. Whatever happened that week? Ruth told me when she and Stephen got up on the Tuesday morning, they were having a row. Alan punched Margaret in the eye. She threw a teapot and broke it. I was always too mean to throw anything. Besides, when it was smashed I couldn't afford to replace it, so better not to throw it in the first place.

Alan then punched her again. Ruth said they were terrified. Suddenly, he grabbed them and ushering them out of the door took them, left, right around the streets until they came to a park.

"Stay here until I come back for you," he told them.

But he didn't come back. Cold, hungry, thirsty and frightened they decided to try and remember their way back to the bungalow, scared of what they would find. My stomach turned; anything could have happened to my children. They were never out of my sight. I was appalled and desperately unhappy thinking of my two little ones abandoned in the park. I couldn't get it out of my mind. I would have his guts for garters. But as things were the children never mentioned their dad. So, while things were quiet, leave well alone. The weeks passed, not a word from him, birthdays there was nothing, Christmas came and went not even a card. Time stretched into years there was nothing, complete silence. Even the old grandad down the road never got in touch. The children never mentioned him, he was completely out of their lives.

I had a large photo of Alan in the lounge which always took centre stage. I had always, even in my darkest hours, kept the picture in pride of place in the house. It was my way of reminding the children who their father was. It is very important to know you have parents and who they are. I was never sure about Sheila and I found it difficult to believe she was my mother and my father was unknown. So I was determined the children would know they had a father and not suffer as I had done. I hoped they would grow up without any hang-ups. Not that the children ever mentioned him, nor did they hear me slag him off. Why this picture is being mentioned is because when we were married, every time he came home he would bin the picture. It started a row every time. He accused me of taking the piss and putting it up to wind him up when I knew he was coming home. Most of the time, I didn't know when he was coming home but he couldn't work that one. Anyway, the picture makes its final appearance years later.

Harold had achieved a lifetime's ambition shortly after marrying Mum. They bought a newsagent's and tobacconist's shop in Thundersley, about half an hour's drive from Southend. Secretly I don't think Mum was too thrilled, she hadn't married at her time of life to work one hundred hours a week. Gone were her card-playing days, she really missed the gang of ladies she had being doing battle with for so long. Their card schools seemed like a battle to me, winning was the name of the game. Gone were her visits to the casino, gone were her dog-racing nights. Gone also were her gin-swigging days. In return she had stability, after her life with Dad that had to count for a lot.

Out of the blue they got a fantastic offer for the shop if they could move in twenty-four hours. It wasn't a problem for me, they were welcome to my bedroom for however long it took, so they moved in with their baby – that was a whippet called Nobby. To be honest I was glad to see a few extra pound notes around. Considering Harold had been a bachelor until he had married Mum – he had lived all his life with his old mum and could be described as being a bit stuffy – he was really laid back with the children. Stephen and Ruth had their own dog – a Chihuahua called Tommy Tucker, even they enjoyed the company, they played for hours and had us in fits.

Harold would take Nobby for a walk every morning, stop and get the paper, then just relax and have a read. He soon learned the shop around the corner was for sale. They bought it and quick as they had arrived they were gone. There was mixed feelings on my part, having Mum live on my doorstep. But I threw my lot in with them and went to work for them.

We were still struggling to fit in with the neighbours, some of them were a rough lot. There was one family of drunks; they would shuffle up the road, one of them would shout abuse at you as you quickly tried to pass. They were a disgusting lot, swearing and spitting. Just across the road the lady earned her living in the bars on the seafront; she would prop the bar up one end of the pub and her fourteen-year-old daughter would be in competition propping up the other end. Next door was a young family with seven kids. Neither of them worked, no disrespect to anyone being genuinely unemployed but they were bone-lazy, sat on their fat arses all day smoking. I had worked my socks off getting my garden straight for myself and the kids. Flowers were in bloom, I had some lovely dahlias; their garden was a wilderness. They had a brainwave one day, only they could have thought of it. They got a goat in to eat its way through the weeds, it wouldn't enter their heads to tie it up. It cleared my fence and ate all the tops of my beautiful flowers. I yelled at the scruffy bitch next door, "Get this bleeding goat out of my garden, it's eaten all my flowers." Her reply is unprintable, but it boiled down to the fact that I was making an awful fuss over a few weeds.

I had another barney with them; we had a new family move in across the road and the two men struck up a friendship straight away. Gossips had it our new neighbour had just come out of jail, he had a list as long as your arm for robbery, burglary, you name it, he had done it. I was disturbed one night and looking out my bedroom window saw the two men push something through the back door into next door's kitchen. At that moment I was pleased to see them, God alone would know what they were doing in the middle of the night, it didn't interest me, I would get back to sleep. Many hours later just before dawn, I sat bolt upright in bed, in shock. There had been a bang. It would have woken the dead. Still none of my business, don't get involved I told myself. My task was to get us all up, get the kids to school and get myself to work.

I hadn't been at work five minutes when the police were in making enquiries. Last night there had been a robbery across the road, did anyone hear or see anything. My big mouth was in overdrive before I could think, "I could tell you a story," I said. I hadn't seen a safe but it didn't take too much working out. The police went around to them and the safe was still in the kitchen, they hadn't managed to blow the door off. When I walked home for my lunch break the police were still there. The two wives were standing on the driveway, "If we thought it was you who bubbled us, we would tear your guts out and stuff them down your throat," they said in front of the police. I looked at them and said, "So you reckon I'm scared of you, you can tell," I said smiling and very cocky, "I'm scared to death," but believe me I was, I was shaking like a jelly. I was so frightened I sat on the stairs and cried.

Hard as I tried to mind my own business, mainly keep out of trouble with the neighbours, there was always something. Our house was almost on a crossroads, over on one corner were the Murphys, now they were a tough lot, another large family, eight in all, parents ex-jailbirds. On the other corner was a lady on her own with four kids. Ivy was quite a character, she was very tall and imposing, her dyed blonde hair was always well combed and she was always neatly dressed be it she got all her clothes from a jumble sale. She never looked clean however hard she tried. It was probably the cigarette in her mouth non-stop that did the damage. If she asked me in, the white cupboards in her kitchen were dark brown stained by the smoking. Ivy spent her whole day gossiping, she knew everyone's business; what she didn't know, that was her task for the day, find out. She could swear for England. Her eldest was the same age as my Stephen and as thick as two planks. None of her children went to school, on the rare occasion when they did she gave them instructions on how to play up the teachers. Simple things like lining up in the playground to go back to class. Ivy would tell her kids to walk in a zigzag line, anything that would annoy those in charge.

It was difficult really for us in as much as Stephen and Ruth had both passed their eleven-plus and were both at grammar school; they were away from the estate all day and in the evening they had homework or school activities. We didn't mix, that was the way things were, we were not being stuck up, I was a nobody, just trying to get on with my life and do my best for my kids. Ivy was into all sorts of mischief, funnily I liked her, but you couldn't trust her. She liked to stir things up a bit but obviously hadn't learned not to mess with my family.

On this particular day Stephen had his best friend from primary school home. They had gone out on their bikes for a ride; it hadn't been many minutes when I saw the two of them running for their lives across the road pushing their bikes. A gang of kids, led by the mouthpiece the Murphy brat, had pushed them off their bikes and had started hitting them. There were quite a few kids and the number that had come along had frightened Stephen and his friend. My first task was to phone Mum and say I wouldn't be back to work that afternoon. She was as cold as ice, "Are you working here or not, because I can soon get someone else." I was frightened to leave the children but I couldn't afford to feed them without working so I told her I would be along, to which she replied, "and don't bring your troubles into the shop."

My mum worked in strange ways; days later the Murphy brat came in for some sweets, he was a real tearaway and looked it from the top of his head to the tip of his toes. His hair looked as though he had stuck his finger in an electric light socket, it stood straight up. Shirt adrift, tear in his trousers and holy socks hanging around his hobnailed boots. He stood with his halfpenny, pondering how to get the most sweets for his money. Mum had been waiting patiently for him and approached him nicely. "Why did you terrorize my grandson last week?" she asked. He wasn't a bit put out by the question, he was frightened of no one and an old biddy like my mum wouldn't phase him. In his Cockney accent he replied, "Weren't me, Missus, Ivy asked me to do it."

"Well," said my mum, standing outside the butcher's is Ivy's son, "I'll give you fifty pence" (a fortune to a kid like him in those days) "if you go out there and kick him in the shins." Out went the Murphy brat and landed an almighty kick on his friend's shin. It's OK for their kids to go around in gangs, aided and abetted by the parents, but return the favour and they squeal police.

In walked two big burly police to Mum. Now she had a really tough time and was a real hard nut. "Is it true you gave the Murphy kid fifty pence to kick a boy?" they asked.

"What nonsense," said Mum. "Can you honestly think that a lady in my position would do such a thing?"

"WE wouldn't have thought so," was their reply. Apologies all around and that was it. I could imagine Ivy – she would be plotting all sorts of revenge, but perhaps she realized she had met her match. It was a message to the urberts on the estate not to mess with us, we would fight fire with fire.

Stepbrother John was around but not so much, Harold had no time for him as long as he made no effort to repay his debts. He was selling second-hand cars for a living; he offered to look out for a car for me, years earlier I had acquired an old banger and it had passed its sell-by date. True to his word he found me a "Beauty", and I parted with my hard-earned cash. Arriving home one day, there was this beautiful Austin Cambridge Estate on my drive, "Wow!" What a treat, John had done me proud. I couldn't wait to get the keys off the mat and get going. There wasn't a squeak from it, so I hurried around to the garage, asked if they would be good enough to drop by and have a look.

When the mechanic had a look he laughed and said, "You're having a joke with me, aren't you?" It was missing a Starting Motor; now I admit I wasn't quite sure what that implied but I was furious. Mum was next – I told her what had happened and asked if she had an address. She was as mad as could be, how dare I criticize her wonderful boy and she bellowed at me, "John doesn't understand cars, he only sells them." Then I had a dose of the old chestnut. I was having hallucinations again and she had to put up with it all. There was nothing I could do but pay the garage for the repairs. The children were all over the place in the evenings and weekends and a car was essential. We would just have to tighten the reins a little for a while, they didn't have a lot anyway.

Shortly after that incident the phone rang at home one evening and two detectives from Southend Police Station asked if they could come around to see me. They wanted to speak to me on a very delicate matter. "What matter?" I wanted to know, but they would say no more other than it was delicate. Obviously I was at home and not too happy with strangers calling after dark. They said they would be round in minutes. Immediately they got off the phone I dialled the station and asked if the two detectives were genuine. "Why?" asked the copper on the other end. I told him about the call and he replied, "and you are going to be out before they get there."

"No I'm not, you cheeky whatnot," I said. I was concerned, what would they want with me.

"We want you to look at a photograph," they said, "and tell us if you know this man. Before you look we want to tell you he is dead. We also want you to know he has been in the sea for some time." I stood there trying not to be alarmed as they asked, "Are you ready to look at the photo?"

They handed me a large picture of just a face, his eyes were closed and the face was very clear. I stared at it for some time before asking, "Who is it? Isn't it your brother John?" they asked.

"Never," I said, "who told you it was?" It was so unlike John it was laughable. The body had been washed up on the beach and the police had published the photo in the local paper. Betty had identified it as her brother, said no more. But John had disappeared; rumour had it he had to get out of town – why wasn't I surprised? Eventually he turned up in Bristol, he never came back to Southend, not even for Mum's funeral.

John and I didn't write or phone for the next twenty or was it thirty years, not until 2002. With Colin (my second husband) we were staying over in Bristol so on the spur of the moment I gave him a call and just said, "Hi how about me buying you dinner?"

He was just thrilled to bits and we hugged for ever. The first thing he said after all those years was, "I wish I had never sold you that car."

"God," I said, "that was a lifetime ago," and sadly it was. Colin had laid the law down as men do, happy as he was to have dinner, he reminded me we had already had a long day and were due an early start, this wasn't going to be a long evening. Getting on for two o'clock in the morning I was yawning my head off, dying for my bed, while the two men were talking their heads off. Finally I had to insist we went home but that wasn't the end of the night. No need for a taxi,

John would drive us and then he proceeded to give us a tour of Bristol until three o'clock. It was too late to sleep so we sat quietly discussing the evening. Colin thought John was terrific, charming – a real character. For me it was unreal, sitting there with John I could have been sitting with Dad, they were so alike. Colin wouldn't have a word said against John.

"I know," I said, "I totally agree with you, he is all you say he is, lovable, silver-tongued, just like Dad." Memories came flooding back, I know all about silver-tongued lovable, charmers; sadly for me that's the way to lose all your money.

As quickly as Mum and Harold had bought the shop they had sold it and had retired to Thorpe Bay, and I was job-hunting again. It was a desperate daily search looking through the papers and visiting the job centre; in despair I took a job as a delivery driver in a feather factory. Yes, feathers, millions of them. They had to be delivered to ladies at home making Indian head-dresses. I had never given much thought to Indian head-dresses, although I had bought a few for Stephen. They have the main feather in the front and the feathers are left and right as they go round the head getting smaller, each side matching in colour. The outworkers would phone up for one thousand head-dresses that week. The feathers were in holding bays as high as the ceiling and I had to count the feathers out starting from the main one in the front. One thousand main feathers, one thousand next size down left, blue, etc, etc, it drove me bleeding crackers. But I had to stick at it for the moment, you can't be without money when there are two kids at home depending on you. Even working as many hours as I could there was never enough money.

The children always had a cooked meal in the evening, I told them I had already eaten, I missed my café dinners and in the evenings was quite hungry. When the kids left their dinner I would rush into the kitchen and practically lick the plates. If it was a pork chop I would suck all the juices out of the bone, "lovely".

When my delivery duties were finished for the day, it was my task to help out on the benches, pressing bleeding feathers. I was bored to distraction. I prayed that my kids were keeping their side of our bargain, they were going to work as hard as I was to make sure they didn't end up like me. Both of them were holding their own at grammar school, so I couldn't be prouder. It was worth the effort I was making to see them doing so well.

Surprising news – Mum and Harold had come out of retirement and they had bought a third shop. I had never been so pleased to work with Mum. Mum said I was to have nine pounds a week but Harold had a quiet word with me and said it would be twenty pounds. And not to say a word to Mum, and I never did.

The children and I settled down to a quiet period. Many a time my day would start at 3.30 a.m. – if there were particularly heavy magazines to be delivered, I would do that first, then I would help Mum and Harold mark the papers for the rounds. Then it was home to get the kids to school. They always had their breakfast in bed, much quicker and it saved any tidying up afterwards. Once they were dropped off at school, it was back for a full day in the shop. Mum and Harold lived upstairs so the children made their way to me after school. Their dinner was always ready; prepared between the rushes, it was dished out and with the words, "Get on with it" I had to fly downstairs to carry on serving. On one occasion when I dashed back upstairs I noticed their plates hadn't been touched, dinner was awful, they said. They were left in no doubt what I thought of being messed about. "Make sure those plates are clean next time I come up." Later when I was washing up I didn't like the look of something on one of the plates, I put it to my nose to smell and it was soap. It must have slipped off the draining board into the saucepan in my rush and I had forced them to eat their dinner, it must have tasted awful. Sadly life was at full stretch for all of us, there was no time for anything, no time for the children and certainly no time for myself.

The years were passing as they do; it was 1974, Stephen was fifteen and six feet tall, Ruth was coming up to being a teenager. There was never a birthday card or a Christmas card from Alan, he was totally out of their life. He must have come to Southend as his parents lived not far away but they were never mentioned. It was Mothering Sunday and when I returned from my morning in the shop I was surprised to see there were no parking spaces. "I'll just stop here for a moment while I check the kids are alright," I said to myself. I knew it wouldn't be many moments before there would be a knock on the door and some irate neighbour would be complaining. Sure enough there's the bell, opening the door the words, "Yes, I know, my car's—" was coming out of my mouth as I looked at the stranger standing on the step. Shut your mouth my brain was saying as I looked at the grey-haired, fat-faced man, I couldn't remember how many years it had been and I only just recognised Alan. He was shown into the lounge, his first words even before he greeted the children were, "So you do keep that photo there."

Sitting on the floor looking up at him was his clone. Ruth had his hair, eyes, skin, nose, mouth and teeth. Never will I forgive Alan, how dare he suggest the day she was born when we both almost lost our lives, how dare he suggest she wasn't his. I didn't think straight away he would be out of the navy now, had done his twenty-two years and had received a golden handshake It was 1974 and he was paying two pounds fifty for each child, he didn't ask about Stephen's blazer bought in his first year now the sleeves stopped at the elbow, or Ruth's shorts bought so big to grow into she couldn't wear them. No he couldn't even go to a packet of chewing gum. Nothing changed after the visit, it was years and years before we heard from him again.

When he left I removed the photo, the children were in no doubt about their father, they were old enough now to make up their own minds. I didn't want that miserable looking bastard staring at me anymore. Then I went upstairs and cut up every photo I had of him, especially our wedding photos. The ringing of the doorbell had ended an era.

Chapter Twelve

It started off as just another normal week. Monday Mum and
Harold seemed their normal self. I had long regarded Harold
as a friend, someone who was on my side. Someone I could
trust, we had always talked to each other. Tuesday I thought
Mum was fussing about a bit, tidy this, sort that out.
Wednesday she was being even more fussy and I was
beginning to smell a rat. Thursday a small boy came in for a
comic; on the shelf was a pile of out of date comics.
Thrusting them into his arms she said, "Here take these."
Mum never gave anything away; with her behaviour during
the week, it was very odd. Friday afternoon she started
tidying out a cupboard, big time. "Do you know, Mum," I
said to her, "if I didn't know better I'd think this shop has
been sold." But of course it wouldn't be sold, I was working
practically 24/7 with her and she would have told me. I'd
have seen the people coming and going, heard something, a
phone.

Not only was it sold, the new people would be moving in
on Saturday, the very next day. They had their own staff and
I wouldn't be needed. I was surprised Harold had let me
down. "So what's going to happen to me next week?"
reminding her I had two grown-up children to support. Not
even stopping her chores to speak to me she replied, "You
will soon get another job." They had bought a bungalow not
a mile from where we lived and would be moving out as soon
as the shop shut on the Saturday. So when did they do all
that? The mind boggles, not a whisper to me. It went back to
my old thoughts. Mum owed me absolutely nothing, why
should she, she had given me shelter of a kind when I was
young, after all she wasn't my mother. Harold didn't think I

172

was entitled to know, it was none of my business. He did think I deserved a handsome reward for the years I had supported them. He bought me a brand new car – UJN 191S – lovely, but I couldn't feed the kids with it. The funny thing was Mum honestly expected me not to mind a bit and got me involved with the moving. Helping her carry her bits and pieces into her new home she said, "This is my last move, you will be carrying me out of here in a box." It wasn't quite like that in the end, the question was, "Who are they going to carry out first, her or me."

It was back to Paul again, just like the old days, nothing had changed. He had a new manageress called Mary, although she was quite matronly she was great fun. Stephen had joined the T.A.S. in the Parachute Regiment, he was enjoying his weekends away. He had taken his Maths A level a year early and was studying hard for his Physics and Chemistry. Ruth was at the Convent just up the road from me; dinner times I would hear a little, "Hello, Mum," and she would be there with her friends. They would have the best table and whatever they wanted, which wasn't much, on the house. For me the struggle was getting harder, two children at grammar school, they were both bigger than myself, I had no choice but to work longer hours.

One Sunday evening a party of six men came in for a meal, they were down from the North on a six-week engineering contract. Nick was a Paul Newman lookalike, those blue eyes with his dark hair and smile, he was gorgeous. He chatted me up and this time I was ready and willing. Our first date we walked the length of the pier, it was a cold misty night and I snuggled up, feeling like a schoolgirl on her first date.

As the weeks passed I knew on my part it was love and returning home one evening Nick said, "Lets go." If Stephen and Ruth had been that few years older I would definitely have thrown caution to the wind and gone, I wouldn't have given it a second thought. Life had been a continuous slog so a little recklessness now wouldn't have gone amiss. But the kids and I had come a long way and I had vowed to see it through. I would rather have cut my throat than rock the boat now at this stage of their lives.

The six weeks flew and before Nick left Southend he bought me a ring for my engagement finger, I was so thrilled. Parting was so tearful, with all the promises to love each other forever. It wasn't long before he was back for the weekend, I met him off the train in London on the Friday evening and took him home. We went to bed with a bottle of whisky and a bottle of vodka and got stoned out of our minds. We stayed in bed the whole weekend, too drunk to get up; I did surface now and then to see the kids were still alive. Finally the weekend was over and Nick was gone. The kids went mad, they were so ashamed of me, I felt awful. Stephen was outraged and told me in no uncertain terms, "While I'm here and head of this house, I won't tolerate such behaviour." I didn't know whether to smack him one on the chops for being so cheeky. I knew it wasn't going to work out and over the next six months I gained the strength to make the break but I will always be grateful for the lessons he taught me, which were to play an important part in my life later on.

Stephen had passed his A levels and was off to Manchester University. Not bad for a kid from a violent broken home and a council estate in the 70s. Remembering my own school days I tried as hard as I could to see he wasn't too short of bits and pieces. He didn't want me to run him to Manchester, just the station in London, he didn't even want me to come on the platform. I could tell how pleased he was to be on his way, away from the poverty and the council estate. Driving home I was so upset I cried buckets, at times the tears flowed it was a wonder I didn't crash. My little curly-haired baby had made it, he was on his way. That had been my ambition, that was what I had worked so hard for, my heart was bursting with pride.

It was all getting too much at the café, Ruth would be alone for too long if I continued. Harold in his retirement was doing the books for a friend who owned a baker's shop. There was a vacancy there for an assistant five days a week, Mondays off, I could do something else that day. I was pleased to get the job after Lord knows how many years, I was finally away from the seafront.

Getting back to that old chestnut, "Respectability", It was a decent job and I felt a lot cleaner doing it. No longer did the whiff of fish and chips come over me as I moved about. I was still plodding along with the Conservative Party. "Why the Conservatives?" people would ask me. Living on a council estate, one parent family, poorer than a church mouse. There was no support when I was being beaten and abused. There was no support when I was evicted from my own home. I was never very political, people are so political and clever but not me. All I can say is, "I felt safe." There's nothing else I can say, "I felt safe." Now I wanted to appear a bit more respectable, the shop was a step in the right direction. The past would be behind me, none of it would ever be mentioned until I was old and grey. Then one day it would all be put down on paper and when my children are old and grey they can read it.

Now I needed some extra money and was looking hard when I ran into a very old, long-standing friend. Colin had just moved with his two sons, who had been at St Helens with my two, into a large block of flats on top of the cliffs at Westcliff. The agents wanted someone to scrub the miles of landings and stairways once a week for five pounds. That would do me, still no time to be proud.

The first Monday I started Colin was waiting for me. "I'll leave you a set of keys to my home, treat it as your own. You may need the bathroom or to get yourself a drink," That had to be the lousiest job on the earth. The stairs had a strip of red lino down the middle and on each step there was a strip of black rubber, the red of the lino ran everywhere if too much water was used. I just hated the job more than I had ever hated any job. It was like being back in Dickens' time with my bucket of dirty water and rag. Funny that! on my hands and knees scrubbing just like my grandmother and maybe my own mother. Now I knew how they felt; at least I wasn't pregnant, I had my two – that was exactly what this was all about. No way would they have to do what I had to do. They would have the best education going, be able to get the best jobs.

During my first day at the flats I decided I didn't have a degree in scrubbing so I hurried along – spent the time making an apple pie for Colin's tea. He had been good to me that morning – I wanted to repay his kindness.

We were now in the 80s, Stephen had spent the summer in the United States teaching Judo at summer camp. His graduation day was really great, Ruth and I sped up the motorway to take him out for a well-deserved meal. He had accepted a job in Kent and had found someone to share digs with, I was pleased he had done so well.

Ruth had passed her A levels in Maths, Physics and Chemistry and in her final year had won "The girl of the year award". It was a wonder my heart didn't burst I was so proud. I wondered if anyone told Madam Mildred what waster of a Merriman's girl had won the award. Ruth chose to go to Nene, in Northampton.

Now I really was alone but not quite, I still had to keep a roof over the kid's head. I felt as though I was nearing the end of the road, it had been over sixteen years since the divorce. Sometimes a bit stressful but however tired I was, it was always a joy to be free. No one knows and words can never explain how lovely it is not to be afraid.

Ruth was back and forth and she seemed very settled. I was busy in the shop and still scrubbing stairs. Saturdays when Ruth was home she would come to work with me to earn pocket money. It was the Christmas just before her twenty-first, birthday, she put her arms around me, hugged me tight and sobbed and sobbed. "Whatever is it?" I asked time and time again. She assured me it was nothing, she just felt like a good cry and afterwards she seemed her usual self. But she had sobbed as though she was distraught and I couldn't help but be worried. She was going back to Nene just before her birthday at the weekend, Saturday night all her friends were eating out at a restaurant, which was already booked. On the Sunday it was open house. I was upset I hadn't been included in the arrangements but grateful to have had her home all over Christmas and the New Year. Mum had baked a big fruitcake and I had it iced professionally. I packed two boxes of goodies for the Sunday. That Saturday night Colin had a Builders' do to attend and he asked me if I would keep him company. I felt quite sad and lonely and I asked the band if they would play something for Ruth. They announced, "The next number is for Ruth who is celebrating her twenty-first birthday away from home." They played, "Take the ribbons from her hair". Now it was my turn to sob, I wanted so much to be with her, give her a hug.

It was the following Wednesday evening, there was a letter from Ruth waiting on the mat. I walked into the kitchen and leaning against the sink hurriedly opened it. *Mum, my birthday was wonderful, something I shall remember all my life.* I was thinking, that's how it should be and was feeling so pleased, when there was a knock on the door. Opening it, I was amazed to see Ruth standing there. We all think we know our daughters, I knew Ruth so well, I knew she wasn't involved in drugs, I knew she wasn't pregnant. I just looked at her and asked, "Why have you run away?" It was a good thing I was numb with shock and for once kept my big mouth shut, I might have said something I regretted. The kettle went on and we settled in the kitchen, she was quite calm and not at all upset.

"Mum," she said, "I got up this morning and I knew I couldn't face another day studying. I went to see my tutors, told them I was leaving. Went out and got a job selling lampshades in an electrical shop. Caught a train home to tell you, I couldn't put it in a letter. Now I am going back to Northampton on the next train."

I was dumbfounded, I took her back to the station, praying to God to give me the strength to act correctly. Struggling for something to say that would sustain her, in the end all that came out was, "Promise me you will keep yourself clean." How naff can you get. I waved her off with a big smile after a hug, but my heart was broken. Not because she had left Nene but she had chosen not to come home. When I got home I sat on the stairs and cried my eyes out, I wondered how many times I had sat on those very stairs and had cried over my children.

It must have been what I didn't say, on the Saturday morning there was another letter from Ruth. She was ready to come home as soon as I had the time to come up and help her with her luggage. She didn't explain anything, why the change of heart, just a short cheery letter. I was pleased the post had been early, I was able to plead a sickie at work. Ruth wasn't on the phone, so I couldn't tell her I was on my way. When I got there she was out, no problem, I'll just wait, however long it is. Finally she came strolling along the street, she looked as though she didn't have a care in the world and that is how it should be at twenty-one. Her bits and pieces were packed in minutes and we were on our way home.

One of my customers ran the jewellery department in Keddies in Southend High Street. There was a vacancy there and she offered me the job. I had started in jewellery, making it, designing it, I had always loved being with pretty things so I grabbed the chance to work there. My first problem was Wednesday afternoon was now the only free time I had for my stairs. Wednesday it would have to be, one old bat opened her door wanting to know what all the banging was about. Seeing me she said, "You are supposed to be here on Mondays." Explaining that it was the only free time I had, I thought she would understand. She really was a sour-faced old witch, she talked to me as though I was a piece of dirt. Sorry to let down people who pay me, but she really got up my nose. Handing her the bucket with the wet rags I said, "Here you do it," and walked off. Everyone gets a strop and that day it was my turn; my children had finished their education, I had finished my scrubbing.

My lovely son was getting married, the happy couple invited me down for lunch. They wanted a quiet word about the wedding plans. Foremost on their minds was not to have me upset on the day. They were assured anything they did was OK with me. After all, the bride knew nothing of the past and when it came to the crunch that was where the past should be, in the past. They had to accommodate Alan and Margaret and if sitting them on the top table was the way things were going to be, it was alright. When Mum heard she went ballistic, no way were they sitting them on the top table, she would have everyone boycott the wedding. Mum could always be trusted to start a fight.

The happy day arrived, Ruth was bridesmaid, so we travelled down the night before and stayed in a hotel. Mum drove down in the morning with Harold, lovely cousin Maureen was there with her four children, so was lovely cousin Sheila. The Harold Wood mob were there, no one was left out. It was a beautiful wedding, top hat and tails, the bride was gorgeous, the weather glorious, nothing could spoil anything for anyone. It was a wonderful family day. The top table looked scrumptious, there in her place of honour was the new Mrs B, then there was me, still Mrs B, and the place setting for the third Mrs B just said, *Margaret*. It didn't enter her head that she was sat at the top table, and should be pleased, she just went mad. The bride, bless her little heart, said, "I felt we had enough Mrs Bs at the top table, I just didn't want another one." But she vowed her revenge – when Ruth married she would turn the invitation down.

Ruth got herself a part-time job in a newsagents and then a full-time job in a sandwich bar. She insisted she gave me housekeeping which I turned down. I didn't want a penny from her, she had very little for a girl of twenty-one, I wanted her to get herself straight. To make her feel that was acceptable I told her if she had any money over at the end of the week save it until I needed it. She had arranged to go to summer camp in America to teach swimming and she still wanted to do that. I tried not to worry about her choice of jobs or lack of ambition, I figured the trauma of leaving Nene was still with her, and she was still a bit lost. One day I told myself she would work it out, for the moment I wouldn't nag or fuss.

They have a great time our kids who go out to summer camp in America. I waved her off at Gatwick with a lump in my throat. Ruth wrote home about seven of them piling into an old banger and driving down to Washington, D.C. They bought lobster and cooked it, something I couldn't afford to do at home. Summer camp was over and Ruth still had time to spend in America, she wasn't coming home a minute too soon. She phoned home, "Mum, your cousin Brendan lives in Canada, do you have his address?" she asked. I told her I hadn't been in contact with him for years and the address I did have was probably out of date. "That will do," she said with great determination, "I'll start there." Now I was really worried, Canada was a big place. Brendan was at home – lucky for Ruth, not so lucky for Brendan who had broken his leg so he was able to give her time. Finally Ruth's visa was running out and she wrote home. *Dear Mum, I'll be landing at Gatwick, etc. etc. What am I going to do in that boring old place Southend?* That summed up her frustration, she got herself a job in a record shop and settled down to a boring old life.

The Conservative Party was taking up a lot of my time especially at elections, delivering leaflets, canvassing, always fund-raising. It was at a cheese and wine evening in '82 I met a lovable old rogue, Ken Cater. Over a glass of wine (six glasses for him) he invited me to join his committee, Milton Ward. He told me in five years he would be the Mayor and he wanted me to be his Mayoress. We never became friends, I think if we were friends the relationship, if that is the right word for it, would never have survived. Ken was quite mature in years, was at the front of the queue when they handed out the Oomph and he always had a lady in tow. Whatever he did was no skin off my nose, we rarely spoke and no way was I in his circle and the Mayoress bit was never mentioned. What he had said that night I had taken quite seriously and thought about it quite a lot. I still had to keep a roof over my daughter's head and I wondered how would I manage if it ever happened. But for now I can dream, "Mayoress of Southend". It was a long way from that barefoot little girl of eight who had lost her way on the death of her grandmother.

Lucky, lucky me, if you can call something that keeps your daughter close I was lucky. Ruth and a friend went to a disco in Basildon, and there was the love of her life. Rob was her first real boyfriend, I think it was love at first sight for both of them. Just five months later they were engaged; he told her at the same time he would marry her when West Ham won the F.A. Cup, I thought we are in for a long engagement here. Two or three weeks had passed and Ruth told me she and Rob wanted to live together. I didn't say anything there and then, I waited a few days and then I asked her to come and sit down, I wanted to have a chat. "Now young lady," I said to her, "are you seriously wanting to live with Rob?" She assured me she was very serious, but they had no idea where they were going and neither of them had any money. Our little house was now a palace, I asked her how she felt about it. Everything she needed was there, linen, crockery, cutlery, etc. She said it was very nice, "but you live here," she said. "Here are the keys, my bags are packed, I'm off," I told her.

It was '85, Colin had a lodger – me. We had just had a very serious conversation, where both of us said we would never marry again. I had been on my own for over twenty years, a lifetime, I had no idea at that time Ruth's bombshell was coming and suddenly I would find myself redundant. The two kids and myself had kept the bargain we made when I was first divorced, all three of us had given it our best shot. Whether or not I had made a good job of it, well – the jury's still out on that one, but I couldn't have worked any harder.

Meeting up with the children was now the most important part of my life, especially my weekly glass of wine and a bite with Ruth. "Mum," she declared one day, "I don't fancy selling pop records when I'm fifty, I think I'll get myself a career." She and Rob had bought the little house, so there was the question of finance. Now she thought she couldn't afford to go back to studying. I assured her she could afford it and I said to her, "You have no choice, otherwise you will end up like me." Ruth fancied a career in banking and applied to Barclays. He asked her what happened, Ruth explained to him that things were wrong from the start, the wrong A levels, the wrong course at University. "I knew," she told him, "if I had stayed until I was one hundred I would never have passed." Then he asked her, "What do you think about Barclays sending you back to study?" They wanted Maths, which she had, Bookkeeping, Accountancy, Law and Economics. She stuck it out and now has the career she wanted and I'm very very proud of her.

It was coming up to election time, '87, and in six weeks Ken Cater would be the Mayor, he had been the Deputy for one year. I saw photos of him in the paper opening this, going there, still not a word. I was on my way to the supermarket, latish one night, it was dark and suddenly I decided to knock on his door and just ask. He stood looking at me for a few moments trying to work out what I was doing standing there, then he said, "Don't tell me you have come to tell me you have changed your mind, because I'm counting on you."

"No, no," I said almost in disbelief and went on my way, puzzled, they were the only words we ever spoke about such an important matter. I got back from the shopping on cloud nine. I was absolutely thrilled but Colin wasn't so impressed, "I didn't need it", whatever that meant. I tried to explain what being born a bastard in the 30s did to you, I tried to explain what being in a violent marriage did to you. I tried to explain that this was something I definitely "did need". In the end Colin said if I wanted to do it I should, but he thought it would be nice for me to be married. "We can't have our Mayoress living in sin," he declared. There are many including Colin who say I only married because I wanted to be the Mayoress, that old chestnut "respectability". Not true, not true at all, I love him more and more as we have grown old together.

It was a very quiet wedding on a Tuesday morning, no flowers, no photographs no cake. Just the four children and their partners and my mum. I wondered if my lovely grandmother and grandad were watching. Afterwards we went to a local pub and had a meal, it was just a perfect day.

The first task for Colin was to take me shopping; he bought me six of everything – suits, dresses, evening dresses, hats, gloves, bags, and a couple of coats. It was upsetting for Colin as Ken had gone to the Council saying he needed more money to carry out his duties. They doubled the Mayor's allowance that year which made the headlines on the front page of the local paper. Then it went on to say the Mayor had to buy the Mayoress clothes. People would say to me, "You do look lovely. Ken has been very generous." The truth was "His Worship" wouldn't buy a cup of tea, to put it politely, he was a mean old bugger.

Finally the great day arrived. Mayor making, 1987, it was very nerve wracking. I went to a Mayor making this year 2003, Colin had been invited and I was amazed to hear him say it was the first time he had been to such an event. I hadn't realized that he, along with my mother and children, hadn't been to mine. Then I had no idea that guests could be invited and it further added to my opinion of old Ken, he was selfish and thoughtless. After my Mayor making there was a grand ball and Colin had a table for ten, a rerun of our wedding, then with a crowd of friends we went back to our flat and celebrated until three in the morning. The Mayor had gone his way with his cronies and that was how it was from day one to the very end. A friend of Colin had just taken part in the American Cup Yacht Race and had been presented with a commemorative bottle of whisky, which he had passed on to Colin. I ran out of whisky and just opened it, I don't think Colin will ever forgive me.

For me it was a wonderful year, I would never knock the Mayoralty, it is a great institution. I was and still am very grateful for the invitation. You learn so much about people and it gave me an inner confidence that I sorely needed. I came out of it a much more rounded person, ready to take on the world. But for the Mayor himself he gave me nothing and I needed something to achieve for myself. I asked Ken if I could have my own charity in my spare time. I launched my appeal for the Prem. Baby Unit at Rochford Hospital. It was hard work and great fun and at the end of the year I had raised eight thousand pounds.

After a really brilliant year it ended as it began – on a sour note, my fault entirely, not being aware of procedure. It is customary at the end of the year to present the borough with a gift with your name on it. Once again I'm probably totally wrong but I would have liked a little something with my name on it, I hadn't done much in my life to be proud of and I was very proud of myself at this particular time. When the presentation came it was a surprise to me. Ken's gift was supposed to be a silver centre piece, actually I thought it was appalling but the point was it didn't have my name alongside his. Now people will say he was the "Mayor"; he was quite right but if we had known Colin would have organised something for me, silly me, it was important to me. Later in private I told Ken I was disappointed; he was dribbling as usual, sniffing as he always did and he was very upset. He said he was disgusted with the piece and do you know what he said, "They wanted seventy pounds off me for it, I wouldn't pay." Why didn't that surprise me? I hadn't seen him pay for anything the whole year. "Who did pay?" I asked, someone must have paid. He replied, "The money was taken out of my charity fund." I was well pleased I had no association with the gift, I thought that was appalling.

After the year in the Mayoralty which was a very high profile one for me, I was offered the opportunity to stand in Milton for a seat on Essex County Council. It wasn't a Conservative held seat but I relished the challenge. I just loved the whole packet of an election, the canvassing, the whole show. Many a time I would hear Nick in my head giving me advice. One sad note, two weeks before the election Harold died, I was really upset. He and Mum had been married nearly twenty-five years, he had been a true friend to me and the kids. For two days I couldn't go out, I couldn't trust myself not to burst into tears.

Harold had a proper Jewish funeral at Finchley. That was a wonderful service and I felt privileged to have been part of Harold's life. It was still strange to me being a Catholic growing up in Ireland to have had two Jewish stepfathers, both of whom I loved, especially Jack. It wasn't that I bonded with them, I felt this strange bond with both of them, I felt something, if I could explain it better I would. I knew Harold would want me to get on with what I was doing so I did.

At the count I couldn't look, I would just hate losing. I had put my heart and soul into the campaign. Even my legs went to jelly and I had to go and sit down away from it all. I was giving myself a good talking to and telling myself I had to see things through whatever the result. Finally Colin came over and said, "You can come and look now." But I was frozen with fright in the chair. He took my arm, lifted me off the chair and said, "Trust me." We approached the table, me trying to look cool as I glanced at the piles of votes being stacked up. I couldn't believe my eyes, I was well ahead, I was winning. I did win and I was so pleased. That started a ten-year roller coaster ride which gave me the ten best years of my life and at times plunged me into despair.

Mum was seventy-three now, widowed for the second time. She was a woman of substance with her own home and a healthy bank account. She told me she was going to associate only with people who made her laugh. Was she having the usual go at me, because I still made her cry? We spat at each other just as we had always done, she soon forgot the many kindnesses I had shown her. My life had been geared to finding my mother and who I was, it was something that caused me great anxiety. As time was getting on both for Mum and me I was beginning to think that time would run out altogether and I would never find "ME".

Colin was really good with her, they got on like a house on fire. He was quite happy on a Sunday to take her out for a drive in the country and a bit of dinner. Mum hadn't been home to Moortown all the years she was married to Harold, so the first thing Colin and I did after his death was to take her home. We took our own car so we could drive all over; we visited Mum's brother Joe in Galway, as many of her nieces and nephews as we could. "It was grand," she said, seeing how well they were all doing. She had a few gin and tonics in Jim Burke's and put flowers on Mick and Lizzie's grave. It was a great time for all of us but no matter how close we seemed to be I never forgot not to step over that invisible line and ask the question, "Who am I?"

Life for me was the best it had ever been, the flat was lovely and Colin had bought me a brand new car. We were both very busy people, I absolutely loved being at County

Hall Chelmsford. I never got over the feeling of pride every time I walked through the door. My fellow councillors were wonderful, one thing you never had to watch your back, everyone was so helpful and supportive. It all seemed a long way from that barefoot little girl of eight walking along the bog road confused and unhappy. It seemed an even longer way from that distraught person who had been evicted from her home, abused and beaten and practically driven mad.

Out of the blue Stephen's wife ran away with another man. Just when everything seemed to be going right for me. My son was devastated, no more than me; I thought the pain would kill me. It was like having a death in the family. Mind you when I first met the girl she told me she had been engaged three times while at University, I thought that was a bit over the top for a young girl. This bloke could offer her nothing but sex, as we all know that has the strongest pull.

Life was getting tough for me on the political scene locally and my Conservative colleagues made sure they gave me a hard time. The trouble for me was Southend wanted Unitary Status and I thought we were better off under the umbrella of the County Council. After all I felt I was entitled to an opinion, that's why I was elected. In my ward there were three Conservative councillors who had served about sixty-five years between them, they thought they were God and you crossed them at your peril. On the grapevine I heard they were going to deselect me. This was at a time when the Conservatives were at an all time low. My ward now had three Labour councillors locally, the voters had thrown out anything that called themselves a Conservative, the voters were sick to the teeth of the lot of them. Glad to get rid of the whole shower, I still held the seat at County for the Conservatives and you would think I would be put on a pedestal and be treasured, not knifed in the back.

At a party one night at the Mayor's home, there much to my surprise was the Chairman of my ward, Geoffrey Baum. He was a nothing of a little man, he had cement in his brain and concrete in his heart. He was totally pissed with power and the vanity oozed out of his veins. Flatter him and tell him how wonderful he was and he was putty in your hands. Life had been tough here and there for me and a little rat like him wasn't going to beat me. So I slid up close to him and with my best and biggest smile almost cooed, "Good evening, Geoffrey." He gave me his usual sickly imitation of a smile. Smiling even broader I asked him, "What's this I hear about me being deselected?"

"Nothing to do with me, Dearie," he said. I could feel the knife pierce my back, "It's your committee."

"Now then, Geoffrey," I said still smiling, "You know what you say, goes." I wasn't going to let him wriggle of the hook, I considered myself a much stronger person than he was and I could fight just as dirty. I could feel the knife twist in my back, but I wasn't going to let this little rat get away with his games. "Well," I said with great confidence and authority, "I'm very surprised with your MBE in the pipeline that you would allow this to happen." I continued, "Mr Major wants the Conservatives united and deselecting a sitting councillor might upset him."

The little nothing of a man puffed up like a peacock, "Am I getting an MBE?" he asked. I thought he would explode, all I had to do now was keep a straight face; as if I knew anything about an MBE – he would be the last person on this earth to deserve an MBE. I feel no guilt in my behaviour, you have to fight fire with fire.

Of course I was reselected, the fact that I worked hard and cared passionately about the Conservatives should have protected me from those three at Milton but it didn't. At a time when the Conservatives were almost wiped of the face of the earth and with three Labour councillors in my ward, not only did I win but I was only three votes adrift from the previous election. But there was major trouble ahead, the petty little man didn't get his MBE. I sounded so surprised when he phoned to tell me, I couldn't understand why not.

He was gunning for me now and he would make sure my political life was at an end.

There was some fabulous news on the home front to take my mind off my worries. After over five years together Ruth and Rob were getting married. West Ham hadn't won the F.A. Cup but I guess Rob got tired of waiting. Rob had always said he couldn't face the big traditional white wedding – a wedding like Colin and myself, quiet, no fuss was perfect. It was the register office with just Rob's parents and grandparents and his best man. Ruth had Mum, her friend Marlesse and husband Hank with their baby, they had flown in from Holland. Lovely cousin Maureen was there with Stephen and Alan. After the service we had a meal in the best restaurant in Southend. In the evening there was a disco for 150 at a posh hotel in the country. Alan and Margaret had been invited to the wedding in the morning. We wouldn't lower ourselves to her level and not send an invitation. Of course she refused, she had waited all those years to get even; she was so thick, if she really wanted to upset us, what she had to do was turn up – now that would really would put our noses out of joint.

Marlesse and Hank were staying with Colin and myself so after the meal we went home to change the baby. Ruth phoned to say Alan had found out about the evening do and he was coming. I assured her that was OK by me. "But Mum," she said, "nobody's coming back to Southend and he wont be able to get back."

"OK. OK," I said, "I promise you I'll give your dad a lift at the end of the evening. Colin hadn't been seen all day, he was busy looking after Ruth's guests, although he loved Ruth like a daughter he never changed his stance about not wanting to be in the same part of the world as Alan.

When it was time to leave for the evening affair the baby was restless and Hank decided to stay at home with Colin and the two men could have a few quiet beers. It was a lovely evening, we had an open bar, then Mum had always been very generous, she wouldn't have had things any other way. Alan hadn't changed, he propped the bar up all evening, I heard him encouraging people to have triples, "After all he said to our guests, they're paying." Normally Dads help out with the expenses at their daughter's wedding, but I wouldn't have wanted him to spoil the habit of a lifetime.

Time for the journey home, Marlesse sat in the front with me, we chatted together most of the time. It must have been about one o'clock in the morning when we pulled up outside Alan's hotel. "How about a nightcap?" asked Alan. Well I thought that was a lovely thought, and was pleased to accept. It had been over a quarter of a century, a lifetime, since our divorce, time to let bygones be bygones. It would have been nice to have had a quiet word with him, after all we had just married our only daughter. Time for him to say how proud today had made him, etc. It was a small lobby, just a few tables, the night porter-cum-watchman asked Alan what he wanted. For me it was a really weird feeling being shown to a table by Alan and being asked what I'd like to drink. I can't remember what Marlesse had but I thought I'd have a brandy. I was quite relaxed, it had been a very proud day, the bride had looked lovely and this was a fitting end.

Thinking Alan was in the same frame of mind as myself, I raised my glass to give a toast. I looked at him and found myself looking into the same face that sat opposite me on the train the day I married him. His face was evil and white with temper and he almost hissed at me, "Don't you ever forget I know you, I know what a lying, conning, cheating, conniving, fucking bitch you are. You may be able to con the people of Southend but you will never be able to con me."

I was absolutely dumbstruck, Marlesse had put her drink down and had picked up her bag and left after bursting into tears. Alan continued in his venomous, spiteful way, "I'll never understand how you've got where you've got, how you have achieved all you have achieved, but I can imagine."

He didn't have a chance to say anymore, I was gone. We both arrived indoors in floods of tears, Colin and Hank wanted to go after him but decided he was rubbish and not worth getting their hands dirty.

Chapter Thirteen

Sheila had always suffered from arthritis. Now Harold was gone she no longer had to get up in the morning. She used to take him out in the car as she was the driver, wash, cook, and clean the bungalow. She could now take things easy. As the first year of widowhood came to an end, she had stiffened up considerably. It was odd she didn't have any friends to go shopping with or go on holiday with or an away-day. This fantastic life she had planned for herself wasn't materialising. She never had any interests in life other than cards and gambling. She often said how she missed her many brothers and sisters. They were all long gone, she had outlived them all. Her only friend was the old lady next door who shared her love for gin. There was always a glass being passed over the fence, usually one way – from Sheila. The second and third years passed and the stiffness with the arthritis became more and more noticeable.

Still doing my best to establish a mother-daughter relationship. We would be making good progress then something quite trivial would happen and Sheila would destroy all the good that had been done. It couldn't be that she was jealous, mothers aren't jealous of their own kids but she was trying to be totally in control of our lives. We went abroad for a two-week break. Colin and I were working very hard, Sheila was well, we deserved it. We were relieved to arrive home without incident. Ruth was soon on the phone to tell us Nan had been quite ill while we were away and had demanded our return. Much to Nan's annoyance she made the decision to let us have our holiday. Next morning, I went straight round to my mother. It didn't take long to work out what had happened. Sheila was so determined to ruin our holiday, she had drunk two bottles of gin and taken some tablets. She had laid in bed for eight days without eating because she had nearly killed herself. Her weight had plummeted and she looked half dead. It showed the lengths Sheila would go to to spoil things for me. This time she had almost gone too far and in my heart I knew she would never recover from the damage she had done herself.

It was time for me to begin saying my prayers. The ideal situation would have been for Sheila to go into a nursing home. Sheila had her own home, money, she could afford it. She would get the care she needed even at this stage. But she was determined to stay in her own home. She thought it was my duty to care for her. She came from that old brigade who thought children should care for their parents. She had conveniently forgotten abandoning me all those years ago. Care in the community was now law and there was nothing that could be done if it was the client's wish. We still hadn't even had a chat about things but I had long realized she was my mother. I could see myself in her every move, her smile, hear myself when she laughed. We were two identical peas in a pod, the only difference being my colour. Strange as it may seem, I never liked my mother, but I loved her dearly. You have to love your mother, you might not like her, but you love her. The decision I made in the end was almost one hundred per cent made because I had a deep desire to find that mother I never had before it was too late. Even if it was on Sheila's deathbed, if we could just hug each other close and say "Sorry" even that would be wonderful. I would never give up trying for that breakthrough. It was the most important thing in my life. I wanted to put the past behind me and move on before it was too late for me.

It hadn't yet come to the stage where I went round to check her every day. Sometimes, it would be three days. One Sunday Colin and I popped in on our way out for a meal. I was all dressed up, fit to kill, wearing the latest shade of lavender eye shadow. Never one to miss a chance to exercise that sharp tongue of hers, she asked me: "What do you think you look like? I've seen people who have been dead for days looking better."

It was always a battle trying to be a good daughter, doing all the things expected of you. One day I thought I had everything under control. I felt I could approach her. Trying to explain how I felt the odd one out with my cousins and was there anything she could tell me to make me feel any different. Perhaps not the best way to put things but how else do you put it. What came next sent me reeling. Sheila appeared to have a fit.

"How dare you speak to me like that! You horrible, rotten little cow. Don't you ever come near me again or touch me. I never want to see you again. Get out! Get out!"

I was shocked and just stood there looking at my mother in amazement.

"Get out!" she screamed.

It took me three quarters of an hour to walk home. Walking along sobbing openly, tears streaming down my face, I wondered what it was all about. Over the years, I've talked about this big secret a lot. Was it a terrible rape when I was conceived? What was so awful to make her react like that? When Colin came home that evening he found me distraught. Three days passed without a word from Sheila. She would rather rot in hell than let her guard down. Finally, Colin couldn't take my distress any longer. He knew I was frightened to death of her so he phoned.

"Look here, Mum, she is your daughter and she needs you and you need her," he said to her. Sheila wasn't in the least bit bothered. She showed no emotion.

"The trouble with Leila," said Sheila, "is she's mad."

Colin replied, "Mum, you know she's mad, I know she's mad, but we have to put this quarrel behind us, I'll bring her round to see you."

So Colin bundled me into the car and presented me to my mother. Now I am almost an old age pensioner myself. My hair was thinning and grey, the lines etched on my face and they weren't all laughter lines. Yet I was being treated like a naughty child. All I had done was ask a question and I was being made to feel I wasn't right in the head. Sheila sat there, all cool, calm and collected and made me wonder what it was all about as she continued her act. "This is the cross I've had to bear all my life," she told Colin.

To me things didn't look that way. I had seen Sheila for two days when I was two and again for a few moments when I was eight. We lived together for about six years from the time I was eleven. After that it seemed to me I was always the one to support her. Certainly she forgot a lot, once again she got away with her act. Colin thought she was a sweet old lady, which in reality she was. If only she could come to terms with this awful burden she carried all her life. Easier said than done, who knows what goes on in a person's mind.

Southend was about to gain Unitary Status, I was going to be redundant. That's fair enough, it's how the cards fell, but the three past councillors at Milton in their jealousy and spite couldn't just let it be. Oh no, being the muppets they were they passed a vote of no confidence in me. It was a put-up job; there were only six people at the meeting and the other three all told me it was a put-up job, down to the three, who had long passed their sell-by date. I was distraught, was there no end to their nastiness but every cloud has a silver lining, in my darkest hour I was offered one of the safest seats for the new Authority. But there is always a snag; in my new ward was another of the little rats, he had lost the last election, like those in Milton the voters had made their feelings clear, they didn't want him. All these past councillors were tarred with the same brush, they were a load of has beens, they hated each other's guts, but united they kept each other in and everyone else out.

My selection didn't go down very well with them, next thing I read letters in the papers asking the voters not to vote for me, of course there wasn't a name to the letters. There was so much bad feeling out there that I offered my resignation. One thing I am not is hard-faced. I felt awful for the lovely people who had adopted me, but they wouldn't hear a word about me quitting. They said they thought I had more fight in me than to give up. But it got worse; one of the little rats stood against me. Conservative against Conservative. Well that's new with the Conservatives. It goes without saying, "I WON." I never had to bother about the opposition, the Labour or the Liberals, my main opposition was always my own party.

Having got safely on to the new authority, it was nothing like County, you had to watch your back all the time, I didn't need it, so I served my time with as much good grace as I could muster and then retired. At least I can say I retired under my own steam, nobody got rid of me. I still support the Conservatives and I am so grateful for those wonderful ten glorious years at County Hall.

The first shock and the start of a nightmare came all too suddenly. It was winter, freezing cold and Sheila had turned her fire off to go to bed. Clad only in her nightie, she fell by the side of her bed. She laid there for eighteen hours before her chum next door wondered about her. The police had to break down the door to get in. At the hospital they were amazed she had survived. If I knew anything about it, she would have been pickled when she fell, that would have saved her.

The next incident that concerned her neighbours was when they hadn't seen a light on all evening and decided to check. They found her in a flower bed, drunk. They put her to bed as she was. It seemed she had been eating dirt, it was all in her mouth when I checked her the next day! That evening Colin said he had something very serious to talk to me about.

"What are you going to do about your mother?" he asked.

"Not a lot," was my answer.

"Now it's time to be serious," Colin told me. "Your mother came to see me today and with tears streaming down her face asked me, 'What is going to happen to me?'"

She wouldn't talk to me but Colin was a real softie and she fancied her chances. At the end of the day I wasn't going to turn my back on my mother, I never had and I wouldn't now. Sheila was determined she was staying in her own home. After months of discussions, Colin and I agreed we would keep an eye on her if we could build an extension to her bungalow in her back garden. She very reluctantly agreed. We put our home on the market. Whatever mixed feelings I had, my gut instinct told me I was mad, totally crazy, a leopard never changes its spots. But I was full of hope. I was a great believer in fate, this was all planned in the stars. Now I would find the mother I never had and had desperately needed all my life.

Colin being in the trade drew up our dream home. We were going to build most of it ourselves. It would be no bigger than a doll's house with one bedroom, lounge/diner, bathroom and a kitchen – so small you couldn't swing a cat. It would be very modern, central heating and double glazing. Sheila had neither and Colin suggested while ours was being done we could keep going and do hers. Sheila wasn't having any of that, her big old storage heaters plus her free-standing fires were good enough for her. She was going to stay in the dark ages. Our only problem was we weren't allowed to put a front door on the side. It was one plot, one building, so one front door. We would always have to come in and go out through Sheila's place.

Finally, we sold our home. We have been married five years. While our new home was being built, we rented a flat for three months which went over Christmas. We were both flat out at work and getting our home up would make each day a long day. Hopefully, in the evening, we would have five minutes by the fire to relax. It would be good having that little time to ourselves. How long were we looking at keeping an eye on Sheila? She was only seventy-seven. It could be fifteen years or more before we would be in a place of our own again.

Everything was going well, the foundations were dug. Sheila's garage had to come down, a big tree had to be dug up plus her blackberry bushes. She made no secret of her distress. We had survived the trauma of giving up our home. All our furniture had been passed through the family. It was far too big for the little place we were building. Sheila never gave one thought to our distress. We had already spent a considerable amount of money, but whatever happened now it was too late to turn back.

Arriving one morning, I was surprised to see how ill Mum looked.

"What on earth has happened to you?" I said.

"Haven't you heard?" asked Sheila.

"Heard what?" I asked.

This time when she fell she let out such a scream the neighbours heard. The police got in through the kitchen window and the door through to the hallway, which we had just mended, was broken again. She had been taken to hospital and after an examination brought home. That night when it was time for us to go home Colin was surprised I had my coat on.

"What about your mother?" he asked.

He thought she didn't look fit to be left and after talking it over, it was decided Colin should go back to the flat alone. It was more important for Colin to get some sleep. I would doze in the armchair. The next day Sheila didn't seem any better. It was difficult getting her up and she kept crying out in pain. A week went by and she wanted to go to the toilet. I had almost got her out of bed, she had her bum on the edge, feet on the floor, legs apart with a bucket between them and she couldn't move. I called an ambulance and she was taken into hospital. A young doctor called Sam came to see her.

Looking at Mum she folded her arms across her chest and in a very arrogant tone said, "So you've got a pain have you?"

I stuck my shoulders back and glaring at this young doctor said, "No, she hasn't got a pain, she's got more than a pain."

Another X-ray (mind you I couldn't swear she had had an X-ray when she fell a week earlier, but she had one that day). Nothing wrong was the verdict. I had had her at home for a week, I certainly wasn't taking her home again. I stood so firm the hospital agreed to give her three days' bed rest. That stretched to a week and then fourteen days. Mum was a terrible patient, abusive, hated everyone but she looked desperately ill. On one occasion, she protested that she was in such pain she couldn't walk to the toilet. The nurse asked her, "Are you going to play me up again?" Mum stepped forward bravely and fainted. Another X-ray was taken and still nothing wrong. She asked for the phone, and then phoned the police. She asked them to investigate, saying she was being slowly murdered.

Sheila was due to be sent home on the Monday when the fourteen days were up. On the Saturday, she looked so ill I thought she was dying. Concerned that she might die, I phoned the grandchildren and they visited her on the Sunday.

Making it quite clear to all concerned that Sheila lived alone and making it quite clear that Colin and I worked full-time, there was no one to support Sheila. Monday came and Sheila arrived home in a wheelchair with two occupational therapists. I sat quietly in a chair and watched.

"Jump onto the bed, let's see if you can do it," they echoed to Sheila like a pair of parrots.

"Go into the kitchen and make a cup of tea," they asked.

"I'll cook bacon and eggs if you like!" joked Sheila.

Anyone with a brain, and these two occupational therapists obviously didn't have one, could see this pathetic, frail, old lady was very ill, she was hanging in there by the skin of her teeth. She was determined to get home so I told her not to worry as they pushed her in the chair out to the ambulance.

"I'll see you this evening," I told her, convinced that she wasn't coming home. So I was amazed to be told that evening her living conditions were excellent and she would be home in the morning.

It was late the next day when the ambulance arrived, about 7 p.m. Colin went in to see Sheila full of good cheer.

"Well, Mum, you've made it. Nice to see you," he said, planting a kiss on her cheek.

"Yes! I'm here despite the efforts of that fucking cow, that bleeding bitch who didn't want me in my own home, but she won't get it."

"Who are you talking about?" asked Colin.

"That fucking mare there," pointing at me as I arrived with a nice cup of tea for her. I stood in her kitchen for ages, totally stunned. It had nothing to do with not wanting her home. I wasn't a medical person but anyone with a grain of sense, doctors, nurses, occupational therapists could see she wasn't fit to be out of hospital.

"What have I done?" I asked out loud, banging the table with my fists. Deep down in my heart I always knew it wouldn't work.

Colin interrupted my thoughts: "Come on now," he said cheerfully, "show your strength of character, go on in and cheek her."

I walked through with a heavy heart to find my mother collapsed on the settee. She had got up to answer the phone.

"Up you get," I said cheerfully putting an arm around her and pulling her up. It was the start of a nightmare that was to last four years and almost take my life.

Chapter Fourteen

It was now mid-December. Luckily, my workload was easing off for the Christmas recess. I saw nothing of my little flat. My days were spent with my mother who, in my eyes, was as ill as ever. TV was showing Audrey Hepburn films. Some days we watched four films. Finally, I managed to get a physio to visit. As usual that day, Sheila had decided to stay in bed. The physio threw back the bedclothes and looking at Sheila's body said:

"You have a broken hip."

"I knew it," shouted Sheila, "I knew it."

At last she would be proved right.

"Don't start all that nonsense," I told the physio, "Mother's had two or three X-rays and her hip isn't broken."

The lead up to Christmas was dramatic, the building was progressing and Sheila wasn't improving. Christmas had always been my favourite time of year so I tried to keep my spirits up. I managed to get Mum in the car and take her to visit the grandchildren. Christmas dinner was subdued. If the truth be known, I was in total shock. We hadn't even moved and we were stressed out already. After her Christmas dinner, Sheila took to her bed and seemed to give up. She had been assessed, there was nothing wrong. There was no support at all. I was worried about the future and now Christmas was over I was taking drastic action. I phoned Social Services at Southend and explained my mother's plight. I was completely dazzled by the description of support available.

"Sounds absolutely wonderful," I said. "I'll have just a little bit of it, please."

"Who's the client?" came the question and that was the problem, Sheila didn't qualify.

I then asked them, were they sure they had got it right and I would like a second opinion.

It was a bitterly cold day a few days later. I was outside sweeping up the building rubble and putting it into a skip. I had a woolly hat pulled down over my ears, an old coat, jeans that had seen better days and a pair of old wellie boots. I was a good advert for a tramp. A car pulled up and out stepped a young man from Social Services.

"Come round the back," was the invitation and we stood amongst all the rubble in the half-built extension. I explained I was quite happy to do all my mother's housework for nothing, money didn't come into it. I would do her washing, ironing, cooking and shopping. All I wanted was someone to check she was up, washed and had eaten in the morning and put her to bed in the evening.

"Can't you wash your mother yourself?" was his first question.

Firstly, I doubt if the relationship was there to have me wash my mother. Secondly, everyone involved, every prat (i.e. jumped-up official connected with Social Services who thought they were something) connected with my mother had it explained to them.

"I WORK. You haven't been listening," I said. "I might be at work."

"What hours do you do?" was his next question.

"Enough," was my reply.

It wasn't a nine to five job. Most days I liked to be on the road by 7.30 a.m. To do that, I had to be up by five. Colin had to be fed and his lunch box for the day prepared. Mum needed her breakfast plus a tray with all her needs for the day – a flask with a hot drink and sandwiches, etc. I liked to have most of the preparation for the evening meal completed and potatoes and vegetables prepared. Then I had a bath and got myself ready for work. Sometimes it was evening work, sometimes I was away two, three days – Birmingham, Leeds etc. I didn't know what hours I'd be working.

His next question was: "Why doesn't your mother walk?"

Who knows the answer to that one either. "She just doesn't," I replied.

Next question: "Is your mother lazy?"

Now that was out of order, the interview was going nowhere. I looked down on the ground and there in the dirt was one of my cards. I picked it up, rubbed it on my sleeve and handed it to the young man and said, "There, that's me, that's my job."

That to me was what you call pulling rank and it was something I hadn't wanted to do.

"Right," I said, "Shall we go and meet mother now?"

Sheila was up, sitting in her armchair. She didn't need any help she told the young man, she was quite capable of looking after herself. If she did she certainly wouldn't go to Social Services. Her friends were queuing up for the privilege of caring for her. The young man told her, "I'm not so concerned about you. My only concern is helping your daughter."

I was very grateful for the support I was promised. I only needed the minimum but it would enable me to continue some sort of life for myself. After the young man's departure, I would now get a second opinion on my mother's health. I would take her privately. A nearby nursing home lent me a chair. The task of getting my mother out of the house and into the car was horrendous. Now I'm no shrinking violet but I just stood in the street and cried. It was the same the other end. I had this pathetic, sick, frail old lady who had been through hell (thanks to Southend Hospital, Rochford Hospital and all the doctors, nurses and occupational therapists) trying to get in and out of a chair and car. It couldn't have done her any good, it certainly hadn't done me much good. Finally, we got there. The surgeon had my mother's notes in front of him and there was the broken hip. Be it a subtle break, that's what the surgeon said and hard to detect, nevertheless it was a broken hip. Mum had her operation, six weeks overdue, the very next day.

This time Sheila was an even worse patient. I asked what drugs my mother was on because they didn't seem to agree with her. But I was assured she wasn't on any drugs. According to Sheila, there was a dungeon under the hospital. If a patient had been moved, it might be because they had gone home or had been sent for other treatment. To Sheila they had been taken down to the dungeon and murdered. Sheila told everyone they were killing the patients off, one by one. I told her she was hallucinating and none of it was true, her response is unprintable. The doctors and nurses held wild parties at nights and raped all the patients. I checked again what medication mother was on. One night Mum asked if she could use the phone.

"Of course you can," she was told, "You're not in prison."

The phone was brought to her. She quickly dialled 999 and said she was being held against her wishes.

Her stay in hospital gave us time to do things while she was out of the way; make a bit of noise and get things straight. We moved in and spent our first night in our new home twenty-four hours before she was due out of hospital. It was going to be four long weary years before we were going to have a night on our own again.

Chapter Fifteen

Tucking my mother up on her first night home, I put on a brave face. Stroking the turned-down sheet across my mother's chest I talked brightly about the future. "Now the operation is over, you can get on with your life," I told her. "As soon as you are strong enough we'll have a day out with the grandchildren."

"Yes, that would be lovely," said Sheila.

I had to do my best, it was my life as well. This is now my home, we had sunk a fortune in it, there was nowhere else to go so I had to make it work.

Soon Sheila recovered but she wasn't the same person. The six weeks with the pain of a broken hip had taken its toll. She had lost a lot of weight and was quite frail. She was well enough to go home to Ireland for a holiday. She was well enough to accompany me to the shops, come out with Colin and I for a meal. If anything was going on in her large family, she never missed it.

We had received some fabulous news, Stephen was getting married again. His bride to be, Lyn, was in her mid-thirties; this would be her first wedding so she wanted to the whole white affair, top hat and tails. Stephen asked Colin to do the honours, he said he had been more of a father to him than his real Dad. Colin is a very private man and had to be persuaded to step into the role. Ruth was Matron of Honour and Mum and I were just thrilled to see Stephen settled. It was a lovely day, the newly-weds looked wonderful and very happy.

It was well over a year when I became a grandmother for the first time, I had waited long enough. I was an old-aged pensioner myself and had began to think I wouldn't live to see the day. Of course the Christening was going to be magic. Auntie Ruth was going to be Godmother. Then right out of the blue, after over three years without a whisper, Alan phoned the children. He didn't know Stephen had re-married, he didn't know he was a grandfather, he wasn't a very happy bunny. But I was more unhappy when I learned he was coming to the Christening; as always I would behave myself, not one unkind or snide remark would pass my lips. I had kept my mouth shut all the years and even though I would feel like kicking his teeth in I would rather die than upset my children.

Mum was very frail now, she was nearing the end of her life, but she wouldn't miss the day. Colin stood firm, now Alan was back on the scene he wouldn't come with us, he never changed in his attitude, he refused to be in the same room as a man who physically and mentally abused a woman, he would have to give him a smack where it hurt. So Ruth, Mum and I set of on the drive to Kent, I pulled up outside the church in my brand new bright red Hurricane Hyundai. The car looked lovely and I thought bright red was just the right colour, it sent out a signal on a day when I needed a boost. With Mum and Alan together and remembering the way he spoke to me last time we met I felt I was sinking fast.

When Mum and I arrived at the Christening party, it was in full swing. I had a job getting her out of the car, you could see how frail she was and even a blind man could see the end wasn't far away. She was driving me bleeding crackers but that was between Mum and me, nobody had the right to upset my mother and would do so at their peril. Suddenly the pig – can I think of a worse word than pig, because I'd hate to upset a pig – anyway I'm talking about Alan, he was standing in front of us. Anyone with a mind, and it was always doubtful if Alan did have a mind, anyone with an ounce of compassion, decency, humanity in their bones could see this frail little lady's time was limited. You would think having been snubbed and not invited to Stephen's wedding, warning bells would be ringing and he would have worked out it was time for him to behave himself, as I was having to do. All he had to do was walk away, if he didn't have the strength of character, but then how can one expect someone who hasn't got any character to have any strength to just be polite and say "hello", that wouldn't have hurt. But no, not Alan, rubbing his hands and sniffing, with that evil leer on his face he said to this frail old lady almost on her death bed, "So you're still alive then." Leering even worse he continued, "Of course you would be, you're too wicked to die, you must be the wickedest woman on the earth, even the devil wouldn't have you."

My heart went out to my little mum, Alan's mind was still in the dark ages, we are now in the 1990s, we had long learned that was how things were years ago when children were born the wrong side of the blanket. It was an enormous shame, the women and the babies were reviled, the cruelty and abuse they suffered was unbelievable, many women were locked away in asylums for the mentally ill; women didn't get over the shock and kept quiet about the experience all their lives, even taking their secret to the grave. Even I understood that, I didn't appreciate it, my life had been scarred by the silence. There were times when I could have rung my mother's neck with my bare hands, not knowing who I was. But having a dogmatic, pathetic little squirt like Alan talk to someone who had more guts in her fingernail than he had in his whole body disgusted me. Perhaps this is where I should say, "May God forgive him," but no, there will be quite a few people of his type down in hell; he seems to be fond of the devil, wouldn't wish my mother on him, perhaps Alan can be in charge of the whips, that would suit him.

On Wednesdays, Mother went to the day centre and once a month she went to church. She was now back in the folds of the Catholic Church.

Luckily, for me, from day one I set down some ground rules. Remember Colin was in business and very busy. When he came home in the evening, he was lucky if he got his meal in peace. There was the post to deal with, phone calls, and all the chores of just living. I was probably worse, my post every day was enormous, plus phone calls etc. It would be lovely for Sheila if we both flopped out on her settee and argued about the TV all evening. Life wasn't like that for us, everyone knew the set-up, we went to great lengths to explain it. So from the start I explained to Mum that we would eat in our own place during the week and at weekends we would all eat together. The first time I served her her dinner alone I noticed a tear in her eye, but that was the only way it could be.

Our next task was to sort our position out with Sheila with regards to our home. Care in the community was law but if a person couldn't be contained in their own home that home would be sold to support them in a nursing home. I totally agreed with that and voted for it. Now I found myself in the position where my mother owned my home. We had spent our money building an extension in her back garden which she owned. I went in despair to Social Services and they said I hadn't a leg to stand on. If my mother had a stroke my home would go. I approached Sheila and explained the situation and she agreed on our Solicitor calling. The Solicitor told Colin and I that she was a sweetie. Hang about I thought, something's wrong here, sure enough a couple of mornings later I heard Sheila yelling.

"Look what that crook has done."

Going in to see what the noise was about I said, "What crook, who are you talking about?"

"That Solicitor," said Sheila, "He has suggested I give you half of my bungalow."

"Well," I said, "We are going to give you half of ours."

Knowing that if we laid one finger on one brick she would have us for damaging her property.

"You can take that building down, I didn't want it there in the first place. I'll tell you something now," she continued, "you won't get one brick of my home."

Worse still, it gave Sheila the ammunition she craved for. She gained great sympathy with her mates at church and at the day centre. We were living in her home rent free and we had even had a Solicitor in to try and get her home from her. Talk about being caught by the short and curlies. We were both getting older ourselves and our total frustration cannot be described.

The day centre was concerned because Sheila was always crying. She was totally dependent on support. The Social called in the morning to wash her, check her at lunch and put her to bed in the evening. I worked long hours and when I got home there was endless washing, the cooking had to be done, housework, ironing, shopping, sorting out Mother's problems and all the time the Social geeing her up. It didn't matter how many times I said, "Mum, I know differently, I make the rules," she would give that false laugh knowing she had us tied up in knots. Her big mouth never let her down and she felt she could always afford to go for broke.

One day she was really taking the piss out of Colin. I turned on her angrily and told her not to keep doing that and Sheila, as always, thought she held the trump card and could go for broke. Her reply stunned me, she really had gone too far but still there was nothing we could do.

"I've been to Social Services for advice," said Sheila, "and they have told me I can get an injunction against you to stop you abusing me in my own home."

I was rigid with shock. Abuse *her!* – it was she who was abusing us. I got straight on the phone and called Colin home from work.

"Now then, Mum you really have gone too far."

"I've got two words to say to you," was her reply, "Good Bye."

There was nothing we could do, we weren't going to give up our home. It was a turning point in our lives we had to take drastic action. Knowing what we were facing, we decided to buy ourselves a second home. Sheila was never to be told, it was another nail in her coffin. Many a time I would have loved to have had a chat with her, loved to have confided in her, loved to have shared my worries with her, but I couldn't trust her anymore.

As the third year passed, Colin's health was deteriorating. Having his own business, he had two more years to go to sixty. He came home washed out, racked with pain. My mental and physical health was beginning to worry family and friends. I was losing weight and beginning to look frail. It was starting to look like Sheila would outlive us both.

Part of our agreement when we built the extension was to keep Sheila's home up to scratch. Her windows were so rotten you could put your fingers through the wood and the front wall would have fallen down. We reluctantly agreed at our expense to double glaze her bungalow and while we were doing that get her front wall removed, what was left standing, and crazy pave the lot. We had the usual problems of getting our cars off the road. While we were at it we might as well go the whole hog and modernise her kitchen. That way there would be hot water for the Social Services. Sheila went bananas. "You leave my home alone, no way are you taking over."

"Look here," Colin said, "If the health people came in they would condemn your kitchen and I'm fed up seeing Leila have to cook in there."

"When does she cook?" asked Sheila.

"You have dinner every day, don't you?" said Colin.

"Oh, call that cooking, do you?" replied Sheila.

One afternoon I was feeling so low I got out the whiskey bottle. Time to have a few and drown my sorrows. I must have had about three doubles and all the time I was drinking I was getting more and more wound up about my father. In the end, I stood up, just about brushed myself down and decided that after over fifty-five years I was going to walk into my mother soon and ask her about my father. This was it, I had to steady myself and I faced Sheila.

"Who's my father?" I asked.

"Whatever are you asking a question like that for?" asked Sheila, completely taken aback.

"I did have a father didn't I? Most people do," I replied. "Who was he or was I a virgin birth?"

Sheila was still looking totally amazed. "You don't know?" she asked me.

"No, I don't know," I said. "How should I know?"

"Why" asked Sheila, "do you think I keep the photo of my little great-granddaughter on the TV? Because when I look at her eyes I'm looking at Jack's eyes!"

"You're not telling me Jack was my father!" I could hardly keep my voice down as I replied to her.

"Of course he was," came the reply.

I stormed out of the room back to my lounge. I didn't believe that for one moment, not one moment. My parents, my mother and father, were married all along and nobody thought to tell me! FATHER UNKNOWN stamped across my birth certificate AND wedding licence. That has to be even richer than being called a bastard! All the pain, all the suffering, my children being deprived of a father all their life. The hard life we all had to survive after the divorce and all unnecessary. How do I come to terms with this? I walked unsteadily back to my mother.

"I wish you had told me years ago," I said.

"Why did you want to know?" asked Sheila.

I looked at my mother and thought what a stupid cow she was to ask a question like that. I still hadn't taken in what I had just been told and I replied to her, "Because, Mum, just once I would have liked to put my arms around his neck, give him a big hug and say, 'Daddy Dearest, I love you."

One consolation, Jack knew I loved him. Why? God alone knows. Besides being the world's biggest gambler he was the world's weakest man. Well, all gamblers must be weak not to be able to say "No" to putting the very food from their children's mouths on a four-legged creature. We were always so close but he was so weak he couldn't tell me he was my father. I didn't believe Sheila for a moment. Anyone so weak as Jack couldn't possibly be my father. I felt there was absolutely nothing of him in me. Once again I asked, "Why didn't I ever know?"

Sheila then told me she and Jack made a decision when I came over from Ireland when I was eleven. They both agreed a Jewish name would be a disadvantage to an Irish Catholic. Jack had wanted to adopt me but after lengthy discussions they made their decision and agreed not to ever tell me. So being labelled a bastard hadn't been a disadvantage then! Sheila looked at me.

"I can't take the blame because you were inadequate as a wife," she told me.

"What!" I shouted at her, "Inadequate on my wedding day, you really are the pits, Mother!"

It was awful that this frail old lady should be shouted at but hard to explain the depths of my frustration. Sheila looked upset. It wasn't very often she got upset but even then an apology would have gone a long way. She thought for a while as though she didn't know what to say, then she muttered, "I thought no one would notice."

"You thought no one would notice. Of course they would notice. What did you think no one would notice – FATHER UNKNOWN – on a wedding certificate."

The old lady dropped her chin on her chest and still muttering said, "I took a chance."

"YOU took a chance," I said looking at her and for once I felt really sorry for my mother. She had taken a chance. Of course it would be noticed but who would say anything. What man in the whole world would have behaved like Alan and I understood exactly but could never understand why she never had the backbone to talk to me.

Sheila's health continued to deteriorate. She was now too frail to be dressed, so she lived in her nightie. She was becoming incontinent and beginning to get bed sores. Morning, noon and night when the Social Services came in they would slip off Sheila's woolly, nightie, socks and sheets and place them in the bath for me to wash. Finally, I went bananas.

"But," said the Social smugly and speaking to me as if I were a couple of jelly babies short of a quarter, "we have a laundry service, there's no need for you to do the washing."

"Right I'll use it," I replied.

"We will pick up your washing on Tuesday and, wonderful as we are, we will return it on Thursday."

"So what happens when my mother shits (because that is what it is, SHIT) all over the bed on Tuesday after your collection. Am I supposed to keep the soiled clothes in the house until the next Tuesday?"

I told them I thought their "wonderful" laundry service was crap.

The good news was that Colin and I were going to have a holiday, on doctor's orders. It was March and we decided on a two-week break in Cyprus the following January. Sheila agreed to go into respite for the two weeks and treat it as a holiday for herself. We had long since stopped going out. All parties etc. were cancelled. As much time as possible was spent at home. Shopping was always done in a rush although a lot of thought had to go into it. I had to buy the right stuff to leave for Sheila when I was out. Rushing around Sainsburys as always, one day I bumped into Margaret a friend from the old days. There's nothing nicer than bumping into an old friend, in a rush or not, it was time to catch up on some gossip.

"Amazing," was Margaret's greeting, "Pat and I were just talking about you last night saying we hadn't seen you for ages. Whatever has happened to you?"

I explained about my mother. We stood for ages reminiscing about the good old days. Did we enjoy ourselves! We painted the town red many a time. We had some wild times and drank gallons of whiskey. "Isn't it a small world?" I said innocently, "Pat's daughter is the manager of the team caring for my mother."

"Yes," said Margaret, "and I've never seen her sober!"

We laughed. It was a good joke. If I had thought anything of Margaret's remark I would have gone straight away to Social Services and had the lady in question suspended while an official enquiry was conducted into the allegation. But it was a joke, even if it wasn't, even if she was paralytic, so what. Looking after people like my mother, good luck if you had a drink.

Returning home, the two lunchtime ladies were changing my mother. What I actually want to call them is unprintable. Laughing – and there wasn't much laughter in the house these days – I said, "I've just been talking about your boss. She, like the rest of us, apparently is never sober. It's amazing with all the stress in the world and all the effort looking after our elderly, people have nothing better to do than run around telling tales." When I was little, we would sing, "Tell tale tit, your tongue shall split and all the little puppy dogs shall have a little bit." I'd like to have fed those two ladies' tongues to a Rotweiler.

A couple of days later when the post came, my world took a tumble. There was a letter from Sir Teddy Taylor, a letter from the head of Social Services (Southend), a letter from this lady's (I'll call her a lady for the purposes of this story) Solicitor. She, this lady, was going to have my guts for garters. She might have thought she had good advice but it wouldn't match the advice I had at County. Dropping everything, I jumped into my car and headed for Chelmsford.

The Solicitor saw me straight away. He told me I wasn't in any trouble. I may have given myself a bit of hassle. Whatever this lady did she would get nowhere and the Solicitor assured me however hard she tried I would hear no more. No Solicitor would touch it. As I got up to leave he leaned forward and said, "Whatever you do, don't apologise. It will look as if you have done something wrong and you haven't." Happy with my situation, I headed home. The lady was determined to fight, for what I don't know, until the bitter end.

My mum was now in a pitiful state and she needed full-time nursing, not care in the community. I went to the Head of Social Services again to see if I could override their decision to keep her at home. Mum was being totally neglected and abused by the system. She was actually in the last few months of her life. I felt even more stressed out with the situation with this lady. I felt I was on trial. I'd get letters – *Dear Mrs S, would you please not turn your mother's heating off before you go out. We found your mother frozen at lunchtime...etc. etc.*

The health visitor was as concerned as I was. They felt Mum was being allowed to rot away in her bed. One day they spent an hour on the phone to her doctor asking the reasons why she wasn't getting better care elsewhere. Sheila had used the threat of suicide all her life now she was too weak to even do that.

"But YOU know what to do," she said to me one day.

I thought back to my ex-husband when I'd have dearly loved to knife him. It was the same now. I was determined there would be life after Mum. No way was I going to do her in. In fact, it caused me real concern. You get no training on how to cope through the night with the numerous sleeping pills, painkillers, medicine etc., the loneliness and this lady just waiting for me to slip up. Ruth was concerned and she asked me, "Don't keep giving Nan all those tablets. If anything happens they will have you for manslaughter."

Sheila was a very difficult patient. She would try to get out of bed. I understood the problem. She was still of sound mind and wanted to go to the toilet. No way was she going to just shit in the bed. I tried to explain to her that was how things were but she was having none of it. One morning, frightened that she would hurt herself, I just flung the front door open and yelled for help. The next door neighbour came rushing in and helped me put my mother back to bed. Mum's mouth was in full flow. She told the fucking woman to stop fucking trespassing on her fucking property and get out of her fucking sight. That was one more person I couldn't call on for help. Two hours later Mum was at it again. I rushed to stop her trying to get up. With a face full of hate and vindictiveness, Mum shouted at me: "You come near me and I'll kick your fucking teeth in."

I ran from the room to my own place and dialled 999. The operator asked me where my mother was. I replied I was too frightened to look.

"Stay where you are," said the operator. "We will be with you straight away."

Thank goodness it was the end of November and getting near our holiday in Cyprus. It was a Saturday morning and I woke quickly aware of my mother yelling.

"Leila, Leila."

"OK, Mum, what now?" I asked gently.

Looking at her closely I saw death in her face. Waking Colin I told him I thought my mother was dying.

"Why think that?" asked Colin.

"I can see it," I replied.

Worried out of my life, I called the doctor. It was still not 7 a.m. He was already out to another emergency, so he came straight away. Examining Mum he couldn't agree with me. Standing in my mother's lounge the doctor said, "We're not looking at a crisis here, your mother hasn't even got a temperature."

He prescribed more medicine. This time with a touch of morphine and told me to give her a stronger dose. Six weeks later she was dead.

Chapter Seventeen

After the doctor's early morning visit, the Social Services called lunchtime and said my mother was cold and dehydrated and they thought I should call the doctor. He's already been I told them. Mum was so ill the doctor was called four times that Saturday. I asked every time if she could be taken into hospital. The doctor said she wasn't a hospital case.

"She's *dying*," I kept saying.

"No she isn't," said the doctor.

"No," said the Social Services, "She's just having a bad day."

I knew the score, she was just an old lady, cheaper to let her die in her own home. That way it wouldn't interfere too much with their budget. I felt with all the criticism I was getting from Social Services they thought she was being neglected by me, but she was being neglected by them. She was being neglected by the system and it was criminal that it should be allowed to happen.

Colin and I cancelled our eagerly awaited holiday. We stopped switching the TV and radio on and just read quietly. All Christmas parties and outings were cancelled. We told the kids and grandchildren to have a bloody good time without us. Our thoughts would be with them. Night times I stayed up to be near Mum. I would put on my pyjamas and dressing gown, close our bedroom door so Colin would get some sleep. Sometimes I would have a doze on our settee, sometimes I would doze on Mum's settee. It didn't matter how much medicine I gave her throughout the night nothing settled her. The ideal situation would have been for me to have curled up in bed with her and hugged her close. You only have one mum and they only live once. But the pain in my life had gone too deep. The anger, frustration and humility of it had left its mark. I knew soon it would be too late and I would no longer have one of life's most priceless gifts – a mother – but the wall between us just wouldn't crumble.

The days and nights passed. It was getting embarrassing "Yes," I would reply to enquiries about my mother's health, "She is still with us."

The neighbours were concerned at my appearance. I had got very frail myself and they were convinced Mum would still outlive me.

All was calm one night when she quietly asked me, "Can't you just put me in your car and take me home."

"You are home," I told her.

"Can't you do anything I ask you, you stupid fucking bitch!" she screamed.

I tried to tell her gently that she was home.

"What!" she shouted, "at number eight?"

"Mum, you have never been anywhere but home."

Her reply to that was unprintable or just plain boring as there were so many F words all rolled into one. She was so rotten to me that next morning I re-booked the holiday. On January 14th, come hail or come shine, I'm going to be on that plane. Social Services still had a respite bed for her and yes she could be moved.

Not all of Social Services were at war with me. The young girls who had to clean up my mother's shit had my full support. They were wonderful, as were the people from the health department. Mealtimes were difficult. I would lift my mum's head off the pillow and try to get her to eat a spoonful. I knew she wasn't getting enough food. When I tried to spoon some tea down her there was an awful hollow sound. She was so empty. I would say to Social Services, "This is ridiculous." They would reply, "She is just having a bad day again."

Mum still had the strength to have a go. "How much longer are you going to let me suffer?" she would ask. "You know how to end this, you fucking cow," she would hiss.

We had a quiet Christmas and New Year had passed. The doctor gave me his home number to ring day and night but when I called in the past he always said double her dose. It was almost a week into the New Year and I hadn't been to bed for a month. I was worn out and frail myself. Mum wouldn't shut her mouth for a minute.

"Leila! Leila!"

"What is it now, Mum?" I would ask.

She would say, "Give this bloke ten shillings and ask him to leave."

"Right, Mum, now try to sleep."

Minutes later, "Leila! Leila!"

"What is it now, Mum?"

"Who are all those people in the lounge? Who's paying for the fire?"

"Don't worry, Mum, try to sleep."

It went on all night. By 4 a.m. I thought I would explode. I've got to get help. No use phoning the doctor. I'll phone and take whoever is on call. It was past seven the next morning when he got to me. As I opened the door Sheila shouted at the top of her voice: "Leila! Leila!"

"What's all the shouting about?" asked the doctor, "Don't you think your daughter needs a break?"

"Have a break?" said Sheila, "She does nothing else."

The doctor turned to me and very sympathetically said to me, "This is care in the community gone completely mad. I'll have her taken away today."

Somehow, stressed out as I was, I felt a great sadness at the words "Have her taken away" as if she were a sack of potatoes. She was my MUM. Colin took the necessary papers to her doctor. He was very put out.

"What's all this about? Why wasn't I called?"

As far as I was concerned, he could take a running jump. I got no support from him and now I was having his decisions overriden.

It was five o'clock when the ambulance arrived and ten o'clock before Sheila was settled in a ward. Having assured my mum she was in hospital to get better and come home I said, "Good night."

"So, you're Leila," the nurse said the next morning. "Mum has called for you all night."

What's new, I thought, it wasn't necessary for me to ask anyone how she was, I knew. It soon got around that I was there, strange a doctor came in, introduced himself and asked could he have a word in the corridor. He looked at me with suspicion.

"Your mother is very ill," he told me.

"I know," I said, "in my opinion she has been close to death for the last month and I've tried everything I could to get her into hospital, but care in the community wouldn't have it."

His expression changed completely to one of kindness and he asked, "How have you managed?"

"Just look into my face and you will have your answer," I said.

"It's over now," he said.

She wouldn't be allowed to live in the community in that state again. With a bit of tender loving care Mum rallied. She had enormous strength. I firmly believe if she'd had expert help a few months earlier she would be alive today. As it was, fight as hard as she could, she was very weak and the mountain was too high to climb. But she hung in there. I was sitting by her bed when a large coloured nurse came in. Mum beckoned to her and signalled that she wanted the nurse to bend over so she could whisper in her ear. I wondered what she was up to now.

"Please give my daughter a hug for me," she asked the nurse.

Standing up immediately I went over to my mum and said, "Don't be silly, I'll give you a hug."

Bending down close and trying to slip my hand under her frail body, "Don't do that," said Sheila, "you're hurting me."

So it was too late to hug her. The days passed, getting nearer to the 14th.

What should I do?

"Go," said the doctor, "you need some tender loving care. I don't want your funeral on my hands."

"Go," said the children, "you are exhausted."

I was torn in two. I changed my mind every few minutes. The night before I left, Mum was lucid and I brightly reminded her that I was away in the morning. If it had been just Colin and myself things might have been different. We were going with family; I felt a responsibility to them, I couldn't let them down.

"People are in place to visit you every day," I told her. "The time will fly and I'll be home before you know," I told her, bending down to kiss her and holding her frail hands I said, "Now then you just hold on till I'm back."

"I'll try," said Mum, "I'll try."

Sunday came and I had been away nearly a week and had phoned regularly. Ruth told me she had just visited. Nan wanted a box of Black Magic, nothing else, to pass around and some drinking straws to make it easier for her drinks and she was out of soap. Sounds OK, please God I'll make it home in time. Tuesday would be my next phone call. That day we all went to visit a monastery. It was gloriously peaceful and beautiful. We strolled quietly around the cloisters where the monks walk in the evening. I visited the chapel, the statue of the Blessed Virgin Mary, my mum's favourite, was made of gold. She would have loved to see it. I lit a candle and prayed with all my heart for her. Just outside the monastery was a taverna and we decided we would have some refreshments before the long journey back to our villa. The boys dropped us two girls outside on the pavement while they went to park. A waiter rushed out and I explained we were waiting for our men. Understanding very little English he explained, "I'm a man."

"No! No!" I tried to explain.

You've pulled, I said to myself, there's life in the old girl yet. We were just having a snack and being the only wine drinker I ordered for myself a carafe of wine and some dry bread. The waiter didn't understand dry bread so I indicated, leave it. The others wanted soup which was served with dry bread.

"Ah!" I said pointing to the dry bread and then myself.

"Ah!" said the waiter and quickly brought the bread.

We were concerned with the time, leave it much longer and Colin would have that dreadful drive home in the dark. But for now I was at peace sitting there with my wine looking out over a vast vineyard. I felt alone with my thoughts as if the others didn't exist. Glancing at the clock it would be exactly 5 p.m. at home. It had been a long time since I have felt so at peace. I would always remember this moment. When we arrived back at the villa, dinner had to be cooked and it was too late to phone that night. Get it done early tomorrow I thought to myself.

Colin walked down the hill with me. But as we neared the phone box I suddenly couldn't go any further. Actually standing in the middle of the road, I froze. "It's too late," I said.

Colin made the call home. From his conversations I knew it was all over and eventually I was able to talk to Ruth. Nan had died at 5 p.m. yesterday she told me. The hospital phoned her at work, she got stuck in a traffic jam and was ten minutes too late. My first thoughts were for my daughter who was very distressed. I should have been there to take the responsibility of it all and comfort my children. I would never forgive myself. After that I knew I would never get over the shock of my mother dying when I wasn't there. I would never forgive myself for that either. My little mum died alone. I held back when I left her, I couldn't say the words, "I love you, Mum", now I'll never have the chance.

Everything was in place, just in case. I wasn't going to have a Requiem Mass, just a cremation with a Catholic Priest. I couldn't face all that Catholic mumbo jumbo after the pain of the life Mum and I had shared. This was my mum and I was dealing with it my way. I had to endure another week on holiday and when I returned home there would be another week before the funeral. That's good I thought, time to get organised and give Mum a good send off.

On returning home my first task was to go and see my mum in the chapel of rest. She looked so small lying in the coffin. The flesh had left her face. Her skin was like porcelain, white and drawn tight. A frown crossed her brow. I gave a small gasp in surprise. I had always thought people died peacefully. Mum's thick black eyebrows almost met at the top of her nose and it was definitely a frown. I was so taken aback that I had to speak to the undertaker about it. It was almost as if she was reluctant to go, things had been left unsaid and records had to be put straight. Making myself comfortable by the coffin I held her hands.

"Mum what the hell has it all been about? Couldn't you ever have found a word of comfort?" I said to her out loud. "Remember the time when I was dressed to kill and you asked me 'What do you think you look like? I've seen people who have been dead for days look better!' Well, Mum," I said, "You've been dead for days and I can tell you you don't look that bloody marvellous!"

I sat for ages talking to her. Perhaps she was listening, you never know. She never listened when she was alive. "I bet you always planned it this way," I told her. "I don't think you ever intended having that great moment when we hugged and let all the pain flow out of our hearts. When we came together and said all our, 'Sorry's' There were many times but you always let your big mouth get in the way. Now you have gone and left me with an aching heart, a great pain that I know will never go away; there will always be a great sadness in my life, an emptiness that nothing will fill. I realize your pain was such you couldn't break the mould and my anger was deep between the two of us we dished it out and just couldn't bridge the gap. I can't think of anything to make it up to you for letting you die alone only to take you home. I'll take you home, Mother dear, after the funeral. I promise you. There wasn't much more to say. I held her frozen hand in mine, such little hands, I didn't want to let go. Suddenly I had a weird feeling, if I held them any longer they would thaw out and Mum would come back to life. It was unreal sitting alone in the chapel of rest, knowing it was the end of a life. It had been a very painful life for Mum as it was for me, but I hoped her great faith which she had rekindled in the last stages of her life would sustain her. I stroked her hair. It was soft and warm.

"Goodbye, my old dear, I'll see you in heaven."

Searching for a copy of her favourite hymn proved unsuccessful so I had to settle for second choice. New curtains were put up at the windows. Her home was scrubbed and polished. Her spare room was emptied out and her big oak table was placed there with just a few chairs. The food would be in that room. She would always put on a show so she wasn't going to be let down. All her photos were put on show. All the doors to my place were open so people could wander through. Everyone would be welcome. One last item – flowers. I wasn't going to get Mum a wreath. Just one single rose and I wanted it left on the coffin. Mum was to take that with her to heaven.

It was amazing the years I had spent with Mum, now she was dead I was looking for answers. I could have asked her myself but never did. All I know was when she came over from Ireland as a fourteen-year-old she lived with Lily. I thought I would phone lovely cousin Sheila and ask her if there was anything she could tell me. It was the first she had heard about Mum staying with her mother.

"When was that?" Sheila asked me.

It turned out to be the year cousin Sheila was born. Her father was away in the army. Her mum was pregnant and Lily had a haberdashery shop to run.

"But," said cousin Sheila, "Mum wouldn't have been able to pay your mum any wages. The recession was still biting between wars and the big stores were coming into their own. In the end Mum went broke."

"Where was this shop?" I asked.

"Barkingside," said Sheila.

Barkingside to me was like a bomb going off. Auntie Lily had a shop a few doors away from where Jack had a fruiterers and greengrocers. Mum would have gone in there for her apples and potatoes etc. So they would have known each other. Perhaps the story that Jack was my father was true and not the rantings of a dying woman.

Still busy clearing out her things it took four trips to the tip with junk to make an impression on the rubbish she had collected. What's this, I thought, as at the bottom of a drawer I found an old brown envelope addressed to Leila Merriman. It had been well over forty years since I was Leila Merriman. They say they always leave a clue, was this my mum's clue? I sat down at her old oak table and, feeling very pensive, opened the envelope. It was full of certificates – birth and marriage. Some were so old I was almost afraid to open them up. There was her marriage certificate to Jack. His birth certificate, his parents, etc. etc. Was this the other half of me I had been searching for all my life? I was always really looking for all of me because I had never been one hundred per cent sure of Sheila, but at the end of the day I was sure she was my mother. I always hoped when I found the rest of me I would be looking at names like Smith or Brown from say Dagenham or Plaistow. Here I was looking at names like Lazarus and Abrahams from the suburbs of Russia. Looking at this lady, I haven't yet worked out who she is. She signed her marriage certificate with an X. Hannah obviously couldn't read or write. What was her story? What is the story behind all these immigrants in the eighteenth century? For now, I shall put this envelope away. I have a mother to bury.

For me personally I have a thing about Jewish people. Ask me if it is a good thing or a bad thing and I couldn't answer. I think they have an amazing charm but I go back to my very strict Catholic upbringing when anyone other than a Catholic was doomed and, of course, it was the Jews who crucified Christ.

For now there was no definite proof for me. Luckily Jack was buried so if it meant digging him up and doing a DNA test on his bones so be it. Of course, there are his two children. It pleases me not to think they are my flesh and bones no more than they would want to think that I'm their flesh and blood. I thought of Betty and her hatred for the very young girl who married her father. Could it be sixty-five years on that that young girl not only married her father, she also married my father. For now I can't get my head around all this. In years to come I'd like to get the records straight for my grandchildren.

Now I understand the silence. In those days brother and sisters didn't know if a sister had a baby out of wedlock. It was such a shame on them all she would be sent away with some cock and bull story like she had got a job working for a duchess, etc. etc. They never knew, but Sheila was here in England with her brothers and sisters so everyone knew I had been born. But who was the father? Not one word from Sheila. It was a total secret and now I knew why. I thought of Auntie Lily with her hand-rolled fag in her mouth stuttering when I was born "b-b-b-bastard why hasn't she been drowned?" If the family had known I was half Jewish they would have taken me for a ride in my pram to the River Deel and let the handbrake off.

The Priest phoned to ask if someone would give the eulogy. On the morning of the funeral, all the cousins arrived including Michael from Kent, Tom's son. I had only seen him once in the forty years since his father had committed suicide. I was very grateful for his presence and sad that the family had been estranged for almost a lifetime. There was a large whiskey for those who felt the need, that would be Mum's way. Who was going to do the eulogy was my query. There were loads of excuses but no offers. As we arrived at the cemetery, I couldn't believe the people there. Who the hell were they? They were probably all Mum's church cronies come to see this wicked daughter, who wouldn't give Sheila – that wonderful, good devout Catholic – a Requiem Mass. Life had been too painful for me to go through all that load of rubbish. I was doing this my way. God would understand. Once again, no offers for the eulogy from the crowd. I told the Priest I'd do it. I sat shattered at the thought of doing it and tried not to get too emotional. All too soon the Priest nodded and it was time for me to stand up and step forward. I stood up in front feeling very conscious, looking at the congregation. I was almost in a daze, out of it. I looked at Colin sitting in the front row with my lovely son and beautiful daughter, their eyes focused on me. Time to begin. Time to start, take a deep breath, I told myself and take it slowly.

"My mum, Sheila, is the last survivor of twenty-three children. She outlived her brothers and sisters by many years. If we believe what we are told they will all be together up there and they will be looking down on us. The cards will be out, they will have a few rolled fags and a bottle or two or three if anyone trumps my mother's ace. They will know she's arrived because there will be a fight. If the good Lord gives my mum pocket money for good deeds done, she will find something to bet on. Mum was never interested in material things – vases, plates on the wall, etc. As long as she had the money for a bet she was happy. She worked hard and played twice as hard. Sheila married twice, both her husbands were of the Jewish faith. I was brought up on Jewish history, customs, food etc. That is why I find this so hard to cope with but if it has brought her peace at the end of her days I'm happy. I'm an only child…"

I wanted to say she left two grandchildren she adored and two great grandchildren who were the light of her life. Most importantly, I wanted to say she was dearly loved, but emotion struck and I sat down quickly. The Priest stood up probably shocked at what I had said. Colin said his face changed colour.

He began with: "We shall quietly pray for a couple of minutes for our dear departed sister Sheila. May God forgive her her human faults and frailities."

I smiled through my tears.

It had been a good service and now it was time as Michael was with us to put some of Mum's flowers on her lovely brother Tom's grave. I always felt he was there. He could have been taken home to Sheerness. He had a widow and three grown-up sons. We were amazed to hear Michael say he had no idea where his father was. So he, with Colin and Ruth, went to the office. I was shocked when I was told they couldn't give the exact spot as he was in a communal grave with twelve others. That was awful, no one would pay for a spot of ground to bury him. It's beyond belief. What now for the holy Roman Catholic faith who chucks on a heap a lost soul who commits suicide? Where's their compassion? Their humanity? Their forgiveness? Where's the love of God for all his children? What for his widow and three sons? He had been a bloody good husband and father to them and me when we were small. Even a dog would have been given a decent burial. What of that bitch Mina who put so much energy into beating my mother up and verbally abusing the rest of us? Pity a little more energy couldn't be put into seeing Tom had a resting place of his own. Tom wasn't a tramp, he was part of a large, loving family. There were dozens of us. I hang my head in shame when I think of it.

One of my regrets in life was that I didn't phone Michael, Sean and Tommy that day. After Mina's intervention on their behalf I was totally shell-shocked and the anger of that day is still with me. Tom was closer to me than anyone else. It was he who held me in his arms on my first night in Ireland. It was he who walked me down the aisle on that dreadful day I married. After his death, with my small baby I had to work for almost a year to pay off his debts. If I had known about the community grave I would have seen to it that he had a proper grave even if I had to work as long as there was breath in my body.

Colin and I walked round to the cemetery yesterday, May 2003. I had a map with a cross that marks the spot roughly where he is. We put a few flowers on the grass. I thought of the other poor souls there with him, they probably had no one. I'd like to dig Tom up and rebury him but how do you sort out who is who out of twelve of them? It's appalling. In the circumstances, I was glad I hadn't put myself through a Requiem Mass for my mother. All that hypocrisy and two-faced rubbish. Those wonderful, devout, holy Catholics who turn their backs on a lost soul who ends his life expect the business when their day comes. They want all the blessings on offer. They will have the Priest shaking incense over them, chants of hallelujah for the good, pious life they have led. I'd like to think they get a couple of turns on the devil's barbecue as he gets to give them a few pokes with his red hot poker. I'd be there to watch. I booked my place by the fire when I was eight.

The grief and pain of losing a mother is traumatic. More so for me because we had never really settled our differences and now it was too late. You only have one mum and I had lost mine. Colin and I set out on the sad, sentimental journey home. We made our way to Moortown. Passing over the crossroads, down the road to the little cottage where Sheila was born. She wouldn't have recognised the old road now. It was quite posh and well used by cars, not at all like when Mum and I were young! We drove slowly past the old home and carried on down to the river. I got out of the car and leant over the bridge. The bridge there now is wooden and dull, the lovely stone bridge with the three steps, carved out by loving Grandad had long gone. The river had been drained and was just a little trickle now. Although it was early summer it was cold and the rain was falling gently. Time for a wee dram. It was going to be a difficult time ahead and I felt in need. Sipping the whiskey, my thoughts went back to when I was child and the river flowed. The fun all of us had fishing, swimming and just running wild and free. It would have been the same for Sheila. She would have played and fished here with her many brothers and sisters, they would have been "Grand" days free from the pain that was to envelop her in later life. They were definitely the best years of her life and it was here in Moortown she always longed to be. I thought of Mum that beautiful young girl who never had a chance and now she was just ashes in the boot of the car.

Time to make our way back. We went past the little cottage again. It had changed. The old hay barn wasn't on the opposite side of the road and the cottage itself was quite posh. This was the road Sheila walked to school every day of her young life. Like her brothers and sisters she started and ended her school days at Ballinvalley School.

Next stop in Delvin was to buy a large bunch of brightly coloured flowers, and then in to see the Priest. I had a ten pound note handy to give him. He was such a lovely man I felt my offering was inadequate. Discreetly, I reached into my bag for a second. The Priest refused my offering so I just left it on the table. After all I've said about the Catholic

Church, he was so kind and comforting. I wondered did he have a direct line to God?

The final stop was in the church itself. I lit a candle for Mum and recalled in my mind the incident with my grandmother when I was just a child. I was probably standing on the same spot where I stood as that eight-year-old. That day was probably the last day I knew peace. I lit a candle for Lizzie and Mick as well. I took a seat next to Colin. We were in no hurry. There was plenty of time for me to be alone with my thoughts. This is where Mum had been baptised. This is where she had made her First Holy Communion and where she was confirmed and Sheila, until her dying day, liked to tell the story of her First Holy Communion. She was one of the brightest pupils and had a one hundred per cent pass. So she had to wear a different coloured ribbon from the rest of the girls. So did I, I thought. Looking back there was very little in Sheila's life to be proud of. This is where she had probably spent the happiest, most contented years of her life and that's why she is back here, hopefully to rest in peace.

Colin and I looked at each other. We had sat there for ages and now it was time to go to the cemetery. It was just a short ride in the car. Taking the casket and flowers, we made our way to where my beloved grandma and grandad lay. I knew the way as I had visited in the past. Now I was alone, except for Colin, the funeral had been so crowded and I was surrounded by family. This was such an unknown area no one explains how you are supposed to feel coping with scattering your dearest ashes. I felt quite panicky, this was very final, scattered the ashes and placed the flowers on top all was calm. Now my mum had her flowers, not on a cold winter's day in a cemetery in Southend but here in the privacy of her birthplace. Now Mum was home where she longed all her life to be. I watched the rain fall gently on the blooms, roll down the leaves and rest gently on the ashes. I stood close to Colin, his arm was tightly round me for support. Feeling emotionally drained, I chatted away to Mum:

"You will be in heaven now, dearest Mum, so you will know how much I've loved you all my life. You will realize how desperately I needed your support and longed for your affection. You will know how much I wanted to be like you and have your personality and charm and sense of humour. The way you could twist everyone round your little finger so they thought you were a lovely lady, which you were. It was only me who seemed to be a real trial to you. I realize now how upset you must have been when you conceived me. You must have been so upset that it turned your mind against me. You never once put your arms around me and hugged me. You never claimed me as your own. You've kept me at arm's length all your life and now you are gone. If only you knew how much I needed you. I don't know what happens now, I've not been there, you are. If God lets you take a peep down on me I'll be trying to be nice and kind to people and lead a good life.

Well, Mum, I think that's it. I'm not just dumping you here. I couldn't think of anything else to demonstrate my love for you. One day I'll bring Stephen and Ruth, Hannah, Adam and Georgina here. I'll try to show them the beauty of this place and demonstrate the happiness and peace of mind you and I experienced here. I doubt if I could ever do that, but I'll try.

Till we meet again, dearest Mum, God Bless."